To: Rita

When It Raynes

An Erotic Suspense Trilogy

Thank you for the
support. Much success
to everything you
touch. Much love!

J. Asmara

Cover Design: Doneen Johnson
djdesigns@artlover.com

ISBN: 978-0-692-76153-3

To Contact J. Asmara:

Email: theasmara@yahoo.com
Website: www.authorjasmara.com
Facebook: www.facebook.com/authorjasmara

Disclaimer:

This book is not suitable for younger readers. There is strong language, adult situations, and some violence.

When it RAYNES

There's no escaping karma...

J. ASMARA

Prologue

Sweat beads sat on her face as Rayne stood in shock looking at the blood splatter on the wall. How did she get there? That moment was far from the happy home she worked so hard to build; loving husband, beautiful children, and a successful career.

Tears began to fall as the reality of what just happened swept over her. It was true what they say, "Skeletons don't always remain in the closet."

Everything she knew was disrupted in the course of a week. The only thing she could think of at that moment was David and how much she loved him.

Rayne, what have you done? Lord please forgive me, she thought as she shed tears.

Chapter 1

Friday May 18th

It was a normal Friday morning in the Smith household. Rayne was awakened by the buzzing of the alarm clock. She let out a soft yawn and prepared to get up to start her day.

She looked around her beautifully put together bedroom and thought of her accomplishments, such as her career, home, and family. At thirty years old, Rayne was Agent of the Year for the third time in a row at Brunson Realty. Not to mention, she was putting things into place to begin her own agency in the near future.

Rayne loved the feeling she got when she helped others find their perfect home. With her knowledge, skills, and ability, she worked nonstop and found her beautiful five bedrooms, four and a half bathrooms, finished basement, three car garage, and pool all in a secure gated community home. It was truly amazing.

The icing on the cake though was her husband David,

Mr. Tall Dark and Handsome. He made her heart skip a beat every time she was around him. His muscles, baby face, and gorgeous smile commanded any room; he was six feet two inches of pure sexiness.

At the ripe age of thirty-five, David was the youngest Branch Manager at Trust Bank Atlanta for the past seven years. Surprisingly, his brains were so much more attractive to Rayne than any of his other attributes.

David Smith was much different than any of the men from Rayne's past. She'd come such a long way from that lost broken girl from Jackson, Mississippi. She had not only found herself but built a wonderful new life in Atlanta, Georgia. How had she got to be so lucky?

Rayne smiled, looked at her husband, and greeted him with a good morning kiss. He smiled as he opened his eyes to the most beautiful woman in the world.

David watched as Rayne got out of the bed and started her morning routine of singing and dancing to the music playing. He thought back to the moment when he realized she was the one for him. From the first moment he saw her he knew that she was special and he had to get to know her...to love her. Nine years later, and he still felt the same sparks that he did on day one.

The more David reminisced, the more he desired her. The image of a morning quickie, before getting the kids up, started dancing in his head. He got off the bed and went into their bathroom where Rayne was in the mirror getting her *Beyoncé* on to *Dangerously in Love*. David stood behind her and whispered in her ear, "I want some breakfast, I woke up a little hungry."

She responded, "Ok baby, I'm almost done here. What do you want me to fix?"

"What I want, you don't have to cook," he announced with a smile.

Before Rayne knew it, David had turned her around, sat her on the counter, removed her panties, and began eating his breakfast. He gnawed, sucked, and licked until Rayne's juices were all over his face and on the counter. She moaned softly and sensually with his every motion. David loved the way his wife responded to him. He was aroused and wanted to feel her warmth by sharing the hardness of his love with her.

Just as David was about to enter her, there was a soft knock on their bedroom door. Rayne gathered the strength to ask, "Who is it?"

"It's Eva mommy," a small voice replied.

"Hold on baby, mommy's coming," Rayne replied as she kissed a very disappointed David.

"We will continue this later honey. I promise," she said with a wink.

Rayne went to the bedroom door and was greeted by a mocha chocolate little girl with beautiful brown eyes, dimples, and long ponytails.

"Good morning love bug. Let's go get you ready for

school," she said with a kiss.

Rayne and David's children, Eva and Evan, were her world. The twins, who were four years old, had been a joy since birth.

Her prince, Evan, was handsome with his smooth caramel skin, green eyes, and head full of big loose curls. He did not have dimples like Eva, but he had a smile that would melt any heart.

Rayne had gotten Eva ready and was in Evan's room when David entered fresh, dressed, and ready to go. *Damn, he could wear a suit,* she thought.

"Baby, finish getting yourself together and I'll get Evan ready," he interjected with a smile, as if he read her mind.

Rayne couldn't have asked for a better father for her children; he was always so helpful. From the moment their children entered the world, David was always there to lend a hand. They had a system so tight that mornings in the Smith household always ran smoothly; children dressed, coffee made, and briefcases packed. He helped her load the children in their SUV and a feeling of contentment filled him as he kissed them goodbye.

Since David was a young boy, he knew that he wanted a family. He actually enjoyed playing house with the neighborhood girls. He always played the daddy and would never let them make him the son. He made a vow to himself that he wanted to get it right the first time, like his parents, who had four decades of loving one another under their belts.

David had met Rayne just a few months after she moved to Georgia. She had recently started at Brunson Realty, when he laid eyes on her at a local deli that was conveniently located in walking distance between their offices.

She was standing at the counter placing her order, looking lovely in a black pencil skirt, blouse, blazer, and pumps. Every hair in place pulled back in a bun that showcased her beautiful face. The confidence she displayed was so sexy to him.

He watched as she sat at a nearby table. David, being the shy guy, couldn't build up enough nerves to say anything to her. It was something unexplainable that was drawing him to her. He went to the deli every day during lunch in hopes of running into her.

It was a week later when David finally saw Rayne again. He was determined not to let another week past and walked up to her table and said hello. She looked up from her book, smiled, and returned the hello. They ate lunch together that day and many days after.

David asked himself, at least a thousand times throughout his and Rayne's years together, how did he get to be so lucky? He dated many ladies before Rayne but none compared to her. She was the most caring and compassionate woman he'd ever met. Rayne did everything in her power to ensure that he and their children were happy and well taken care of.

*****

David finally made it to work after his thirty-minute drive. He enjoyed his job at Trust and started with a smile as he did every day.

Meanwhile, Rayne had reached the twins' preschool, gotten them settled in their classrooms with a kiss, and was off to work. Rayne smiled as she thought about her morning. She loved when David was spontaneous; one minute she's singing, and the next, she's cumming. Since the twins were born, they had to become creative with their sex life, but they made it work; be it when the children were asleep, playing hooky from work, or shipping the children to their grandparents'. Rayne began thinking that it would be a wonderful weekend for the kids to see their Grandma and Papa, especially after the morning's episode.

*****

Nothing but loving thoughts danced through David's head as he was on the way home after his long day at work. He smiled as he imagined the greeting he would receive from his loving wife. The more he reflected, the quicker he wanted to get home. After what felt like an eternity, he finally pulled up into their driveway.

Still filled with warm thoughts, he began to the front door with keys in hand. The door was opened before David was able to insert his key and he was greeted with a vision that always melted his heart. There stood his chocolate queen in a black tank top and pink yoga pants that showed every curve of her body. Rayne had a body that any man would want, D cup breast, small waist, hips, and an ass that was perfect for cupping.

As David admired her beauty, he was embraced with a passionate hug and kiss. He smiled because that was what made him want to come home every day.

She led him into the kitchen where he was greeted with the aroma of roast beef, potatoes, broccoli, and fresh rolls. They sat at the dining room table and filled each other in on their days.

David suddenly realized the house was silent and asked, "Rayne, where are the children?"

"Baby, it's just you and me. I sent the children to your parents' for the weekend. I figured we needed some alone time."

She straddled him, kissed him gently, and whispered, "Now, go upstairs, take off your suit, and unwind. I have water in the bathtub waiting for you."

Without hesitation, he went upstairs, after being sent off with another kiss. He noticed the rose petals leading into their room to the bed, on the bed, and towards the bathroom. As he entered the master suite, he knew it would be an exciting night. Rayne carried herself very well in the streets, but her freak factor was through the roof.

David undressed and got in the bathtub. Shortly after, he was joined by Rayne, who stood before him butt naked.

He watched as she entered their glass standup shower. It turned him on to see the water run down her body. The more David admired her, the more he became aroused. He got out of the tub and joined her in the shower. He pressed his body onto hers from the back and began kissing her neck. She moaned in pleasure as his manhood grew.

He turned her around and passionately kissed her mouth as he played with her nipples. Her breasts were the ultimate hotspot, so he began sucking, rubbing, licking, and nibbling; that drove Rayne crazy. The more she reacted to his touch, he more aggressive he became. He enjoyed bringing her pleasure and pain. Though the water was running down their bodies, he could feel her juices that had begun flowing.

David pinned Rayne to the shower wall, placed her leg on the built-in seat, and began eating her out. Rayne braced herself on the shower wall as she moaned and groaned. David was so in tune with Rayne's body that he knew when she was about to have an orgasm. He enjoyed watching her cum more than anything. He felt that the look that came across her face was priceless.

Her kitty purred and David knew that it wouldn't be long. She grabbed his head as he tickled her clit with his tongue as he buried his face in the pink palace. Rayne let out an orgasmic moan while wetness dripped down David's face, but he was not satisfied with that. He licked and chewed on her clit until she shook uncontrollably from ecstasy. David used his big arms to hold her thighs ensuring to give her indescribable pleasure.

Rayne had reached her fourth orgasm when David turned off the shower and carried her out of the bathroom onto the bed of roses, where he continued to kiss and caress her body.

"Lie down and let me please you," Rayne said seductively. Once he laid back, she stroked the shaft of his penis while her tongue danced around his body until she reached her destination. Her tongue tickled his penis from the head, to the shaft, down to the balls, and back up as she caressed his chest.

Rayne slowly placed his penis into her mouth. He let out a soft groan that turned her on and she deep throated it. The tightness of her throat around his penis drove David crazy. It took talent to be able to do the things Rayne did with her mouth, the kind he had always appreciated. The more Rayne sucked, the harder he became and the harder he became, the wetter she got.

David got so turned on by watching her ass bounce as she pleased him that he grabbed and pulled her into the 69 position. After five minutes, neither one of them could control themselves any longer.

Rayne slid her body down and began riding David backwards. He watched with amazement as she rolled her hips, enjoying the pleasure he felt with every motion of her body. They moaned as their bodies made music, up and down, round and round, and back and forth she went; riding him, her black stallion.

David loved when Rayne took control but wanted to bring her pleasure much more. He flipped her over and made love to her. The deeper he went, the more she wanted. Screams of ecstasy could be heard from their bedroom, as she came over and over again.

David knew just how to reach Rayne's "G" spot; one leg in the air and hit the sides of her wall. She responded to every stroke in perfect rhythm with his body. He could feel her insides contracting and knew she was ready. He began thrusting harder and faster until he was showered by her wetness.

Her small frame shook with uncontrollable moans and groans as her pussy squirted all over his penis. After the third set of multiple orgasms, he knew it was time for him to get his.

He asked, "Are you ready for me to cum?"

She softly whimpered, "Yes daddy, cum for me."

"Where you want it baby?" he whispered, as he went deeper.

"In my mouth," she said, as she moaned through the words.

He loved when she was nasty! He got a few more strokes in and pulled out. She sucked and stroked his penis and less than a minute later, his desire exploded. He felt like he was having an outer body experience.

Rayne watched David with cum running down her lips.

Mission accomplished, she thought, *and all before dinner.* He kissed her on the forehead and laid down, attempting to catch his breath. After a few minutes, they finally got up and got cleaned up.

With nothing but robes on, they made their way downstairs for dinner. The dinner Rayne prepared was absolutely delicious. They ate and then laughed and talked all night until they fell asleep, wrapped in each other's arms. Their bond was so tight that neither one of them could ever imagine anything or anyone ever coming between them.

Chapter 2

Saturday May 19th

Rayne woke to an empty spot beside her; she had not heard David get out of the bed. She glanced at the clock on the nightstand and saw that it was seven a.m.

David never gets up this early on a Saturday, she thought.

"Babe!" she yelled. There was no answer. She went in the kitchen as David came in from the backyard.

"Good morning, baby," he said with a smile.

"Morning, babe. You're up early. What are you up to?" she interrogated.

"Well, my love, I was setting up something special for you," he stated.

"Oh really," she said with a flirtatious smile and stance.

"Yes, really. I need a few more minutes, so you go back upstairs and I'll come get you in a few."

"Okay honey," she responded with excitement as she

ran up the stairs. Rayne loved surprises. She went into the bathroom to freshen up; she washed her face, brushed her teeth, combed her hair, and put on some lip gloss.

Rayne was reading a fitness magazine in bed when David walked in and asked, "Excuse me beautiful lady, would you do me the honor of escorting you to the lovely backyard?"

What in the world does he have up his sleeves? Rayne grabbed David's arm and walked out to the backyard.

Inside of their screened gazebo, David had decorated a table with a bouquet of pink, purple, yellow, and white roses and a fragranced candle. He also had soft music playing in the space. Smiling from ear to ear she asked, "What is the occasion?"

He kissed her on her forehead and said, "Just wanted to show you how much I love you and hell, after last night, I thought you deserved a nice breakfast."

"It's beautiful and I'm starving. Thank you sweetheart," she responded with gratitude.

David served her a bowl of fresh fruit, bacon, eggs, toast, coffee, and freshly squeezed orange juice.

Rayne was truly grateful for her husband because he was always so thoughtful. They didn't get too many days when it was just the two of them, so those moments were cherished.

She sat and allowed him to feed her fruit because she felt there was something about his fingers that made her strawberries taste better.

Chrisette Michele's *Golden* came on the radio, which was the song they danced to at their wedding. David grabbed Rayne's hand and they danced and sang to one another. She drifted into lala land in his embrace.

"Sweetheart, I have to get ready to go to the office and run my monthly audit reports. It shouldn't take but a few hours. I should be home by noon," he said as he looked at his watch. He kissed her and then continued, "I have more in store for you Mrs. Smith. You have a nine a.m. appointment at Sherrie's for a massage, manicure, pedicure, and facial."

Like any other woman, Rayne enjoyed being pampered. She ecstatically said, "I love you so much, sweetheart. You make me so happy."

*****

David left the house before Rayne did. As she reached into the center console of her Mustang (her weekend "me" car) to grab her sunglasses, she saw a little white box with a red bow. Rayne opened the box and saw a sapphire and diamond bracelet and earrings; blue was her favorite color. She called her husband to thank him and went on her way to Sherrie's House of Relaxation.

Rayne felt like a new woman by the time she left the spa. She was driving along, grooving to Jill Scott, when her cell phone rang.

She answered to hear her mother's voice on the other

end, "Hey, baby girl."

"Hey Mama."

"What you up to?" her mother asked.

"I'm on my way home. David treated me to a few hours of pampering at a local spa. I'll have to take you when you come to visit," she responded.

"Ok, that sounds good. Well, I didn't want anything. I just wanted to tell you that I love you and I'm very proud of you," her mother confirmed.

"Aww, I love you too, Mama," she stated.

"Enjoy the rest of your day, baby girl. I'll talk to you later, sweetheart," her mother announced.

"Alright Mama," she said while hanging up.

Hearing her mother say those things made her very happy. She and her mother had just recently started working on their relationship after years of resentment and hurt between them. Rayne had not seen her mother since she left Jackson and had convinced her to get on the train to visit the following month.

Rayne stopped by The Wine Shoppe and picked up some Moscato for her and David before going home. David had not made it home by the time she got there, so she went for a swim.

Rayne had finished her third lap when David came out into the backyard in his swimming trunks. She did her final two laps and watched David from the lounge chair alongside the pool. She watched as he moved gracefully through the pool. David swam like a fish. Rayne admired his big arms alternating from the water. She waited patiently so that she could put her hands on her sexy specimen. The water droplets on David's body glistened in the sun as he stepped out of the pool.

He caught Rayne's eyes as she stared him up and down. He moved toward her and kissed her passionately. His kisses sent a tingling sensation throughout her body.

She wanted him right then and there. Rayne secretly had a fantasy of being watched while having sex. So, the possibility of someone seeing them did not faze her one bit, but David on the other hand was a little too conservative to make love to her right there. Maybe, if it had been night time, but during the day she knew there was no way. There was an electric circuit that she felt with every one of David's touches. She couldn't take it anymore and led him into the house.

They had made it to the stairwell when David sat Rayne on the fourth step, peeled off her bikini bottom, and went head first between her thighs. Every time he ate her, he was on a mission to please like never before. He attempted to suck her dry, to metaphorically pull her soul through her vagina opening.

David enjoyed the closeness he felt with her during those intimate moments. He continued and watched as her eyes rolled upward. Her thighs trembled in his hands as he held them open. He enjoyed tasting the sweet nectar of her fruit. She laid there with a level of zealous that one could only hope for. David brought continuous warmth that moved through her whole body. She anticipated his penetration with every touch.

He entered her with a deep, hard, but calculated thrust. She let out a passionate shriek that surprised her. David grabbed the stair above Rayne's head and started slow grinding. He made sure each side of her walls had adequate attention. He softly kissed her on her neck and whispered, "I love you, Mrs. Smith," before he exploded inside of her.

Life could not get any better for Rayne. Her life was filled with so much enjoyment and love; a love that she never thought she'd deserved. David gave her one of his famous forehead kisses that Rayne loved and got up to get her a towel. He returned and helped her clean up the love that oozed between her legs. He helped her up from the stairs and they went upstairs.

They showered and laid in the bed for the remainder of the afternoon. The only time they got up was to warm up the leftovers and grab the wine. They ate dinner and drank wine while watching Rayne's favorite movie, *Love and Basketball*. The two of them were enjoying themselves when the house phone rang. David reached over to the nightstand and answered it.

Rayne watched as David's face displayed sadness and regret while listening to the person on the phone. She walked over to him as he said, "Ok, we'll be there as soon as we can." David then hung up the phone.

"What's wrong David?" she questioned.

"Sit down baby," he answered, with pain in his voice.

"Who was that?" she questioned again.

"Baby, please sit down," he pleaded.

"What David? You're scaring me. Are the kids ok?" she asked frantically.

"The kids are fine. That was your stepbrother Eric. It's your mom," he stated with his hand on her leg.

"What about my mom? I just talked to her earlier," she said with hesitation.

"Your mom passed away earlier today. She had cancer and didn't tell anyone," he answered regretfully.

"What!" she screamed.

"I'm so sorry, baby. Bruce found her this evening when he came home from fishing."

Rayne's whole world collapsed at that very moment. She vowed to never return to Jackson but how could she not see her mother laid to rest.

So many emotions overwhelmed her at that very moment. Luckily, she had David by her side because she needed him more than he even knew.

Chapter 3

Sunday May 20th

Rayne sat in the passenger seat of their Chevy Tahoe as David drove westbound on Interstate Twenty. She and David picked up the children from her in-law's home and hit the road that morning.

Until that point, David always respected that Rayne did not share much about her family or her past. He'd finally accepted that Rayne did not have a close-knit family like his. As time went on in their relationship, he stopped trying to get her to talk about her family and even going back to visit.

Rayne hoped that she could make it through this visit and keep her sanity. She knew it was going to be the longest five hours of her life; a not so ideal road trip.

Faint memories started flashing into Rayne's head; things that she buried so deep that they seemed like someone else's memories. She could see a clear vision of her mother.

Her mom was a good mother. Rayne's father died when she was ten years old and her mother worked numerous hours every day with two jobs. Rayne always admired her mother's strength. She refused to let anyone or anything stop her ever; she didn't want to become a statistic.

When Rayne was sixteen years old, she got a job to help her mother so that she could go to the local community college to become a certified medical assistant. Later, she continued her education and became a registered nurse. Sonya, Rayne's mother, fought to keep her on the right track; she never wanted Rayne to fall into the stereotypes set by society of being raised in a single parent household. Rayne's academics were superb; she remained on the honor roll throughout school and graduated with a 4.0 grade point average.

Rayne always had the desire to help those less fortunate. She had been active in various outreach programs through her school's honor society as well as the church. Life for Rayne was good and she and Sonya were extremely close.

Rayne was brought back to reality by the faint voice of little Evan. "Mommy, I have to potty."

"Ok honey. Can you hold it until Daddy finds somewhere to stop?"

"Yes ma'am," he said hesitantly.

They stopped at a nearby exit, filled up, let the children

use the restroom, and ate. Rayne looked across the table at her love, who had mistaken her worry for sadness.

She wanted so badly to turn around and go back to their world, but she knew it wasn't possible. She had less than four hours before she had to face the past she fought so hard to forget, some of the good, bad and ugly decisions she made. She wished she had more time to mentally prepare, but she didn't. Rayne prayed God would smile on her and she'd get through the next few days without rustling any dirt, grime, or rubble.

A familiar feeling of helplessness swept over Rayne; a feeling she felt so many times as a young woman. She knew the next five days could possibly be the longest and hardest ones of her life. The Smiths' finished their meal and got back to their journey to Mississippi.

Rayne continued her journey down memory lane as David drove. Sonya's primary focus had always been Rayne. During her senior year of high school her mother met Bruce, who brought a smile to Sonya's face that Rayne had never seen before. Seeing Sonya like that made her exceptionally happy. Rayne decided to go to the local college to continue helping her mother at home.

Bruce had his place but stayed at their house occasionally, which was to be expected. He respected Rayne and her space, so it didn't matter to her one way or another. They were all adults.

Rayne was dating Randy at the time. He wasn't her

mother's choice for her because he was somewhat of a bad boy. Thinking back, Rayne realized that's what attracted her to him.

He was the total opposite of what she was used to in her sheltered lifestyle. Randy was suspected to be one of the biggest drug dealers in Jackson. He knew Rayne was special so he hid that side of him from the then, naïve, Rayne.

Randy's slickness stood out to Sonya and slowly brought a wedge between Rayne and her mother. Their conversations became few and somewhat forced. Little did Sonya know, Rayne had actually been secretly dating Randy since her senior year of high school and was convinced, in her mind, that he was "the one". In order to keep the peace in the home, Rayne began sneaking around with Randy.

Rayne's life was great. She was on the Dean's List at school, promoted to manager at work, and had peace and love at home. Everything was perfect for her. Her journey on the adulthood highway had started as a smooth drive. Thinking back to that part of her life brought a smile to Rayne' face.

It was just before eight o'clock p.m. when they arrived in Jackson. The Smiths' checked into their room at the Hilton and laid it down for the night.

Chapter 4

Rayne woke in David's arms. She had fallen asleep in his embrace after they made love. She always felt safe in his arms. Rayne watched as her babies slept in the bed next to theirs. She got lost in every inhale and exhale of Eva and Evan's breathing. They were so precious when they slept, so innocent. Rayne began reminiscing again. She was taken back to when her innocence was taken from her during freshman year of college.

Her mother and Bruce got married that spring. Bruce sold his house and moved into Sonya and Rayne's home.

That particular weekend, Bruce's sons were visiting; Eric was eleven and James was seventeen. Rayne was up to her normal Saturday routine; homework, house cleaning, t.v. watching, and internet surfing. The weekends were Rayne's time to relax after a busy week. She and the boys had a movie night, while her mom and Bruce went to

Sonya's work function. A good horror movie, popcorn, sodas, and candy were a perfect night, as far as Rayne was concerned.

Rayne and the boys had spent time alone prior to that night. She never had any problems out of either of them before, but that night, James started acting a little strange after he came in from hanging out with a neighborhood kid. She recalled that Bruce and her mother had discussed that the boys' mother was worried that James was drinking and possibly doing drugs.

James had become a little fidgety and started asking off the wall questions like, "Is it ok for stepbrothers and stepsisters to be together?" and "Do you think age is only a number?" The more he spoke, the more she was convinced that he had become a pill popper.

One of Rayne's services to the community had been that she volunteered at a local rehabilitation center. She learned a few things during that time. James was bouncing all over the place with his conversation and was acting anxious, which were both common symptoms of pill popping.

"Look James, I understand that teenage life can be extremely hard, especially when your parents aren't together. But do not ruin your life by doing things that you may regret, like using drugs and/or drinking alcohol. Your mom and dad both love you. I know it's not the easiest thing to talk to our parents about, but you should reach out to someone." She touched him gently on his shoulder in a compassionate manner. "We are not related by blood but our parents are married, and I am here for you if you ever need me. Well, I'm about to take a shower and y'all need to get ready to go to bed," she said with concern, as she got up from the couch.

Rayne checked all the doors and windows before she took her shower. She checked on the boys afterwards and went to bed. Rayne had just found her sweet spot in bed when her bedroom door opened.

She expected it to be her mother, informing her that she and Bruce had made it home, but to her surprise, it was James.

"James, what's up? Is everything ok?" she asked.

"Yeah, I was thinking about what you said earlier about being there for me," he responded.

"Okay," she stated with hesitation.

"Well, it's like this. I want you and I'm tired of you not seeing me as nothing but a little boy. I'm more man than that lame dude you are with," he said, moving closer to her bed.

At this point, Rayne felt very uncomfortable. First because he was in her bedroom and second, his tone was sinister.

She spoke reluctantly, "James, when I said I am there for you, I meant like a big sister; that is all. We are family now. So, you are going to have to put those feelings aside."

"I HAVE to put my feelings aside? I don't HAVE to do a motherfucking thing. You strut around like your shit don't stink with your little ass shorts and fitted shirts. Yeah, you're fine, but you ain't all that," James spat out as he stood over her.

Realizing that James' tone had become aggressive, she attempted to sit up, but James pushed her back down and straddled her.

"What? Little Miss Rayne too good for me!?!" he yelled.

Rayne tried to calm him down with reasoning and declared, "James, I don't know why you are so angry but I don't think I'm better than you. It's just-"

He quickly interjected, "Shut up! Yes, you do. But you're not. I'm enough man for you and I'm going to show you." He snatched the covers off.

She fought and screamed as he raised her nightgown and ripped her panties. She let out another scream but no one came to her rescue. Eric was in the shower on the other end of the house, and Sonya and Bruce had not made it home yet.

Though James was only seventeen years old, he had the strength of a grown ass man. He pinned her hands down as he spread her legs and entered her. She went numb as she felt the pain of his penis being introduced to her dry and inexperienced vagina. Tears flowed from her eyes as she laid there. Rayne was a virgin and had been saving herself for marriage. She wanted her first time to be special, definitely not forced. Her whole world crumbled at that moment. Her soul was truly hurt. She felt like a little girl in need of her mommy. *How could this be happening,* she questioned.

She did not know how much time had passed before James was done but it felt like an eternity. She laid there praying to God until he exited her violated temple. Before he left the room, he kissed her and said, "Now, think about that when you're with your little boyfriend. Princess." Since then, she still had a problem with anyone calling her princess.

Once the door closed behind him, she immediately jumped up and locked her door. She climbed back into bed and cried uncontrollably in the fetal position. She felt helpless as she thought about what she should. There was no way she could tell her mom, and definitely not Bruce. Though she was hurt physically and mentally by James' actions, she could only think of not ruining her mother's happily ever after.

Rayne wept as she thought about the dilemma she faced back then. She was overwhelmed with emotions she had suppressed for over ten years. *Maybe it was a mistake returning to Jackson,* she thought as she felt the beginning of a panic attack.

Rayne eased out of the bed and went into the bathroom to avoid alarming David and the children with her tears. Once in the bathroom, she washed her face and gave herself a pep talk. She knew she had to calm down and pull it together. Otherwise, the days to come would be emotionally unbearable.

Rayne had turned on the shower, to steam the bathroom before she jumped in, when there was a soft knock on the bathroom door. David slid into the bathroom and greeted his wife with a kiss. "Good morning, baby," he said pleasantly.

"Morning sweetie," she answered.

He asked with a hug, "How are you feeling?"

"Honestly, I don't know because my feelings are all over the place," she replied.

"Well baby, that's understandable, your mother just died. I love you because you are such a strong woman, but it's okay not being able to process your emotions right now. Is there anything I can do?"

"Just continue to love me 'til death do us part."

He winked and probed, "Anything less than that is not an option. Do you need any help in the shower, Mrs. Smith?"

"Why thank you, Mr. Smith, but I think I can manage," she said playfully.

"Well, I'll be right out here if you need your back washed," he said, exiting out of the bathroom. He could always bring a smile to her face.

Rayne showered and thought back to the strained relationship with her mom; the strain brought by him. After

James raped her, Rayne shut down. She had not confided in anyone. She did not want to place her mother in a position of having to choose between her child and her husband.

With hindsight being twenty twenty, she knew that she should have said something. Not only had holding it in destroyed her emotionally, but James later went to prison for raping a young lady he had been seeing. When she had heard about it, she felt partially responsible.

The months that followed the rape were pure hell on earth for Rayne. Her grades dropped, she wasn't focused at work, and she hardly spoke to anyone. She avoided James like a plague. The weekends the boys came over, she either requested to work, stayed with Randy, or went to a hotel.

Rayne also became reckless; she'd started having sex with Randy and even took a few drinks. It never dawned on her, at the time, that Randy embraced her reckless behavior and never questioned the drastic change.

One evening, nearly four months after the rape, Rayne was at work as usual. She was in the manager's office finalizing the work schedule when she passed out. She woke up in the back of an ambulance with an oxygen mask on. She laid there falling in and out of consciousness.

When Rayne fully came to, her mother was standing over her in the hospital bed. She felt so weak and asked, "Mama, what happened?"

"You passed out at work. They said your blood pressure

and blood glucose level were high. How are you feeling, sweetheart?" she asked.

"Tired and my body is aching," she responded.

The doctor walked in and said. "Well, hello Ms. Jennings. So glad that you are awake. My name is Dr. Lamb; I've been the physician overseeing your care this evening. We've ran several test and I'm glad to report your blood pressure has returned to a normal level. I've also ordered an ultrasound to check the baby to ensure that he or she isn't in distress."

Rayne had what felt like an outer body experience. *Did she just say 'the baby'?*

Dr. Lamb continued, "We've stabilized your glucose level, but you will need to be seen by your Obstetrics and Gynecology office first thing because you've developed gestational diabetes."

Rayne, still in shock, heard her mother say, "Excuse me, did you say 'the baby'?"

"Yes ma'am. My guess is that she's approximately fourteen to eighteen weeks, but the ultrasound will confirm how far along she is. I apologize but I assumed you both knew. I will leave you to talk. I will be back in about thirty minutes to conduct the ultrasound," Dr. Lamb confirmed.

Rayne heard the door close and immediately her mother yelled, "Rayne, how could you do this? I've worked so hard to ensure that you were given the opportunities that I did not have. How are you going to finish school and be somebody's mama? How long did you think you could hide this? Is Randy the father? Is this why you've been so distant? Rayne, I am so disappointed in you. I can't handle this right now. I need to get my thoughts together."

Rayne tried to stop her mother and pleaded, "Mama, wait, please don't leave." Sonya walked out and did not look back after leaving the room.

She just laid there and cried. *How could this be?* The bigger question that floated in her mind was; whose baby was it, James or Randy?

Rayne got out of the shower and heard the laughter of her children. She always loved children but when faced with the situation many years ago, she knew she could not be a mother. The ultrasound timeline and measurements confirmed that James had to have been the father. Rayne had not entered her second trimester, but abortion was not an option, as far as she was concerned. As she laid in that hospital bed alone, no family or friends, she knew what needed to be done.

Refreshed from her shower, Rayne joined her family in the room. David and the kids were having a pillow fight. They were laughing hard and having a good time. Moments like that meant so much to Rayne. She decided to convince David to give her one more day before she tackled her family.

They spent the day lounging by the pool, relaxing, and ordering room service. Rayne even worked out at the gym.

I'll deal with tomorrow...tomorrow because today is wonderful.

Chapter 5

Tuesday May 22nd

Rayne woke refreshed after her day of much needed relaxation. For the first time since she learned of her mother's passing, she had a peaceful sleep. She was so grateful that David understood.

She'd received several calls from family members wanting to know where she was and when she was coming. Of course, they would not understand her struggle, so she avoided them. She knew they hadn't seen her in over a decade, but the only person she communicated with was Bruce. He not only understood but respected the fact that she needed an additional day.

The morning started off great. She and David got the children ready and ate breakfast. Afterwards, they packed Eva and Evan's backpacks and headed to the funeral home to meet Bruce. The meeting was set for Rayne to be involved in the arrangements that were being made for her mother's wake; which had been scheduled for that Wednesday afternoon.

Franklin Funeral Home was in charge of her mother's arrangements. Franklin's had been the primary funeral home in Jackson since Rayne was a little girl.

When David pulled up to Franklin's, Rayne noticed that they'd upgraded from the fifteen hundred square feet building since she left. In front of their vehicle was a lavish two-story structure with a lovely fountain in front of a wraparound porch with columns.

Rayne and her family exited their vehicle and entered the exquisite establishment. Rayne enjoyed looking at all the contemporary furnishings, wall hangings, and accessories. It was beautiful. If she didn't know it was a funeral home, she could see herself staying in a place of its caliber.

The receptionist, Vivian, was very pleasant and showed them into a conference area. She entered to see an older version of the Bruce that she remembered. Tears welled up in Bruce's eyes when he saw Rayne.

He embraced her tightly with a hug and said, "Oh my God, Rayne you've grown into such a beautiful woman. It's been way too long. You are looking just like your mother and your family is absolutely beautiful."

Rayne introduced David and the children. Bruce shook David's hand and instantly loved on Eva and Evan.

"Hi. I'm y'all Papa Bruce. I'm so happy to finally meet

you two. Eva, you are just as pretty as you want to be and Evan, my man, you are such a handsome little guy," he said.

Watching Bruce interact with the children softened the hardened heart she had for him. Though she knew Bruce was not the reason for James' actions, part of her had blamed him, which wasn't fair. From day one, Bruce entered her life as a father figure; he always treated her as if she was his daughter. Unfortunately, he never knew his son was the motive for her despising him and always thought he had done something wrong. Luckily, time does heal some pains.

The owners, Edward and Christina Franklin, walked in after the hallmark moment ended to discuss the arrangements. The receptionist also entered and offered to take the children into the playroom.

Once Eva and Evan left the room, Edward began to fill Rayne in on the things that Bruce had selected up to that point. Though making arrangement for her mother's funeral was at the bottom of "must haves" in her life, she had to admit that Bruce had done a beautiful job overall.

Rayne checked out mentally, when Christina began talking about the flowers and obituary layout. She became overwhelmed with sadness. *So many years wasted.*

She thought back to the day she broke her mother's heart in that hospital room. She attempted to contact her mother for about an hour after she left the hospital, but

Sonya would not take her calls. Bruce had finally answered the phone and tried to comfort Rayne, as he explained the hurt and disappointment her mother felt, but no words from her.

Randy called Rayne's cell phone that evening as she laid in the hospital bed. Her heart dropped into the pit of her stomach when she saw his name flash on the screen. *What am I going to do?* She had already lost one person she loved and refused to lose another, so she answered.

"Hey baby," she answered nervously.

"Hey Rayne. What's up, you busy? Sounds like you were asleep," he inquired.

"No, I wasn't sleep. I'm actually in the hospital. I passed out at work today," she admitted.

"What? You ok? I'm on my way," he asked with care.

"You don't have to come. I'm feeling ok but I do have something to tell you," she admitted.

"What is it Rayne?" he asked worried.

"I'm pregnant."

There was complete silence on the other side of the phone. Rayne had to look down to ensure the phone didn't get disconnected, but the time was still moving on the screen. Randy always had something to say, so Rayne did not know how to take his silence. She engaged him again, "Randy, did you hear what I said? I am pregnant."

"Oh. Wow. Yeah, I heard you. Am I the daddy?" he questioned.

"I can't believe you just asked me that," she snapped.

"I'm sorry, Rayne. I'm just in shock. It'll be ok. Your mom knows?" he asked with fear.

"Yeah. She's not very happy either; she's probably packing my stuff right now. She won't even talk to me," she responded, fighting back tears.

"Don't worry sweetness, you can come stay with me."

"I might have to take you up on that," she said sadly. "They're gonna release me tomorrow. My car is still at my job. Will you come pick me up?"

"Of course I will sweetness. Just call me when you find out what time you are being released," he said confidently.

"Ok. Well, I need to get some sleep. I'm exhausted."

"Go ahead and get you some rest. Good night," he said.

"Ok. Good night," she responded and hung up.

That conversation was the starting point of her web of deceit and lies.

Rayne was brought back to her current situation when Edward invited them to see the area where the wake was going to take place. She was not surprised to see it was a beautiful area, like everywhere else they viewed.

Once they were done, the Smiths were escorted to the play area to get their children. Eva immediately ran to Rayne, while Evan remained in front of a television and PlayStation and asked, "Mommy, do we have to go right now? I'm having soooooo much fun." Rayne couldn't blame Evan for falling in love with the space because it was amazing. Any and everything a kid could imagine was in there.

"Sweetheart, we have to go, but maybe you can come and play a little tomorrow," she answered.

Reluctantly, Evan replied, "Ok mommy."

They left the funeral home and went to a local family restaurant for lunch. Bruce and David really hit it off; they talked about everything from sports to politics. Rayne enjoyed the feeling of having a normal family. Growing up, it had been pretty much just her and her mother.

Her mother's family was mainly in Brooklyn, New York and her father's family was in New Orleans, Louisiana. When Rayne's father died, Sonya refused to return to New York to raise Rayne and decided to stay in Mississippi. Sonya was the only child so when her mother passed, she kept in touch with her only aunt and uncle and two of her cousins. Rayne had not even met any of her cousins.

Then there was her father's family; the people who deserted Rayne and her mother after her father's death, so any family outside of Sonya was nonexistent. Rayne thanked God every day that she had been strong enough to turn the negatives in her life into positives. But it was a long and hard struggle some days, especially after Randy picked her up from the hospital.

Rayne never told Sonya about the rape, instead she packed her stuff and moved in with Randy. Things started off alright; she was still in school, still working, and had her blood pressure and gestational diabetes under control.

Rayne was six months pregnant when the honeymoon with Randy came to an end. She began seeing traces of his street life. He could no longer hide certain things, such as late night random calls, suspicious looking visitors, and a lot of coded conversations.

Though Rayne had accusations, it wasn't until she came home early one afternoon and saw Randy and his friend Justin sitting at the kitchen table with stacks of cash and bags of marijuana, that she realized her happily ever after was a fairytale.

Randy turned to Justin and said, "Aye man, I'm gonna holla at you in a minute. Let me handle this real quick. I'll meet you at the spot."

Once Justin left, the air was real thick in that apartment. Rayne and Randy argued back and forth until the argument ended with "Shut the fuck up," followed by a smack.

She sat in shocked as Randy collected his drugs and money and went into the bedroom. From the couch, she saw him place the money in his safe and throw the marijuana in a gym bag.

He came and stood in front of her. "Look Rayne. You are my woman and the mother of my child. Know that I love you but I'm gonna do me. All I need you to do is to be pretty and stay out of my hustle. You, me, and my seed in there are my forever. I got some business to take care of, so I hope by the time I get back, you're over this fiasco," he said with force.

He kissed her on the cheek and left. *How dare he put his hands on me?* Rayne never had a man hit her and he had her fucked up if he thought she was going to put up with it. She had no idea what she was going to do or where she was going, but if Randy thought she was going to be there when he got back, he was sadly mistaken. Rayne got out of her feelings and went into the bedroom to pack her things. Her plan A had fallen apart, so she needed a plan B quick.

Once Rayne got into her car, she called her friend Sky. She and Sky had been friends since Sky moved to Jackson from Grenada, Mississippi. Sky moved to Jackson to help her grandmother, after she had a mild heart attack. The girls met when Rayne was in the ninth grade and Sky was in the eleventh grade. They both volunteered at a local nursing home during a service to the community event.

Though Sky was a few years older than Rayne, she never treated her as if she was beneath her. Rayne was instantly drawn to Sky; she had the life that Rayne dreamt of. Sky's father was a pediatrician and her mother was a lawyer; Rayne always called her Rudy Huxtable. Her family lived on a twenty-acre lot, in a plantation style home with personal horse stables and trails.

The girls became extremely close. They spent almost every day together up until the day Sky left for college. Sky went to the University of Southern Mississippi, which was about two hours away in Hattiesburg, Mississippi. They kept in touch and Rayne had even gone to visit her a few times, until Rayne shut her out.

Rayne had allowed that night to control her life by consuming every bit of joy she had. *No more!* Rayne thought, as she sat in her car. Sky answered the phone and was excited to hear from Rayne.

"I really need to get away. Can I come to your place?" Rayne asked.

Sky responded with, "Of course you can. When are you coming?"

"I'm planning on getting on the road shortly."

"Ok. Be safe," Sky said before they hung up.

In true friendship, it never mattered how much time passed between conversations, it always seemed like you just spoke yesterday. Rayne gassed up her Nissan Altima and hit the highway to Hattiesburg and never looked back at Jackson.

*****

The kids loved spending time with their Papa Bruce. Whatever they wanted, he gave. Though the trip was a bittersweet one, Rayne had to admit, it did feel good to be home. They finished lunch and Bruce said to her, "Rayne, I hope this isn't going to be the last visit from you. I look at you as my daughter. I would love to be a part of you and those beautiful babies' lives. Please think about it. They're the only grandchildren I have."

Rayne smiled and replied, "I will take that into consideration. See you later Bruce. We had a great time." She kissed him on the cheek.

Rayne took David and the children sightseeing around Jackson and then spent time in the park, prior to heading back to the hotel. Eva and Evan were exhausted by the time they reached the hotel. Rayne bathed them and put them down for a much needed nap.

She and David enjoyed their few minutes of alone time. They cuddled up on the balcony in the chaise lounge and watched the sunset. Afterwards they went inside to the couch where Rayne drifted into a peaceful sleep in David's arms.

She was awakened by the room door closing. When she opened her eyes, the kids were sitting at the table and David was placing plates in front of them. He glanced and expressed to her, "Hey sleeping beauty. You are up just in time; we ordered room service. Come join us, my queen."

Seafood Alfredo, broccoli, and garlic bread, Rayne thought with a smile. David knew how to please her stomach. Looking across the table at David, she hoped they could squeeze in some time for him to please something else, but for now, she enjoyed listening to the conversation the children were having amongst themselves.

Their imagination had them owning a pizza plant, so they could make the pizza that was on their plates. She smiled at the thought of a pizza plant. Over the years, she'd learned that you must value the "little" things.

The manuscript of her life included some not so good things, but it all built her character. There weren't many days she did not think of the child that she threw away; how much different her life would have been had she kept her child or if it was a girl or a boy. Yes, she ran from Jackson but she could not out run her mind.

David had always told Rayne that she brought him life but in actuality, he had been her savior. He showed her that not all men preyed on the weaknesses of women. Rayne became so bitter after the incident with Randy. It was not easy for her to trust anyone, but David was patient and showered her with the sincerest love.

*****

Rayne arrived at Sky's apartment at about 10:00 p.m. the night she left Randy. Sky was happy to see Rayne but also shocked to see her belly.

"Looks like we have a lot to talk about, Raynee Bear," she said with a sideways stare.

Rayne smirked and replied, "You have no idea, my Rudy Huxtable. I hope you don't have class in the morning because this may take all night." They talked until the wee hours of the morning. Rayne told Sky about being raped, her and her mother's nonexistent relationship, and the Randy ordeal.

Though Rayne never went into the who, when, or where

about the rape to Sky, it felt like she released a ton of bricks.

Rayne could see the hurt and pain come over Sky's face as she shared; Sky was always the emotional one. With tears in her eyes, Sky hugged Rayne and told her she could stay as long as she wanted, and she was going to help her out in any way she could.

Randy blew Rayne's phone up that night; he'd called, texted, and then called some more. Rayne grinned with his every attempt. Little did he know, she had planned to change her number the following morning.

Sky showed Rayne to her guest bedroom, Rayne's temporary home. Sky came from a well off family but was never flashy. Her apartment was warm and inviting but not over the top. Rayne undressed and got into the bed. It didn't take long for her to fall asleep, especially after the day she had.

The following morning, just before dawn, Rayne began to toss and turn. She had a nightmare that Randy had found her. In the dream, she was in Sky's apartment asleep and woke up to Randy standing over her. "Oh, you stupid bitch. You thought you could get away from me? First, you lie to me about that bastard in your stomach being mine. Then, you steal from me. You are dead. My face will be the last face you ever see!"

Rayne jumped up out of the dream as he was strangling her. She was drenched in sweat as she attempted to bring her heart rate down.

She knew she needed to get her plan together like ASAP. She went to Hattiesburg on impulse without a well devised plan, she had no doubt that Randy would find and seriously hurt her. Not only had she taken away his "forever", but she also took his seventy-five hundred dollars.

*****

Rayne finished her dinner. The memories resurfacing had become tiring. She lounged around with her family and watched the Lion King until they fell asleep. *Three days down, three days to go.*

Chapter 6

Wednesday May 23rd

Rayne had a horrible night. She tossed and turned throughout the entire night. She was taunted by James and Randy in her dreams. They were demanding her to own up to her wrongs. Rayne was running for her life but one or the other was behind every door, down every street, and around every corner; regardless of how fast she ran, she could not escape her past.

Out of breath and panicked, Rayne opened a final door and was face to face with the barrel of a gun. Unfortunately, she could not see who was holding it because of the shadows. A muffled voice said, "It is time for you to pay for the pain you've caused." The gun went off and she woke up.

Rayne laid there still; a fear like she'd never felt came over her. She could hear her mother whispering to her, *"Baby Girl, you knew you would have to face your decisions one day. All those secrets you kept have been festering in the minds of those involved."*

Rayne always had the gift of dreams. The things she envisioned always would come to past one way or another, whether it be in her life or in the life of someone close to her. She hoped that dream was a fabrication of the emotions she felt from her return to Jackson and not a premonition of things to come.

Rayne got out of the bed and went into the bathroom. She hopped in the shower and washed her tears and sorrows down the drain. She took a deep breath and said a quick prayer, "Lord, please guide and protect me and my family today." She stepped out to face what life had for her.

Her day consisted of shopping and relaxing at the pool in preparation for her mother's wake. The service began at six o'clock p.m. and she wanted to arrive at five-thirty to welcome the visitors with Bruce.

Mrs. Franklin greeted Rayne and her family with hugs as they entered the funeral home. She announced, "Mrs. Smith, your father has not made it yet but the area is set up, and your mother is prepared for viewing. Would you and your husband like to have a few minutes with her before the visitors arrive?"

Reality hit Rayne at that moment and she could not speak. David grabbed Rayne's hand and spoke for her, "That would be great Mrs. Franklin. Would the play area be available for the children this evening?"

"Yes sir, it is. I will get Vivian to escort the children."

They waited for Vivian and then went to the viewing room. David held his wife's hand as they entered the room. There was a soft pink casket sitting in the front of the room, decorated beautifully with arrangements of all different types of pink flowers. A knot in Rayne's stomach appeared, like the size of a grapefruit. She had not seen her mother in over ten years and now, it would be in a casket. Her feet were heavy as she walked up to the casket.

She felt faint as she stood by her mother's lifeless body. It was a good thing that David was there for her to lean on. She had stressed so much about the skeletons of her past that she had not faced the fact that her mother was gone. It hit her like a ton of bricks that she would never see or speak to her mother again.

Rayne's tears fell as she looked at Sonya; she was so beautiful. She truly looked like an angel lying in her white dress. Her hair and makeup were flawless. Regret swept over Rayne as she cried uncontrollably. David comforted her and wiped her tears.

After a few minutes she said to David, "Baby, give me a minute alone with her, please."

David hesitated but asked, "Are you sure you're going to be alright, sweetheart?"

"Yes, baby. I'll be fine. I love you," she answered, while holding back more tears.

"I love you more. I'll be right outside of the door if you need me."

Reluctantly, David moved toward the door as Rayne watched him exit the room. Her heart was heavy with all the things she wished she had said to her mother.

Even after verbal communication returned, Rayne still never told her the truth about James, Randy, or the child she abandoned. Rayne touched Sonya's hand and began sharing through tears. "I love you, Mama. I'm so sorry for all that I've done and all of the headache and heartache that I've caused. You were an amazing woman. I wish I could have been half the woman you were back then. Know that I am striving every day to be that woman now."

She paused, in attempt to hold it together, before she continued. "I'm sorry I shut you out. As twisted as it sounds, I did it for you. I did not want you to live with the guilt that your husband's son raped your daughter. I did not want you to have to deal with your first grandchild being a product of such disgust. I hope you never felt it was anything that you did. I'm so very sorry. I will miss you my sweet, sweet mama."

Rayne kissed Sonya on the cheek and went to her husband outside of the door. When she exited the room, Bruce was standing there with David. Bruce smiled as she approached. "Hey Rayne. You look lovely as usual. I just asked David about those grandkids. I can't wait to see them little beauties. I don't know what those boys of mine are waiting on to have me some grandbabies. Oh well, I'll spoil Eva and Evan, as long as you allow me to."

At that moment, Rayne was tapped on her shoulder. She turned around and to her surprise, it was James standing there. With a grin on his face, he engaged her, "Hello, Ms. Rayne. Nice to see you. Pops, don't be starting that mess about grandkids. For all we know, I may have a kid or two out there somewhere. Just be patient Pops."

Rayne froze; she had not seen him since that awful night. So many emotions went through her, but anger beat out all of them. She wanted to punch him in his face. Lucky for him, it was neither an appropriate time nor place. She forced a smile and excused herself. She watched as James escorted Bruce into the viewing room, but not before he shot her a wink and a smile.

Rayne stepped out onto the veranda to regain her thoughts; she needed some fresh air. A voice got her attention, "Rayne, is that you?"

She turned to see an all grown up and handsome Eric coming towards her. He scooped her up into hug. "Oh my goodness, Rayne. I thought I would never see you again," he said with joy.

"Baby boy, you've grown up and looking mighty handsome I must say," she mentioned.

"Well, thank you. Sorry about your mom. She will be missed. Man, I loved that lady," he spoke with tenderness.

"Yeah, me too... me too," she stated, trying not to break down.

Rayne and Eric walked into the funeral home hand in

hand. David met them at the door. "Hey baby, I was just coming to check on you."

"Thanks sweetie. I'm good. I want you to meet Bruce's other son, Eric." Rayne smiled through the introduction.

They shook hands and did the manly hug thing that guys did. People started to pour in the funeral home. Rayne was greeted by many people, a few she knew, but many she did not.

Sonya had positively impacted many people in her fifty-three years of life. Everyone that Rayne encountered spoke highly of her.

The viewing time had come to an end and Rayne was mentally exhausted. She searched the room for her husband to tell him she was going to get the children.

Rayne finally spotted David. He was engaged in a conversation with a gentleman at the front of the room. He'd done a great job of meet and greet throughout the wake. She approached them and she could see David's face light up. He said, "Rayne, hey baby. I want you to meet someone."

She continued to her husband's side. Then he added, "Baby, this is Randy. He's been sharing some of the history of your wonderful city. Randy, this is my lovely wife, Rayne."

The gentleman turned around. Rayne could have crapped herself when the man turned and she was face to face with Randy Thomas. He smiled and said, "Oh David,

Rayne and I go way back. I haven't seen you in a while. Come give me a hug buddy."

She did not move, so Randy moved towards her. "Looking good," he whispered in her ear and gave her a kiss on the cheek. "Sorry for your loss, Rayne. We must get together before you leave. We have *so* much to catch up on. Y'all have a good evening. Nice meeting you David."

Rayne's heart rate rose and it felt as if someone was cutting off her air supply. All she heard was David call her name before she hit the ground.

Rayne heard muffled voices around her, but she could not open her eyes. She was fully consumed by fear. *Is it possible to really be scared to death?* She hoped not as she laid on the ground. *Lord, please don't let this be the end of me. Come on Rayne open your eyes,* she thought, as she felt herself going in and out of consciousness. She could hear David giving instructions to others, but she could not get her body to respond.

As the voices faded, so did she into her subconscious mind. *"How much longer can you portray this perfect image?"* She heard a familiar voice ask. *Daddy…oh damn, I'm dead,* she thought, before everything went black.

Rayne finally woke up to an I.V. in her arm and a tube in her nose. It was like déjà vu as she looked around the small hospital room. Unlike the last time, she woke up alone. The door opened and David came in with a teddy bear and flowers. "Hey baby, you're up. How are you feeling?" he asked.

"I'm fine," she insisted. "What happened?"

"The doctor said you were dehydrated and it seemed as if you may have overexerted yourself at the funeral home earlier," he explained.

"Where are the kids?"

"They are with Bruce in the waiting area. Now that you're up, let me get the doctor. I love you, baby. Please, don't ever scare me like that again," he said, as he moved towards the door.

"I'll try not to, babe," she said with a soft tone.

David returned to the room and the doctor entered shortly after. Rayne could not believe that the face that was greeting her was Dr. Lamb. She was surprised that she was still working at Jackson Memorial. Rayne owed a debt to karma and she was coming hard for payment.

Rayne thought about the night she spent alone in the hospital. Dr. Lamb had been so encouraging; she informed Rayne about support groups and agencies for young mothers in the surrounding areas. Dr. Lamb gave Rayne her personal cell phone number and also spoke to her about options, such as abortion and adoption. She turned out to be very helpful, especially after Rayne took off from Randy's house.

Here Rayne was many years later, possibly in the same room, forced to face her past.

"Hello, Mrs. Smith. I am Doctor Evelyn James, the

physician caring for you this evening. My diagnosis is that you were severely dehydrated and suffered a massive anxiety attack, which resulted in your passing out. Your husband told me that you did not have a history of fainting or anxiety attacks. Is that correct?" she asked, while going through her records.

Rayne hesitated before she replied, "That's correct."

"Ok, your vitals look good but I would like to keep you overnight for observation." she uttered.

"But my mother's funeral is tomorrow," Rayne proclaimed.

"As long as your vitals remain stable, you would be released first thing in the morning. We cannot make you stay, but I highly recommend it, especially with the events you will encounter tomorrow. I will give you all a moment alone to discuss it."

Rayne could see, by the expression on David's face that trying to plead her case about not staying in the hospital was pointless. When it came to either Rayne or the children's health, it was non-negotiable with him. David looked at her and reassured what she had read on his face.

"Rayne, sweetheart, you need to stay. We...I need to know that you are ok. I will be here bright and early in the morning to get you, unless you want me to see if Bruce would keep the kids tonight and I'd stay with you," he voiced.

"No, you can go to the hotel. I'll be ok. Please, let me see the kids before you all leave."

David left and came back with Bruce, Eva, and Evan. Rayne reassured her children that she was ok and loved on them before they departed.

Rayne channeled surfed the t.v. She had just found a *Criminal Minds* episode, when Dr. James came and said, "Well hello Rayne. I was quite surprised to see you here. How are things going?"

"Everything was better than ever until recently." She filled Evelyn in on what she'd been doing, as far as her career and family.

"You have a lovely family; your husband seems absolutely amazing and your twins are adorable," she expressed. "I'm sorry to hear about your mother. Were y'all able to reconcile your differences before she passed?"

"Thank you, we were working on our relationship. We had gotten to a really good place," Rayne confessed.

"That's good. Have you had any or made any attempts to contact the family who received your baby?" she asked with sincerity.

"No, I stand by my decision. I know in my heart that I made the best decision. I'm sure he or she is better off wherever they are, without me," Rayne admitted.

"Well, I am glad you never had any regrets," Evelyn said with a smile, "I wish you the best, Rayne. Make sure you get some rest. My shift is over in less than an hour but you'll be in good hands with Dr. Michaels. By the way, how is Sky? Have you seen or spoken to her lately?"

"Last time I spoke to her was a few years ago, she was in Florida with her own private practice. I'm so happy for her and her success. She's also married with an eleven-year-old named Jordan," Rayne said proudly.

"Good for her. Well, good night old friend. See you in the morning," Evelyn stated, as she closed the door.

*****

Old friend was an understatement. Evelyn and Sky became Rayne's "go to" ladies the months after she left Jackson. Rayne had decided to give the baby up for adoption, after her and Randy's sudden breakup. She also intended to leave her web of lies in Jackson, but that didn't happen. Like her grandmother had told her when she was a little girl, "Tell one lie child and you'd have to tell another and another to cover up the first one." Ironically, that would be one of the few memories she had of her childhood, but it had turned out to be very true.

She also recalled when her grandma told her, "If you lie, you'll steal, if you steal, you'll kill." *Gramps was right about two of the three; hopefully, the third would turn out to be untrue.*

Rayne had contacted Evelyn about her decision to give the baby up. She gave Rayne a point of contact at a local agency, Sheila Evans.

Mrs. Evans explained to Rayne that the process would go quicker and more smoothly for the baby, if she had a family in mind prior to the birth.

Even though Rayne did not want to keep the child; she cared enough for the child not be in the system or stuck in an orphanage. Sky had spoken to her parents and gave them the watered down version of Rayne's situation. Her father mentioned that he had a colleague who spoke about wanting to adopt a baby.

When Sky told Rayne about the colleague, she felt it was the perfect situation. Her kid would have the opportunity to be the next Rudy Huxtable.

At the point of that decision, until then, things had continued to move in the right direction for Rayne. Once she agreed to allow the couple to adopt her baby, Sky's parents suggested that she stay at their plantation home. They wanted to ensure that she and the baby had a safe environment and adequate care.

The Browns had also suggested a home delivery to keep the adoption more discreet. Rayne hesitated at first, but quickly realized she had nothing, not even reliable healthcare. She consulted Evelyn, who conveniently was a certified mid-wife. Rayne mentioned it to the Browns, who, along with the mystery couple, decided to hire Evelyn.

Evelyn was there for Rayne through every emotional rollercoaster. Sky was still in school, so she wasn't there as often, but she was always a phone call away. Living with the Browns was an amazing time for Rayne. She had her own area. It was the old slave quarters of the plantation that the Browns had remodeled as a guest house.

The atmosphere was perfect for an expecting mother. The majority of the food was grown on the property or purchased locally. There was even a gym onsite that she used regularly. Rayne also took advantage of the free time and signed up for an online real estate course.

Real estate was a major part of the plan she had put together for moving forward. Time flew by and she was nine months pregnant and ready to deliver before she knew it.

The day Rayne gave birth was unforgettable. It was like nothing she'd ever experienced in her sheltered life.

She literally felt like she was dying but Evelyn attempted to keep her comfortable with light anesthetics. After twelve hours of hard labor, Rayne delivered at ten-twenty p.m.

Rayne decided that she did not want to see the baby or even know what it was. She did not want to develop any type of attachment whatsoever with the baby. She was just happy to know that she had delivered a healthy baby.

Rayne signed the adoption forms with Mrs. Evans present. That evening, she watched as Mrs. Evans, Mrs. Brown, and Evelyn walked out of the room with the baby. Rayne briefly felt regret but she quickly got over it, knowing she was not in the place to provide what that child needed. She stayed with the Browns until her six weeks was over and Evelyn gave her the green light on her health.

Rayne was packed and set to hit the road when Mrs.

Brown visited her in the guest house and asked Rayne about her plans. Rayne shared her pursuit of becoming a real estate agent, as well as her desire to finish her degree. Mrs. Brown suggested that Rayne stay, until she at least completed her real estate agent certification. Rayne told her she did not want to impose but Mrs. Brown ensured her she would not. Rayne did just that; she remained at the Browns' for an additional year.

When Rayne was ready to leave the Browns' home, not only was she a different woman mentally, but a certified Mississippi real estate agent who had finished her Associates of Arts in Business Administration.

She always wanted to go to Atlanta, so she applied online at Brunson Realty. She did not have any experience but they had a training program set up that would allow her to easily gain experience, as well as prepare her to get certified in Georgia.

The Browns became her family. She was sad to leave them, but she was excited to start her new career. She was very grateful for them and the things they had done. They even blessed her with five thousand dollars to help with the first few months of living expenses. Along with the money she acquired from Randy, she had more than enough to start a new life.

Chapter 7

Thursday May 24th

It was about seven a.m. when Rayne was awakened by the hospital telephone.

Sleepily, she answered, "Hello."

"Good morning sunshine," was spoken from an unfamiliar male voice.

"Who is this?"

"So, you leave Jackson and get with Mr. Big Time David, and you don't recognize the voice of us country folks," he responded.

"Randy?" she asked, but hoped she was mistaken.

"Ding. Ding. Ding. You win the grand prize," he answered sarcastically.

"What do you want?" she questioned with an attitude.

"I want what is mine and I want what you took from me," he reminded her.

"Randy, I'm sorry for stealing from you. I was young,

dumb, and afraid. I will give it back to you, with interest," she negotiated.

"That's all fine and good, but that's not the only thing you stole from me. Where is my child, Rayne?" he blurted out.

"Randy, I lost the baby. I had a miscarriage about a month after I left you. Sorry, your baby is dead," she informed him.

"I don't believe you Rayne and it's mighty convenient. I will let you have that, for now, but understand that it's not over. Maybe it'll be a good conversation for you, me, and your hubby to have," he reminded her.

"First of all, stay the hell away from my family. Secondly, it is not a matter of convenience, it is reality." she responded with a bitterness.

"You know I did not have a personal doctor and was only going to those fakes at the clinic. Not to mention, the stress you caused, which is a factor of miscarriage. Sorry, but I do not have the paperwork from the hospital anymore, so you are going to have to trust me. Third, I will have a check for fifteen thousand dollars ready for you today. That is double what I stole. I advise you to take that and never think about me and that baby again."

"So, you've gotten tough over the years, I see. Ha. You are not running anything Rayne and I am not one of your little pansies. You are still a liar but that's ok. I will take the money because it is mine, but you will not dictate this situation. I will see you later and I will be expecting my check," he stated.

Rayne jumped at the loud echo the phone made from Randy hanging up. Randy was right to laugh at her; she was not tough. She was no longer that spiteful, angry young lady and she truly was afraid he would hurt her and possibly her family. She thought that maybe it was time for her to come clean to David.

Rayne laid in the bed and wrestled with the million thoughts that floated around her. Dealing with Randy was not what she needed at the moment, especially not on the day of her mother's funeral. She was in deep concentration when Dr. James entered the room with a smile on her face.

Dr. James greeted her, "Well, good morning, Rayne. How are you feeling?"

"I'm feeling alright," she answered.

"Well, that's good. Your vitals have been steady all night, so you will be released within the hour," Dr. James explained.

"Thank you Doctor," she replied.

"Rayne? Are you ok?" Dr. James asked. "I know it's been a while since we've last spoke, but I still consider you a friend, Rayne. You can talk to me."

"Ok...it's Randy," she finally admitted.

"He's the almost but not sure for real baby daddy, right?"

Rayne smirked at hearing Evelyn say, "Baby daddy."

"Yes. He showed up yesterday at the wake and I believe he was the trigger of my panic attack. He called me this morning, demanding his child. I told him I lost the baby, which he did not believe. He threatened to include David in our drama. I am trying to right my wrong, but he has become a thorn in my side," she confessed.

"What are you going to do?" Dr. James asked.

"I'm thinking that I'm going to have to tell David the truth; well, my version of the truth. I still have the paperwork you gave me, documenting my miscarriage. Lord, I'm ready to get back to Atlanta," she acknowledged.

"Well, be careful. I'm not sure what this Randy guy has been up to for the last ten years, but I know from what you told me about him in the past, he seemed like bad news. Let's hope he's not dangerous. As far as your husband, be mindful of the lies you tell because they sometimes come back to bite you on the butt. You don't want to lose what you've worked so hard to build," Dr. James reminded her.

The hospital room door opened and David and the children entered.

"Mommy," Eva and Evan screamed in unison.

Evelyn excused herself and left, but her last words lingered in Rayne's mind. *"Be careful of the lies you tell."*

Eva and Evan would not let Rayne stay in her empty blue place. They ran to the side of her bed and kissed her on her cheek; an instant smile came to Rayne's face. David patiently waited until the children cleared out and then gave Rayne a good morning kiss. Rayne felt so loved.

"You're here mighty early Mister."

"The kids and I could not stand being away from you. They were so determined to be here; they made sure I was up early this morning," he proclaimed.

In less than an hour, Rayne was released from the hospital and into the care of her husband. It felt so good to get back to the hotel; it had begun to feel like home. Rayne sat with her feet up and attempted to relax, but she continued to contemplate her situation. She had a feeling that Randy would be at the funeral, so she had to make sure she was in control of the situation and not him.

When David went to take a shower, Rayne looked into her purse to grab her checkbook. She grabbed the one for her personal checking account; the account that David never questioned the balance. The checkbook was next to her pink handled twenty-two caliber handgun. It had become a necessity, being a real estate agent in Atlanta. Luckily, outside of the range, she never had to use it.

David was the one who pushed Rayne to learn how to protect herself. He'd been shooting guns pretty much his whole life, coming from a hunting family. Needless to say, he was an amazing shot. The range had become one of their bonding moments. She especially enjoyed going through the concealed weapons course together. They were a team licensed to kill.

Writing the check was a bittersweet moment. Part of

her was glad to be closing the gap on the situation, but the other part of her feared it would not be enough to be free of the hold that had been on her for so many years.

Rayne was getting the children ready for the funeral when David came out of the bathroom looking delicious. Even though David wore a suit every day; he was extra sharp in that one. He caught Rayne staring and asked, "Do I look good enough to escort you today, my love?"

She wanted to tell him that he looked good enough to do whatever he wanted to do, to and with her that day or any day. But instead she said, "Yes, my love. Hope I don't have to fight the girls."

"Well, my mind, body, and soul are only for you," he said with his million dollar pearly whites. She smiled as she finished getting the kids and herself dressed.

Even though Rayne was dressed conservatively, she had a little sass with her royal blue top and black bottom peplum style strapless dress, fitted black blazer, and black pumps. She applied light makeup and finished her look with lip gloss; then they headed to the home Sonya and Bruce once shared.

When they got to the house, there were two limousines parked in front of the house. The children were excited because they had never seen a limo up close, let alone rode in one. The yard had a substantial amount of vehicles, more than she expected, considering only the immediate family were riding in the limousines.

They stepped out of the Tahoe and walked to the house. The curb appeal of her childhood home was beautiful. Amongst the perfectly manicured lawn were rose bushes, a lemon tree, and a pecan tree; she smiled because her mother always loved pecans. Bruce met them at the door with hugs and kisses.

Rayne admired the upgrades they'd done as she walked in. It was remarkable. They had completely opened up the space with a concept that worked well. Regardless how hard she tried, Rayne could never take off her real estate hat whenever she's in a home.

Bruce introduced them to her mother's first cousin Betty, and Eric's wife, Crystal. Bruce's parents were there as well. Rayne had met them when Bruce and her mother got married; to her surprise, they recognized her.

Rayne's eyes were drawn to an area that was showcased in the living room. There was a sixteen by twenty canvas picture of her mother on an easel stand. It was beautiful; she was all glammed up, like it was a Glamour Shots photo. There were flowers placed around the stand along with a book that people had been writing their fondest thoughts of her mother. Rayne was taken back to her childhood as she looked at all the pictures of herself.

Rayne saw that her mother had her pageant trophies displayed. Looking at the house, you would have never known that they had not spoken for a ten-year period.

Rayne took a long, deep breath. She knew she needed to remain calm to get through the day hospital-free.

Bruce came to her and asked, "How are you doing?

She answered with assurance, "I am doing alright. How are you doing?"

"I'm making it," he said sadly.

"It's going to be ok. We'll get through this together. As a family," she said with a reassuring smile.

He smiled and then said as he started walking away, "Oh yeah, our lawyer would like to speak with us tomorrow morning at nine a.m. It's in reference to Sonya's will. So, I'm going to need you at the house. Hopefully, that won't interfere with your travels home."

"We were planning on leaving first thing in the morning, but that's fine. I'll be here," she confirmed. They loaded into the limousines and luckily, James was smart enough to stay away from her by riding in the opposite limo. David held Rayne's hand the entire way. That little extra encouragement was exactly what she needed. Eva and Evan sat in amazement the whole ride; they were super-duper excited.

When they arrived at Christ First Missionary Church, there were cars lined up and down the block. Rayne spent a lot of her time as a child at that church; she stayed out of trouble by volunteering in ministries, being part of the dance team, and singing in the choir.

She admired the minor upgrades and changes that

were done to the church, as the ushers escorted them into the sanctuary where they were seated on the front pew. There was a slide show presentation playing on the church's projection screen. It was a reflection of Sonya's life. Since the funeral was closed casket, she and Bruce thought that would be less emotional on everyone.

The service was conducted beautifully. Sonya's closest friends spoke very highly of her. Sonya always told Rayne that, "respect would take you further than money any day." Sonya genuinely had a love and respect for everyone, which was showed during the ceremony. She was truly a remarkable woman. Rayne made it through the funeral with minimal tears and no panic attack.

Once the funeral was over, they moved to the burial site, which was located on the church grounds. They released doves and butterflies at the grave site to symbolize her soul flying free. Rayne had held it together, until her mother's body was lowered into the ground. Everything became final at that moment. All she could do was sit and cry as she thought of the wasted years. Sadly, Rayne could not blame anyone or anything other than her own pigheadedness. She had allowed the demons of her past to dictate her actions.

Rayne lived her life every day, like she had control, knowing deep down that she did not. She allowed the materialistic and superficial things to keep her attention. Sonya had raised her so much better than that.

Rayne decided, at that moment of reflection, that she was going to change and was going to live her life the way her mother expected her to. She wiped her final tear and blew a kiss to her mother's casket.

By the time she and her family got to the repast that was held in the church's fellowship hall, she was mentally exhausted. Between the events of the funeral and the anticipation of running into Randy, Rayne was ready to get back to the hotel. She put on the most pleasant face she could muster up and made it through the repast. The ladies of the church did an amazing job with the repast. It was something about the way southern women put together events. The food alone was to die for; Eva and Evan definitely had their share of cake and cookies.

*****

It was early in the afternoon when they arrived back to Bruce's house. They were sitting around the table chatting when Eric said, "Hey Rayne, let me talk to you a few minutes outside."

Without hesitation, she went and sat on the front porch with him and asked, "What's up Eric?"

"I just wanted to have a few minutes alone to talk to you because I'm afraid that now that your mother's gone, I may never see or hear from you again," he spoke with sadness.

"Don't be silly Eric," she said while comforting him.

"Silly? Is that not what you did for ten plus years?" he

asked with a laugh.

"I guess you're right and I see your point," she admitted.

"I've always wanted to ask you what happened. I never could figure out what made you hate us so much."

"Eric, I never hated you. You were always the little brother I never had. You were my baby and still are," she said with a smile.

"Then, why did you leave?" he interrogated her.

"Eric, it was complicated," she replied.

"Like a baby complicated?" he quickly answered.

Shocked by his response, she asked, "What are you talking about?"

"Don't act like you don't know what I am talking about, Rayne. Your face could never hide anything," he implied.

He was right about that. Rayne had always worn her emotions on her sleeve, as well as her face. She could never hide her true feelings about anything, good or bad and it got her in trouble many times.

He continued, "James and I were here that night you were in the hospital. We heard your mom and Dad talking about it when she got home. She was really upset." Eric paused before he continued on. "James said some unforgettable things, but that's not relevant right now. Rayne, I'm not confronting you to make you feel bad or uncomfortable. I just want to have you as my sister again," he revealed. "I want you to know that you are special to me and I'm here. Just don't shut me out again, please. I've missed you."

Obviously, the secret wasn't as secret as she thought. Rayne wondered about the things James said, but she decided to leave well enough alone.

"I always wanted a sister when I was younger. When my mom and dad divorced, Mom told me that it was not going to happen. That's why I was so happy when Dad and Sonya got married; my wish had come true. You always treated me so good, nothing like how James treated me. It was the little things you did, like helping me with my homework, playing Nintendo, and most importantly, listening to me. You always had my back and I thank you for that. I remember that one time when Billy Thomas was teasing me, and you stepped in and told him that you'd put your foot so deep in his butt that he'd be pooping your Air Jordan emblem for a week," he reflected.

They both laughed at the memory. "That kid needed his ass whooped," she said.

"That is so true. He wasn't trying to have you be the one to give it to him though because he didn't bother me again," he responded with a chuckle.

Rayne had not realized that she had made such an impact in Eric's life. She reassured Eric that she was not planning on disappearing again and concluded with a hug. *Step one in project "better Rayne".* They sat on the porch and talked a little more.

Eric filled Rayne in on his life. She found out that he had accomplished a great deal. Eric joined the Marines after he graduated high school. Rayne never pictured Eric as a Marine. He was always a mild-mannered child. He had served two years when he was wounded during a deployment in Iraq. He was one-year shy of completing his first enlistment when he was medically discharged. Prior to his deployment, he met his lovely wife, Crystal, while he was stationed at Camp Lejeune, North Carolina. They met at the gas station near his barracks. She was working there part time while attending college.

They seemed very much in love and were doing well. They lived in Madison, Alabama; Crystal was a kindergarten teacher and Eric was a house flipper. *We may need to do a house collaboration project one day,* she thought when Eric shared that detail. She was proud of her "baby boy". She was glad he had not turned out to be a piece of shit like his brother.

Rayne gave Eric her brief overview of her life. They wrapped up their conversation and rejoined the rest of the family. Rayne enjoyed watching David interact with Bruce and the family. She wished he could have met her mother; she would have loved him. They ate dinner and headed back to their home away from home.

The children were beat; they fell asleep on the way to the hotel. Rayne and David decided to let the children sleep and carried them into the hotel. They undressed them and put them into the bed. Rayne was getting undressed when David came and pressed his body to the back of hers. "How are you doing, sweetheart?" he asked, as he kissed her gently on the back of her neck.

She responded with, "As well as to be expected on a day like today, but I made it through. I couldn't have done it without you by my side."

"That's my job, sweetheart. I want you to try to relax tonight. Take a shower and then I'll give you a nice massage," he said, smiling.

Rayne couldn't determine if David was plotting on her or if it was genuine concern, but either way it was a win-win situation.

She turned, gave him a kiss and said, "Sounds good, I think I need some help washing my back though, if you're up for the job."

"Always," he stated eagerly.

They hopped in the shower and he caressed her gently, as he lathered her body up with shower gel. She thought back to the vow she made to herself to take control of her life from the demons that inhibited it for all those years. She felt like she had gained a rebirth from her mother's death. She was ready to take life head on, but first, she wanted to take control of her husband sexually.

Rayne took the loofah from David's hands and kissed him in a way she had never kissed him before. The passion and strength behind the kiss paralyzed David for a moment. He quickly got it together and grabbed her ass. She caressed every inch of his back as she kissed him. From his lips, she moved to his pecs. While there, she made sure to give his nipples some much needed attention. She kissed, licked, and flicked them with her tongue; he always enjoyed when she did that.

Rayne watched as David tried hard to contain himself. If she could help it, his fight wouldn't last long. She enjoyed the power struggle; the more he fought to "man up", the more she fought for him to lose control.

She continued her journey down his body. Her tongue explored his well-defined abs, as her hand moved to his already tender nipples. Rayne read nothing but pure pleasure all over David's face, and not to mention, his all the way erect penis.

She knew he was anticipating her taking him in her mouth, but she decided to tease him a little. She cupped his balls as she outlined his "V" with her tongue. He let out a moan that let her know she won that round.

Rayne admired his penis. She hadn't seen many in her life, but it had to be the most beautiful one ever. The veins were perfectly placed along his long thick shaft. He had a curve that always made his head look like a soldier ready for battle, fuckable, by any standard. Still with her hands cupping his balls, she tickled his head with her tongue. He braced himself on the shower wall as he moaned softly.

She tickled his balls with her right hand and stroked

his penis with her left, while she tickled his penis opening with her tongue; multitasking at its finest. His penis grew even harder in her hand as she intensely stimulated his body. She listened as he moaned more and his breathing pattern changed. She then grabbed his ass and took him in her mouth with no hands.

He grabbed her head as he got into the rhythm with her. She knew him well enough, sexually, to understand when he was ready to explode; she was not quite ready for that, just yet. She slowed her rhythm and began giving him a hand job.

She looked at him, turned the water off and said, "I want you to fuck me real dirty." They stepped out the shower and he bent her over the sink and fucked her dirty, doggy style. She watched him in the mirror as he commanded her pussy. She bit down on her lip to contain the screams of pleasure; she did not want to wake the children. David grabbed Rayne's hair as he drilled his dick deep inside of her.

She responded with wetness that dripped down his thighs. He wanted more; he wanted her to shower him with her juices. He turned her over and laid her on the counter, where he did his famous hammerhead move. He took his hard dick and hit her pussy with it directly on her clitoris. Damn near instantly, Rayne's pussy opened up and squirted her sweet ambrosia all over them. David loved it; *the messier the better*, he thought.

He hammer headed her until her cum was all over his chest. With her legs in the air, David re-entered her wet pussy and continued with their dirty love. In mid-stroke, David's muscles tightened and his semen moved up his shaft. He got one more stroke in before he pulled out. His cum shot out like a bottle of shaken Cola. It was everywhere, on Rayne, on the counter, and even on the mirror. They both were panting and attempting to catch their breath.

David kissed Rayne passionately and invited her to another shower. They showered and then cleaned up the aftermath of their love. The night ended with David giving Rayne a full body massage and them going to sleep, bodies intertwined.

Chapter 8

Friday May 25th

Rayne tossed and turned throughout the night. She had the same dream she had a few days prior, except this time, as she ran down the street, David was calling her name. She was trying her hardest to find him, but every time she thought she'd made it to him, James or Randy was there instead.

Silently, Rayne laid in the bed and thought for a while before she got up. She knew she needed to get that monkey off her back. Randy had not shown his face at the funeral as she suspected, so she didn't know what he was up to. Part of her just wanted to leave and leave the past in Jackson, but the logical side of her knew it would be like putting a bandage on a wound that needed stitches. She definitely needed to gain control or she would forever be haunted in her dreams.

The clock on the nightstand displayed seven thirty a.m.

She had a little over an hour to get ready and meet with the lawyer. She showered and got dressed. She was in the mirror putting on her makeup when David walked in. He kissed her on the cheek and asked, "Looking good, sweetheart. What's this lawyer look like? Do I need to be worried?"

"Stop being silly. I'm sure he's about a hundred with gray saggy balls," she commented.

They laughed at that image. "You're all the man I want and need anyway," she said while blushing.

"Glad to hear that," he stated.

"This should take no longer than an hour; then we can get on the road. I'm ready to get home."

"Me too, be safe on the road sweetheart."

She smiled and said, "Ok." David always took the protective role when it came to Rayne, one attribute that she appreciated.

Rayne applied her lip gloss and left the hotel to meet Bruce and the lawyer. When she got to the house, she was surprised to see James and Eric's cars there as well.

As she turned the engine off, she wondered, *what did you expect? Mom loved those boys as her own.* When Rayne walked into the house, she was welcomed by the aroma of a good ol' country breakfast; fresh biscuits, eggs, bacon, and grits. She was excited because she had not grabbed anything from the hotel.

She was in the kitchen eating and talking to Bruce

when her cell phone rang. The number was unfamiliar but she answered it anyway.

"Hello."

"Is this Rayne?" the voice asked.

"Yes, it is. Who is this?" she inquired.

"We must go through this every time we speak? This is Randy, man."

She immediately went outside on the porch to take the call. "How can I help you, Randy?" she questioned while snapping.

"Heard about y'all little will reading today, might need more than that fifteen G's you offering. You know, for pain and suffering," he responded.

"Look Randy, fuck you and your pain and suffering. I'm about sick and tired of you!" she yelled.

"Sounds like someone grew some balls overnight. Meet me at the King Motel on 4th Avenue, room three eighteen, when you finish with all your legal mumbo jumbo," he instructed.

"Ok Randy. Just know when that check leaves my hand to yours, we are done, forever. I don't even want you to part your lips and say my name. Capish?" she demanded.

This time, she was the one who hung up on him. Rayne sat on the porch for a few minutes to regain her emotions. *How did he get my number? Better yet, how did he "hear" about the will reading?*

Her thoughts were interrupted by a black Lincoln LS

that pulled up into the yard. She assumed it was the lawyer.

When he got out of the car, she was surprised to see that not only was he nowhere close to a hundred, but he was a beautiful chocolate man, a detail she was probably going to leave out to David.

She greeted him as he reached the porch. He introduced himself as Phillip Brown. "Phillip Brown", that name sounded familiar to her but she could not place him. She escorted him into the house where they all gathered in the den.

Mr. Brown explained to them that her mother had recently made some significant changes to her will. It seemed that Sonya had gotten wise in the finance department over the years. Mr. Brown started speaking on the specifics of her mother's estate.

Sonya had taken a one-million-dollar life insurance policy out, in addition to the one hundred-thousand-dollar policy Rayne and Bruce were aware of. Out of the million-dollar policy, she left one half of it to Bruce and the other half was divided evenly among Rayne, Eric, and James. Naturally, she left the house to Bruce, but to Rayne's surprise, she had a five-acre plot of land on the outskirts of Jackson that she left solely to Rayne.

Mr. Brown went into his briefcase and pulled out two envelopes. He handed them to Rayne and Bruce. Enclosed were personalized letters that Sonya had written.

They all thanked Mr. Brown for his assistance. Bruce was walking him out when he said, "Nice to see you again, Rayne."

Rayne was puzzled at the word "again".

"Where do I know you from again?" she asked.

"I'm Sky's first cousin. I met you when I came to visit Auntie Sarah and Uncle Bill during the time you were staying with them," he explained. She knew he looked familiar.

"You've certainly grown from that boney knock-kneed little boy," she said jokingly.

"Thank you, I think. You looking like life has treated you well. Last time I saw you, you were waddling like a little duck," he said with a little chuckle.

Rayne quickly changed the course of the conversation and said, "Yes, life has treated me very well. Thank you again for helping my mother put her affairs in order."

"You're very welcome. You all have a good day," he stated.

She dodged that bullet but when she looked up, both Eric and James' eyes were glued on her. She sat on the couch and read the letter from her mother.

Rayne,

Let me start this letter off with, I love you dearly. Ever since the day you were born, you've always been my motivation to succeed in life.

I know we've had our differences and haven't always seen eye to eye, but family is very important. Rayne, please remember that. I need you to look after Bruce for me. He loves you as much as any dad would their own child. He's going to need you, especially now that I'm gone. I've been battling with ovarian cancer for several years. It had been in remission until the beginning of this year. Please don't be angry that I didn't tell you. I just wanted to enjoy having you back in my life.

I was so wrong for deserting you that night in the hospital. I was hurt, but that is no excuse for the way I treated you. I had been extremely selfish. I'd regretted my reactions ever since, but I allowed my stubbornness to get in the way. I'm not sure exactly what you went through during those years, but I am sorry for bringing any misfortune to you. I'm at least hoping that I've gotten to see you and those babies before my passing. Continue to grow, baby girl. You have the strength and knowledge to be a phenomenal woman.

Do not sell yourself short; ever. Continue to carry yourself well and be a great role model for your children. I love you very very much, my sweet Rayne. Now, onto some business.

I recently sold my stock market shares. Enclosed is documentation for three trust funds that I'd set up for my grandchildren. I'm sure you are puzzled on why three. Well, I'm not sure whatever came of your first pregnancy. I've *heard rumors and have also drawn my own conclusions, none of which you've ever confirmed or denied.*

I'd hoped that you'd confide in me, but time was not on my side. The first two accounts are in Eva and Evan's names, with you listed as the benefactor. The third is solely in your name, so that you can do with it what is necessary for the first child; if there is a first child. If you had aborted the baby, hold onto it for your next child. I've set it up for the children to receive monthly installments beginning on their 25th birthday.

They should be able to live comfortably with the interest it would have accumulated by then. I love you baby girl, in life and now, in death.

Forever in your heart,

Mom

Rayne was crying like a baby by the time she made it through the letter. Eric had come over with a box of tissues. He sat with her until she regained her composer. She gave Eric a huge hug around his neck; he had grown into an outstanding man.

Her cell phone started vibrating in her lap. When she looked down, it was a text message from David. **Rayne, I love you more than life itself. Know that I'm here. It's me and you against the world babe.** Reading that reminded her of the business she had to handle for it to remain him and her. She texted David back and told him she loved him too and left to meet Randy.

The King Motel was not located in the best area of Jackson. *Just like Randy's trifling self to be in this piece of shit part of town. Glad I have my girl in my purse because that chick may come in handy on the rough streets of Jackson,* she thought as she continued toward the motel.

The streets along the way were filled with bums, drug dealers, drug heads, and prostitutes. It was obvious to Rayne that Jackson streets never rested because it was barely ten o'clock in the morning.

Rayne pulled up into the parking lot a little after ten. Before she got out, she gave herself one of her famous pep talks, *Ok Rayne, in and out. We don't have time for reminiscing and shit. Give him this money and go home to your sexy ass husband and beautiful children.*

She took a deep breath and made her way to the third floor. The Kings Motel had to have been the center of shadiness. The scent of marijuana lingered in the stairwell as she moved up and she saw the remnants of a condom in a corner. *Disgusting. Note to self: disinfect immediately after leaving this joint.*

She arrived at room three eighteen through the sounds of sex, arguments, and laughter. Rayne knocked on the door and moments later, Randy came. He stood there in front of her with a stupid Kool-Aid smile.

"Well, come on in ma'am," he said.

Once Rayne was in the room, he said, "Have a seat." He motioned her towards a worn seat at the corner of the room.

"No thank you," she said.

She didn't have time for that, plus it was disgusting. *That chair has to be the home for thousands of germs.*

Then he asked if she wanted a drink. *What is he trying to do; being all hospitable and shit?*

Getting a little annoyed with his "kindness" she said, "Look Randy, I don't have time for all of this. I'm here to handle our unfinished business, so I can continue my life...without you."

"Your life started with me, Rayne. You did not know how to live until you met me," he corrected her. "So, I don't care how good you got it now with your house on the hill, perfect husband, perfect kids, and what not. You have me to thank for all those things, in some aspect."

In a twisted way, there was truth in his words. He continued, "You were so quick to judge me, but you weren't as innocent as you pretended to be." He moved closer and said, "I know that you lied about the baby."

"What are you talking about Randy?" She quickly interjected.

"Don't play Rayne. I know EVERYTHING, from the baby not being mine, to you not losing it," he informed her.

Feeling a little uneasy, Rayne asked, "What are you talking about?" Rules of the game; first, you must know what they know and then deny, deny, and then deny some more.

"I know about you lying about me being that baby's daddy, about the baby being dead, and about the fact you gave the baby up for adoption," he continued badgering.

Oh shit, does he really know? But how? she thought.

"I know you didn't give two shits about that little girl," he said angrily.

Little girl?

"Randy, where did you get these so called facts from?" she asked.

"Don't insult my intelligence, Rayne. I'm not that same two-bit hustler from back in the day. I have my ways, plus my source will remain nameless," he confirmed.

"Look Randy. I don't care what you know, don't know, think you know, or want to know. I am here for one sole purpose and that is to square up on my unauthorized withdraw from you many years ago. Anything else, save it for a therapist," she exclaimed bluntly.

Yeah, that was cold, but the world is cold; fuck him.

Rayne looked down to grab the check out of her purse when Randy grabbed and slammed her against the wall by her throat. "You cold bitch!" he spat at her.

She tried to fight him off but he was too strong. He continued on his rant, "I hate bitches like you! You think you can call the shots because you got a little money! News flash bitch, you ain't above me! Look at you now, eyes all bugged, wanting some air! Stupid bitch!" He loosened his grip enough for her to gasp for air. "You came in here like you were going to toss me that check and I would mind you, like a little puppy. You are a user Rayne, but I'm going to use you and toss your trifling ass in the street."

She saw the same look on his face as she did on James' face that night he took her innocence. She knew what was coming next. She looked at her purse on the floor that fell from her hand when Randy pinned her on the wall.

This cannot be happening, she thought, as she felt Randy's pants fall on her feet. She screamed as loud as she could before he moved his hand and placed his forearm across her throat. He pulled her clothes and groped her. She fought and kicked, until he applied more pressure to her throat.

Rayne knew she was going to die as she stood there, needing air. She would never see David, Eva, or Evan again, and she couldn't blame anyone but herself.

She saw Randy in tunnel vision and was seconds from passing out from lack of oxygen when she heard a thud. The door opened from a forceful kick. She saw a bright light fill the room.

She heard Randy say, "What the fuck?" and then, he dropped his hold on her. As she attempted to supply some air to her lungs, she heard scuffling and cursing.

A few minutes later, she heard a gunshot. She looked up and saw the smoke from the barrel of the freshly fired pistol. It was just like her dream. She could not focus her eyes to see the face of the man holding the gun. Was she going to be the next victim of this mystery man?

She took another deep breath and attempted to get off the floor. The man moved to help her up. As he squatted to lift her up, she looked and was cheek to cheek with none other than James.

Talk about ironic; she was saved from being raped by her rapist. He looked at her and asked, "Are you ok?"

"Yeah, I'm ok. What are you doing here?" she responded with gratitude.

"I followed you. I heard you on the phone at the house and had a feeling you were about to do something real green," he admitted.

Sweat beads sat on her face as Rayne stood in shock, looking at the blood splatter on the wall. How did she get here? This moment was so far from the happy home she worked so hard to build; a loving husband, beautiful children, and a successful career.

Tears fell as the reality of what just happened swept over her. It was true what they say, "skeletons don't always remain in the closet." Everything she knew was disrupted in the course of a week.

Rayne stood looking at Randy's brain matter on the wall. James had grabbed a towel and began wiping down everything in the room. Her brain was telling her to move but her legs would not; she had never seen anything so horrific before.

She snapped out of her trace when James handed her

the purse. She looked and said, "Thank you, James."

"Don't thank me yet. Let's get the fuck out of here, so you can get back to your family," he said hurriedly.

Surprisingly, when they left the room, there wasn't anyone on the motel landing or any curtains shifting. It was like no one had heard the noise. *Guess one good thing came from being in an area known for criminal activity,* she thought, as she hopped into her vehicle.

Her mind was racing a thousand miles a minute as she drove away. *You need to get it together Rayne. Find somewhere to stop once you get off this side of town. You need to regain your thoughts,* she thought as the phone rang.

She looked down at an unfamiliar Jackson phone number. Hesitantly, she answered, "Hello."

"Where you at?" the voice questioned.

"Who's this?" she inquired.

"James."

She looked around and said, "I'm on Greenway Dr. near an IHOP."

"Ok. Pull in there. I'll be there in a minute," he said and then hung up.

Not even five minutes later, James pulled up in his Impala, hopped out of his car, and jumped into her truck. She had so many mixed emotions at that very moment. She'd spent her entire adult life hating him. She'd never expected to be in the same room with him, let alone him being in her vehicle. *Damn, he saved my life.*

James asked her again if she was alright. She told him yes, which was a big lie; she was a total mess.

James looked and said, "I need you to snap out this shit if you want to continue your life in Atlanta." He leaned in real close, pulled her chin up, and looked in her eyes. "Fuck that dude. I never liked him no way. Look Rayne, I know you can't stand me because I've done you wrong, but know that I have your back. This will never come back to you. I will do whatever I have to, and I mean, whatever, to make sure of that. Ok?"

She nodded and he let go of her chin and reclined in the passenger seat. James sat quiet for a minute and then switched gears in the conversation. He looked at her and sincerely said, "Rayne, I'm so sorry for what I did to you; please forgive me."

Rayne saw a look of sadness on his face. In front of her was a man so far from the monster she'd painted in her mind for years.

"Thank you for saving my life; we're even now," she said humbly.

He smiled and said, "Thank you. Now, tell me about this baby, our baby."

"What are you talking about James?" she asked dumbfounded.

"Cut the bull, Rayne. I knew about the pregnancy from your mom but I never knew the deal with it. Today, I heard what dickhead was saying about the baby. Please, just be honest with me," he said, matter-of-factly.

All she could hear was her mother's voice saying, "*It's time baby girl.*"

She took a deep breath and said, "I gave the baby up for adoption. I never laid my eyes on the baby. I don't know what it was or where the kid is now. Randy seemed quite confident that he knew a lot about the kid though."

"So, how did he find all of that out?"

"I don't know. I was wondering the same thing."

"Who all knew about the baby and the adoption?" he questioned carefully.

"Just Sky, Sky's parents, my mid-wife, the adoption overseer, and me. Oh, and a few of Sky's relatives, to include Mr. Brown," she answered, while counting on her hands.

"That's a nice list so you never know," he stated.

"But what reason would any of them have to tell Randy?" she asked worriedly.

"That's a good question. Too bad we can't ask dickhead now. Have you ever thought about finding the kid?" he questioned.

"No and up until this point, I hated your guts and wished you'd die; that alone was reason enough for me to leave well enough alone," she declared.

"I understand. I wished I'd died plenty of days too. Things hadn't really worked out in my life and I truly believe it was because of what I've done to you. I was so angry when my mom and dad split; that's when I turned to the streets. Those pills allowed me to escape from my reality. When I was high, I felt like nothing or no one could stop me. I was addicted to that feeling. When the high of the pills weren't enough, I dabbed in powder and then rocks. I've done some bad shit in my life, Rayne. After that bid I did for raping that broad, I vowed to never go back to prison. Let me add, I did not rape that girl. That bitch lied about her age. She had the body of a grown woman but that bitch was only sixteen. When her pops walked in on me giving it to his daughter rough and nasty, he thought I was raping her. I guess she was scared and went along with it. I sat in that damn cell for eighteen months over some bullshit. But, it's all good. I've been clean for three years and outside of what just went down, I've been pretty much on the straight and narrow. What doesn't kill me makes me stronger," he divulged without missing a beat.

They left the conversation at that. He gave her a few minutes to get herself together and then told her to go to the hotel, pack, and get on the road to Atlanta. For once, she and James were on the same sheet of music and she did just that.

Chapter 9

James laid in the bed staring up at the ceiling of his eight hundred square foot loft apartment. He had been reflecting on the events of the past few days; he inherited over one hundred fifty thousand dollars, found out that he had a kid out there, and committed murder.

He had been involved in several deaths, but never by his own hands. Surprisingly, the murder was easier to deal with than him being somebody's daddy.

He was thinking that it is time to be serious with his life and settle down. This was a little ironic because he had Ms. Friday lying beside him butt naked and couldn't even remember her name. Only thing he remembered was she gave good head. She was not Mrs. Right but she definitely was a good Ms. Right Now. Also, he thought about Rayne and their conversation. She was content with not knowing what the child was or where the child was, but he could not leave the situation alone. He NEEDED to know. Rayne already had the family that James dreamt of.

He got out the bed and moved to a desk that was tucked in a corner. He grabbed a note pad and labeled a sheet of paper, "Operation Lost & Find". He jotted several avenues he had intended to take to accomplish his mission. Amongst his list was "Sky," "Sky's parents," "Mid-wife," "adoption lady," and "Mr. Brown."

Ms. Friday had woken up and made her way over to him. She hugged his neck and whispered in his ear, "Good morning, handsome. Looks like you're working hard over here. How about you let April take your mind off all that icky work?"

Oh. April, is her name, he thought.

He turned the chair around and asked, "And how do you propose April will do that?"

She said, "By taking her time and making sure that every single inch of your body has some attention."

"Oh yeah?" he asked with a purpose.

"Yeah. That's a promise," she said while kissing him.

"Well, sign me up," he quickly responded.

She led him to the bed where she made good on her words.

James left the list on the desk but he did not leave his determination there. He was going to find his child, regardless of if Rayne liked it or not.

After April left, he turned the television on to the news

and made breakfast.

"...there are still no suspects in the Kings Motel shooting. The victim has been identified as thirty-five-year-old Randolph Edward Thomas. We are asking anyone with any information to call our Crime Stopper hotline at 1-800-158-STOP."

"Damn, that fool," James said as he grabbed the egg carton. He knew his way around the kitchen. He prepared an omelet filled with white American cheese, spinach, tomatoes, and mushrooms, with a side of some biscuits and gravy. Though he and his mother had a strained relationship, she made sure he had the tools to become independent. She would tell him, "Son, you can't depend on no one to provide your needs. You better know how to wash your own clothes and cook your own meals."

James took his plate and cup of V8 Splash to his desk. As he ate, he reviewed and added to the list. He circled Sky's name. He decided the search would begin with her. He didn't know if Rayne had told Sky about what he'd done but he was hoping she would give him something to work with.

His first task would be finding a way to locate her. An idea came to him as he took his last bite. He dressed, grabbed his keys, and left to execute his plan. He was driving along when his phone rang.

"Hey Pops," he said.

"Hey James. What you up to?" Bruce asked.

"I'm out running some errands. How are you doing today?"

"I'm ok, taking it one day at a time. It's setting in that Sonya's gone, now that everyone has left," Bruce responded with a regretful tone.

"I feel you. Well, I'll stop by in a few and maybe we can grab some lunch. How about that?" he asked, hoping to lift his spirits.

"Thanks Son. That sounds good."

"It's cool, Pops. I'm gonna make sure you are straight; I'll see you in a few," he explained and hung up.

He had planned on heading in that direction to check on him anyway. He knew that since Eric lived out of town, he had to be the one to make sure Bruce was taken care of.

James pulled in the driveway of an old red bricked house. He got out the car and walked up to the front door. The old screen door creaked as he pulled it open. He forcefully knocked on the door. He heard a frail voice say, "I'm coming."

Less than a minute later, an older lady with silver hair hanging on her shoulders appeared. "Yes. Can I help you?" she wondered.

"Good afternoon, ma'am. I'm not sure if you remember me, but my name is James. I'm Rayne's stepbrother," he spoke politely.

"Oh yes, Rayne. How's she doing? I heard about her mother passing; very sad," she said with sorrow.

"Yes ma'am. She's doing alright. She left yesterday; she lives in Atlanta now," he answered.

"Good for her," she said.

"Sorry to bother you Mrs. Brown, but I'm trying to get in touch with Sky. I hoped you could give me her contact information. Rayne had misplaced it and I told her I would stop by to get it from you. I hope that's ok with you?" he asked, while crossing his fingers.

"Sure baby, give me a second. Let me grab my address book; wait right there," she said warmly. She closed the door and returned shortly with her book in hand.

James pulled out his notebook and copied Sky's address and phone number. "Orlando, Florida." *Nice change from Mississippi, Sky.*

He thanked her and started to walk off but stopped mid-step, turned and asked, "How's her parents doing?"

"Sarah and Bill are doing well. I'm expecting them to come to visit for the fourth," she mentioned.

He smiled as he walked to his car. Sky's granny helped more than she would ever know. He pulled out his notebook and wrote "Sarah and Bill Brown. July Fourth". *Not bad for ten minutes,* he thought as he traveled for a father-son afternoon.

Chapter 10

One year later

Life as Rayne knew it was wonderful, but it was not easy. Several major events occurred in Rayne's life since she'd left Jackson. The most significant being the birth of her second son, Ethan Jackson Smith.

She found out about her pregnancy shortly after she returned from Mississippi. Her pregnancy had brought the joy that helped her move past the Randy incident. It took her about six months to shake the horror of what happened in that motel room.

Rayne and David's relationship took a hit during her adjustment period but lucky for Rayne, David had related her emotional turmoil to her hormones. She had recently stopped having nightmares and was feeling great. She'd anticipated the police knocking on her door for questioning about Randy's murder, but it never happened.

James held true to his word. He never sent the cops her

way, even after they harassed him because someone saw his car at the motel. He told the officers that he had met a prostitute there and had no knowledge of a murder. The cops must have bought his story because nothing ever came of it.

Rayne had never spoken of the incident to anyone. She went back to the hotel to her family, as if nothing happened. She grabbed her things, went home to her normal life, and did not look back.

Rayne wanted to tell David about the events on several occasions, but the fear of losing him always stopped her. She hoped to bury that memory, like she had done so many others.

In addition to her bundle of joy, Ethan, she turned the dream of owning her own real estate agency into a reality. She worked from her home office during her pregnancy, but had put an offer on a building located in the Stockbridge area. She also was on track to have two agents working for her. Life was sweet.

One Saturday afternoon, while she was laid out by the pool sipping wine and watching her minis play in the pool, her cell phone rang. *Private Number.*

"Hello?" she answered with reluctance.

"Is this Rayne?" a voice questioned.

"Yes and who is this?"

"This is Rudy," the voice admitted.

"Rudy who?" she continued with interrogation.

"Huxtable," the voice said.

Rayne let out a screech. "Oh my goodness, Sky? Is that you? It's been so long; too long actually. How's it going?" she asked, without catching a breath.

Sky answered, "Rayne, slow down. Yes, it is me; yes, it has been too long, and it's been better but I am good."

"What's wrong?" she asked her without hesitation.

"I'm getting tired of Florida. I decided to move to Atlanta. A buddy of mine asked me to help him in his practice. So, I need some assistance from the hottest real estate agent in ATL," she confidently answered.

"Awesome. You know I got you. When are you planning to make the move?" Rayne asked with excitement.

"Jordan gets out of school next week, so I'm looking at the end of the month," Sky stated.

"Well, that sounds great; that's about two weeks. I'll start pulling listings tomorrow. How many bedrooms are you looking for?" she asked, while making notes on her tablet.

"Well, it's just Jordan and me. My husband left last year, so three bedrooms are fine," Sky reluctantly replied.

"I'm sorry to hear that honey," she spoke with sincerity.

"Thanks, but it's ok," Sky responded.

"Y'all can stay here until we can find something," she informed her.

"I don't want to impose," Sky said.

"That's craziness. You're family. I'll have to talk to

David, of course, but I don't see it being a problem."

"Thank you, Rayne. Can't wait to see you."

"Me either. Love you Ms. Huxtable."

"Love you too, Raynee Bear."

Sky hung up the phone and smirked, as she looked at the phone. *I love it when a plan comes together,* she thought.

When it

RAYNES

Clear Skies

II

J. ASMARA

Prologue

SKY

"Do you vow to have and to hold, from this day forward, for better, for worse, for richer, for poorer, in sickness and in health, until death do you part?" *What a fucking joke,* Sky thought as she packed up the home she once shared with her husband.

Sky and her husband shared fifteen years before that bitch took him from her. That was the ultimate betrayal. *Hoes can be conniving these days. He allowed himself to get caught in her web once again, after all we'd built together. But it's ok, they will all learn.*

A smile came to Sky's face as she sealed the last box. On the outside looking in, anyone would be envious of Sky's life; wealthy family, prominent doctor, beautiful home, and an amazing daughter, but on the inside, Sky was a mess. She yearned for love.

All Sky wanted was him; she'd give everything up to be

with him again. It had been a year, but the hurt still stung like it was yesterday.

How could he leave me like that? Sadness slowly began creeping in. *Not today Sky. You got too much to do besides being sad and crying. Put your big girl panties on and let's handle this business. It's only you and Jordan now, so be strong,* she thought as she attempted to get her emotions under control.

Sky moved the boxes from the house to her vehicle. She had decided to only take whatever could fit in her Cadillac Escalade. Her happy times in Florida were no more. It was time for her to move on and produce lasting memories in Atlanta, by any means necessary.

I hope ATL is ready for me because I'm coming through like a storm, taking what I want, starting with Ms. Goody Two Shoes herself. Rayne, you will pay for what you've done to me.

"Karma's a bitch," Sky declared. The words discharged from her mouth like a bullet from a gun as she slammed the hatch closed on her SUV. Sky got on the road and went to her friend, Johanna's, house.

Johanna had opened her home to Sky and her daughter Jordan during the transition. Johanna was the first person Sky met when she arrived in Florida. Johanna had been her real estate agent and the two later became best friends.

When Sky arrived at Johanna's, she and Jordan were

sitting on the couch eating popcorn and watching *The Princess and the Frog*. "Mommy!" Jordan yelled as Sky walked into the den.

"Hey pumpkin. If I didn't know any better, I'd think you'd missed me," Sky said playfully as she hugged Jordan.

Sky then turned to Johanna. "Hey lady. Thank you so much for letting us stay here. I really appreciate it."

"No problem, dear. You know y'all are always welcome. Shoot, it was nice to have some company for a change. This house gets lonely."

"Well, you need to stop being miss independent and start dating, so you can get wifed up by one of these sexy Florida men," Sky said with a chuckle.

"Ha ha, very funny Sky. I'm not trying to hear that. No man is going to be able to deal with me or me with him," Johanna responded. "I'm going to miss you two. Are you sure you have to leave?" she asked sadly.

"I'm going to miss you too sweetie, but there's something I have to take care of and Atlanta is the only place for me to do it. We'll be back to visit though." She smiled and then continued, "You my girl, you're not going to get rid of me that easy."

They both laughed. "Ok. So, you better not get there and start acting brand new on me. So, what are we going to do on your last night?" Johanna asked.

"I was thinking we go to the Marina to get some dinner and then maybe hit Dave and Buster's," Sky said.

Jordan interjected with, "I love Dave and Buster's. Can we go? Can we?"

Sky looked at Jordan and said, "Calm down young lady. You know better than to jump into my conversation."

"Yes Mommy," Jordan said sadly.

Sky, Johanna, and Jordan hit the streets of Orlando and enjoyed their last night together.

JAMES

"Ms. Arnold, is there anything I can do to change your mind?" James asked sensually.

The woman standing before him began blushing like a school girl. Angela Arnold wasn't the typical woman James went for, but his inner whore didn't care.

James was willing to do whatever he had to, to accomplish his goal. He would not allow Angela, with her boyish figure and timid nature, stand between him finding his daughter.

James contacted Sky and she filled in many of his blanks. She confirmed that indeed his and Rayne's child was a girl. She also gave him the adoption agency that was used; Loving Touch Child Assistance Agency.

Once he arrived at the agency, he was informed by Ms. Arnold that Mrs. Evans, the woman who handled the adoption, had moved out of state. He attempted to get information about Rayne's case by saying that the child was his sister's kid and he wanted to find the child to fulfill his stepmother's dying wish.

Of course, like any good agent at any other government agency, Angela was not able to "divulge" such information; hence James being willing to sell his soul for it. Ms. Arnold looked at him and playfully said, "Anything."

He knew he was in for it as he analyzed her. Angela Arnold was five feet even, one hundred twenty pounds, small A cup breasts, not much ass, but cute in the face. She was more conservative than James was used to. *What the hell, pussy's pussy,* he thought.

"Yes, anything pretty lady. Family is important to me. Finding Rayne's daughter is very important. Please help me," he said sincerely.

James was a master of lies. He knew he had her as he watched her begin to blush.

"Well, how about we start with some dinner and we can talk about getting you that information. I just have to lock up here," she said.

Fuck that. I don't have time for all that, he thought as he moved close enough to her for her to feel his breath on her skin.

"That's nice, but I'm thinking about some more instant gratification." He moved centimeters from her lips and then continued, "I'm thinking about laying you down on this desk and fucking you like you'll never forget." He kissed her lips and asked, "How does that sound?"

Angela was in a drunken daze from James' sexual aura.

Though she was a reserved woman sexually and otherwise, she was taken aback by how gorgeous James was. She thought his body looked like it was chiseled by Michelangelo. That was with his clothes on, she could only imagine what he looked like naked. Angela had never felt a sexual connection to anyone like she had at that moment.

Angela knew that she would not be able to fight her burning desire much longer. Her body was saying yes, but she knew that she shouldn't give into temptation. She looked at him and timidly said, "James, I don't even know you. I can't..." her words trailed off as James picked her up and sat her on her desk.

"Angela, live a little. We're both adults here. I promise you will enjoy everything I do to you."

"I can't."

"Can't or won't?" he asked as he spread her legs and put his hand under her skirt. "Why not let me bring you pleasure?" James felt the warmth of her vagina through her panties as he gently caressed her. "Why not let me help you relieve some built up tension?" Angela moaned softly as he continued, "If you 'can't' because you got a man, that doesn't bother me. Plus, I have a condom. So, what do you say?"

James felt her wetness and knew that he had her. Quietly, she asked, "What about the door?"

"It's just before five, I'm sure no one will come in and fuck them if they do. Stop thinking so much and live a little."

Angela nodded her head yes as James applied pressure to her clitoris area. With the go ahead, James snatched her panties until he ripped them. James kneeled down and placed his head under Angela's skirt. He was happy to smell her soft sweet aroma; it made Angela much more inviting to him. He knew he had to hold back no punches, to get her to talk.

He flicked her clitoris with his tongue and Angela gave up her internal fight. He felt her release the tension she had in her legs. James sucked and licked on Angela like his life depended on it. Angela had knocked her inbox tray, tape dispenser, stapler, and post it notes off of her desk onto the floor as she attempted to run from James' tongue. He placed his arms under Angela's thighs and gripped her ass, so she could not run.

To James' surprise, Angela had a sweet taste that was unlike any other pussy he'd eaten, it tasted like candy. What started as a devious plot suddenly became enjoyable for him. He wanted her to cum for him, so he could get all of the sweetness she had to give.

James placed his tongue into her inviting pink hole and circled her outer walls. Angela let out a soft moan, as she laid back on her desk submissively. He kissed her on her clit and asked, "You like that?"

"Yes," she responded timidly.

"Tell me you like me eating your pussy?"

"I like it."

"No. Say you like me eating your pussy."

She hesitated, "I..."

"Don't be afraid. I won't judge you. Tell me you like it and I'm going to make her cum," he said as he moved up toward her face.

"I like when..."

"Go ahead," he edged her along seductively.

"I like when you eat my pussy."

He kissed her and said, "Good. Now I want you to cum for me. Ok?"

"Ok," she said with a soft smile.

James went back to his mission to bring her pleasure like she'd never felt. He placed his middle finger in her vaginal opening. He stimulated her sensitive flesh with his finger as he licked her clit.

Angela moved her hips slowly and James added his index finger and sped up his motions. James then used his thumb to tickle her butt hole. She tensed up when he first touched her there but quickly relaxed as he continued. He used her juices to move gracefully around her virgin hole.

James felt Angela's thigh quiver and he sucked her harder. Angela's moans became less calculated and more free spirited. She let out a scream as she started to cum.

James put his finger in her butt and gently finger fucked her as she came. Her reaction to that confirmed that she had never had that happen to her before. To his surprise, she held her own.

As Angela laid there enjoying the aftershock of her orgasm, James went into his pocket to grab his condom. He looked at her and said, "I want you to rub on her. Make sure she stays ready for me while I put this condom on."

James watched as Angela rubbed her pussy, which turned him on. He enjoyed watching a woman please herself.

"Taste that sweet pussy." She gave him an unsure look. "Suck your finger. I want you to taste your sweet pussy." She complied with his request.

"Good girl. Are you ready for the main event?" he asked playfully.

Angela looked at James, who had taken off his shirt and dropped his pants. She was totally mesmerized. His clothes did him absolutely no justice. James' body was perfect; chest, arms, and abs all tight. Her eyes moved down to his erect penis. *Damn, he's hung like a horse,* she thought.

Angela was so hypnotized by his penis that she forgot about any and all worries she had prior. She braced herself as James entered her. She was taken away by his strokes; they were made with such finesse.

Damn, James thought as he entered Angela. He was taken away by the warmth that surrounded him. He felt a warming sensation throughout his body with his first stroke; her pussy fit him like a glove. *Get a grip James.*

Control this pussy and stop getting caught up in this shit, he thought as he went deeper. Angela let out a squeal. *Got her ass. Keep it up dude,* he thought with a smile. James felt Angela's walls contract and he told her, "Let me know when you're about to cum."

She said, "Ok," softly through heavy breathing.

James got three and a half more strokes in when she said, "I'm about to cum. Ohhhh...damn."

James pulled Angela's body towards him as he went as deep as he could. She screamed with pleasure as she came for James. He watched Angela as she released her fluids. She bit down on her bottom lip and had a seductive expression on her face. He listened as her breathing patterns returned to normal.

He pulled out and told her to get off the desk. "I want you to turn around and put your hand on the desk." He kissed her neck and then went down her back. He rubbed her hot, wet, and ready pussy, before giving her all of him from the back.

Angela attempted to run when he started hitting her corners. Her small frame wasn't ready for what James had in store for her. James was hitting angles that she'd never had hit before. It hurt so good.

As James danced on Angela's G spot, she felt a tingling sensation that started at her toes and traveled through her body.

James heard the change in the tone of Angela's sounds.

"You about to come for me?" he asked.

The shocking feeling felt so good to Angela that she could not speak, so she nodded her head.

"Good. I want you to squirt for me."

I don't know how to do that, she thought. Between her being embarrassed by her lack of experience and her desire to explode, she could not find words to speak.

James sensed her inexperience and coached her along. "When you feel it coming, I want you to push. It's going to feel weird at first, but just trust me." *Ha, 'Trust me', great choice of words,* he thought.

Angela couldn't fight the urge any longer and gave into her overly stimulated body. She skeptically did what James said and pushed with the orgasm. Nothing happened at first and she felt like a fool for trying. She had a second orgasmic shock go through her body and she pushed.

Wetness shot from her body like she was urinating. Once she started, she could not stop. Her legs began to tremble and tears ran down her face from the intensity.

James smiled. "Good girl," he said as he gave her slow deep thrusts. "Go ahead, push it out for me. Give all of it to me."

The warming sensation of her fluids on his skin took him to a euphoric place. The feeling broke through his strong mental barrier and he could no longer hold his seed. His ass cheeks tightened, his back arched, and he freed himself within her. *Thank god for condoms because that definitely would have been a baby*, he thought, feeling accomplished.

James pulled out and gloated over the sloppy mess he'd produced. He gently bit Angela on her ear lobe and arrogantly said, "Now we can go get something to eat, after you look up that information for me."

RAYNE

"Three bedrooms, two and a half bathrooms, two car garage and pool." *Hmmmm...sounds like one to add to the list,* Rayne thought as she stared at her computer screen.

Rayne had been putting together a listing sheet for Sky. She hadn't seen her friend in years and was excited to reconnect with her. She had less than a week before Sky arrived in Atlanta, so the clock was ticking. Rayne had no worries because she did her best work under pressure. She prided herself on her sharp real estate skills.

Things were going well for Smith & Smith Realty. Due to Rayne's growing cliental, she'd outgrown the above the garage apartment she'd turned into her office. In less than a month, Rayne would be in her own building, something she was excited about.

Rayne had not had much excitement in her life. It had been a year since her mother's unexpected death. Rayne went through an emotional roller coaster and dragged her husband, David, along with her.

Rayne knew she was lucky to have a man who loved her

the way David did. She was also aware that if she didn't get it together soon he may get tired of her shutting him out; which was easier said than done. Rayne carried deep secrets; Randy's murder still remained unsolved, she still had an unaccounted for child somewhere, and the lasting disgust she had for James.

Rayne battled with her feelings about James. Though she told him they were even, there wasn't anything that could remove the years of hatred she had felt for him. She'd only seen him once since the hotel ordeal and she remained cordial. Even though she was able to tolerate James, she knew there would never be more to their relationship than her toleration. Ultimately, she was glad that he was true to his word and she was never connected to Randy's murder.

It had gotten to be difficult for Rayne to carry the weight of her past, especially being a mother of three, running her own business, and being a wife. She knew she was going to have to dig deep for the strength to get through.

Chapter 1

Rayne laid in the bed and watched as David packed his suitcase; three and a half days without her king. David was leaving to go to Charlotte, North Carolina to his annual management conference. He was excited to go this time, which confirmed that they were growing apart. There was no way that three days of Power Points and guest panels should excite him, but Rayne could not blame him with how distant she'd been. Things needed to turn around and quickly. They worked too hard for what they had to be anything other than a loving power couple. Rayne got out of the bed and walked behind David. She hugged him and said, "I'm going to miss you baby."

David stopped packing and turned to face her. "I'm going to miss you too Rayne," he said.

"Are you really? I know I haven't been the easiest to live with the past year or so, but I don't want to lose you."

"Baby, I'm not going anywhere."

"Maybe not physically, but I don't want to lose you

mentally either. It's you and me til death do us part...right?" she asked, looking for reassurance.

"Of course, Honey," he responded before pecking her on her forehead.

"Good," she said with a smile.

Rayne knew she had some work to do, but the added reassurance was good. She sat on the bed and helped him with his packing.

"What day is your friend coming again?" he asked as he packed the last item into his suitcase.

"She'll be here on Saturday. I'm hoping we can have some alone time before she and her daughter get here. Thank you for being ok with her and Jordan staying here," she said. "It's been so long since I've seen her; I'm excited."

"I can tell you're excited. Glad something is bringing you some excitement these days," he said with slight sarcasm his voice.

"I'm not sure I like that tone."

"I'm just saying Rayne. I don't want to argue with you, but excitement hasn't been an emotion that I've seen lately. That's it."

She could not argue with him because he was right, so she simply said, "Ok."

Before either could respond, Ethan began crying and Rayne went to his nursery.

Rayne fought back tears as she stood over Ethan's crib. Ethan was created from love; the love that she allowed her past to slowly strip from her. She couldn't even imagine how David felt during her times of confusion.

Ethan smiled as Rayne picked him up. "Good morning honey," she said as he cooed at her.

Ethan was an adorable chunky baby. When he smiled at her, his dimples peaked through his rosy cheeks. Ethan was a perfect mixture of her and David. Rayne was looking into her own eyes as she held him. He had the same award winning smile that David had, as well as his jet black wavy hair.

Rayne carried Ethan to her and David's room. When she approached the door, she heard David say, "I'm about to leave in a few. I'll call you when I get to the airport. Yeah, you too. I gotta go."

Who was he talking to? Sounding all chipper, Rayne thought.

David had just put his cell phone in his pocket when Rayne walked into the room. Her inner voice told her to leave the situation alone, but she couldn't.

"Hey daddy's boy," David said as he reached for Ethan.

"Baby, who was that?" she inquired.

"Huh," he said with a confused look, "What are you talking about, Rayne?"

"The phone. Who was that on the phone?"

"Ted," he responded slowly.

"Ted?"

"Yes, Ted. What's this about?" he asked.

"Nothing Sweetheart," she said.

"It's not nothing. You never ask me who I've been talking to and we are not going to start now," he said sternly, as he walked out of the room with Ethan.

Rayne could hear David in Eva's room telling her that he was getting ready to leave for his trip. Rayne felt awful as she heard David explain to Evan that he wouldn't be gone long.

She had this amazing man that she was interrogating because of her own insecurities. She knew she would have to make it up to him and she had an idea how.

* * * * * * *

James woke in his bed alone. He decided to chill and he did not take the chick he met at the club up on her offer of taking him home with her. *Those hoes always ready to give it up.*

It had been a few weeks since he seduced Angela into giving him the documentation, rather lack thereof, of Rayne's adoption, but for some reason, he could not get her off his mind.

Since their first encounter, James had gone back two different times and knocked her off. She'd become a pro at squirting for him. *Damn, that pussy's good,* he thought as he shook his head.

It was something different about Angela that James could not shake. Everything he'd learned from the streets said that she was not supposed to be the one to have him caught up, but he was.

James found himself thinking about her throughout his day, which went against all his "pimp shit". *Stay focused,* he told himself as he laid there.

He had to find his little girl and he'd done too much work trying to locate her to let anyone or anything get in the way.

He'd been very calculated throughout his process. He knew with a situation that sensitive, directness was not going to be the best method. He thought back to his encounter with Sky a few months prior.

Once James received Sky's information from her grandmother, he'd come to the conclusion that it would be better to speak with her face to face. He hired a private investigator who followed Sky to get her habits, as well as gave James the name and address to her practice, Lakeshore Family Practice.

James flew to Orlando on a Thursday afternoon, with the intent to fly out that Sunday morning. When he arrived, he checked into the Embassy Suites in downtown Orlando. Though he was there on a mission, he wanted to be in the city's center because that was his first time in Orlando. Plus, Jack, his PI, informed him that every Thursday evening like clockwork, Sky went to ladies' happy hour at a downtown bar. *That bar owner is smart. Talk about a way to bring in customers, cause I'm trying to be where the ladies at myself,* he thought as he chuckled to himself.

James showered and got fresh in his Polo shirt, plaid shorts, and leather moccasins.

Jack said that Sky normally arrived just before six o'clock, so James went at six thirty to ensure she'd made it by the time he got there. *Damn,* he thought as he walked into the bar, *Florida hoes are fine.* He scanned the room and spotted Sky with two other women.

Sky was always fine to him, but she was on her grown woman with a fitted top, high waist jeans, and wedge heels. He could not see all of her because she was sitting, but he imagined that she had a side of ass with all that. Her girls were hot too, but it wasn't about anyone but Sky that night.

James sat at the bar in a location that gave him direct line of sight to her. He'd watched her for about fifteen minutes when she got up and went towards the restrooms as well. *Action,* he thought as he got up and went towards the restrooms.

He waited until she was coming out and then "accidently" bumped into her. "Oh, excuse me. I'm extremely sorry," he said.

She responded with, "It's ok", without even looking at him.

"Sky?" he asked in a surprised manner.

She then looked up and slowly asked, "James...is that you?"

"Yes," he said as he reached to hug her.

She responded by hugging him back, so he was sure

Rayne never told her about what he had done to her.

"Oh my goodness. What are you doing here?" she asked.

"I'm here on a little business and heard this was the hot spot on Thursday nights," he said.

"I bet. You trying to come get some Florida ass coming on ladies' happy hour night. You ain't slick," she said with a giggle.

"How you going to call me out like that? And all within two minutes of our conversation," he said playfully.

"Yeah, ok. Well, you looking good," she said with a smile. *Damn good,* she thought as she checked him out.

"Thank you. You looking rather lovely yourself," he said. *I knew that ass was going to be right,* he thought as he checked her out.

"Thank you. Are you alone?" she asked.

"Yes. Why do you ask? You trying to get fresh with me?" he asked with a big smile on his face.

"No," she chuckled and then continued, "I'm here with two of my close friends. If you don't mind being in the mist of female conversation, you can sit with us."

"I would love to. Sure your friends won't mind?" he asked.

"They're always down for a good looking man," she said as she escorted him to the table in the lounge area she shared with her friends.

The look of surprise that was on her friends' faces when

they walked to the lounge area let him know that there obviously hadn't been a man in her life for a while.

"Ladies, this is James. James, this is Linda and Marie," Sky said, once they reached the area.

"Nice to meet you ladies," James said while turning on his charm.

Sky watched as her friends undressed him with their eyes and quickly said, "James is from my hometown. He's actually one of my close friend's stepbrother."

Linda, the most flirtatious of the group, asked, "So, what brings you to our city?"

"I'm here on business," he responded.

"What is it you do?" Linda asked as Marie and Sky both gave her sideways glares.

"Linda..." Sky started.

"What? You know I be wanting to know," Linda said innocently.

"It's ok. I'm a marketing consultant for an interior design agency in Jackson," James interjected.

With a portion of the money James inherited from Rayne's mother, he invested in Eric and they expanded on his house flipping business. With the interior design branch, they'd managed to keep most things in-house and minimized outsourcing work.

"That sounds interesting," Linda said.

James responded with, "Yes, It's been quite rewarding in many aspects."

James and the ladies had great conversation. He found out that Linda was a manager at a hotel and Marie was a broker. Both were areas that interested him. It was a quarter after eight when James looked down at his watch. "Well ladies, I've enjoyed this time but I have a phone conference in less than an hour I need to prepare for. Sky, I'm leaving on Sunday and would love to get together before I leave."

She smiled and said, "That sounds great. I need to be leaving too; I have to get home to my daughter. I'll walk out with you and we can exchange information."

"Great. You ladies have a good evening," he said, looking at Linda and Marie.

James and Sky exited the bar, and he walked Sky to her SUV.

"Nice truck Doctor," he said as he looked at her pearl white Cadillac Escalade. It was sitting on twenty-two inch chrome wheels and the interior was peanut butter color.

"Well, thank you. I love my baby," she said as she reached into her purse and pulled out her business card.

James took it and handed her his. "You free for dinner tomorrow?" he asked.

"I would have to see about getting a sitter, so I'm not sure."

He moved in closer to her as she sat in her front seat and said, "I would really like to see you tomorrow, so please try to make that happen. Ok?"

"Ok," she said as he closed her truck door.

He watched as Sky drove off; he could see her peeking in her rearview mirror. He was confident he struck her interest and his plan to get information was going to come together. *Now, I need to find a strip club,* he thought. His story about having a conference call was better than the ignorance he hoped to get into on the streets of Orlando. James spent his night partaking in the seduction of Orlando's finest.

* * * * * * *

Damn James is fine, Sky thought as she drove away from the bar with a smile on her face. *He will work in my plan. I don't think for a minute that it was an accident running into him, but I'll play his game and see what he wants. I may even let his fine ass help me with this sexual drought.*

* * * * * * *

The next day, James had flowers delivered to Sky's office. It was a bouquet of thirty-six orchards, her favorite according to Jack's tip.

It was shortly after noon when Sky called him. He smiled when he saw the four-zero-seven area code and quickly answered, "Hello."

"Hey. This is Sky. Are you busy?" she asked.

"No. I'm relaxing. About to go get some lunch. Glad you called," he said.

"Thank you for the flowers. They are beautiful.

Orchards are actually my favorite flower."

"Wow," he said as if he was surprised to hear that. "I'm glad you liked them," he continued.

"I did. I was calling to let you know that I am available tonight, if you still want to do dinner."

"Good. I was thinking about going to Kasa Tapas on Orange Avenue. Several people have raved about that place. Would that be fine with you?"

"I've wanted to go there, so that's great. My sitter will be here at six o'clock, so how about I meet you there at six thirty?"

"I'll see you then," he said and then hung up the phone.

James waited outside of the restaurant for Sky. Sky was a punctual woman; it was exactly six thirty when she pulled into the parking lot. James grabbed the single rose that was sitting on the front seat of his rental car and went to meet her at her vehicle.

As he approached the truck, he first saw a smooth caramel leg come out the truck. He watched as Sky stepped out; the form fitting above the knee black dress she wore showcased her nicely put together body. *Damn, she fine as a motherfucker,* he thought as he tried not to get a hard on.

Sky smiled as she saw him approaching and said, "Hi."

He responded with, "Hello beautiful," as he hugged her. He released her from his grips and gave her the rose.

"Flowers twice in one day. If I didn't know any better, I'd think you were trying to romance me," she paused, gave him a sideways glare, and then continued with, "I'm going to have to keep my eyes on you."

"Please do," he said as he placed his arm in position for her to hold on to.

They spent the time talking and laughing about things back in Jackson. Halfway through dinner, Sky opened the door for James to probe her for information.

"It's good to talk to someone who gets it. These Florida folks don't always see things the way I do. I feel so alone sometimes, being so far from home," she sighed and then continued sadly with, "The only friends I have are Linda, Marie, and my friend Johanna."

"You don't keep in touch with anyone from back home?" James curiously asked.

"Other than my immediate family, that would be a no. Unfortunately, my husband did not approve of my past friends. Now, I don't have him or any friends. How is Rayne? I haven't spoken to her in a few years. Didn't even have her number to call her when her mother died," she said.

"She's doing really well. She just had her third child or should I say fourth?" he said, probing her.

Sky almost choked on the water she was sipping when he said that. "Fourth?" she asked.

He concentrated on her expression as he said, "Yes, fourth. She told me about the first child while she was home for Sonya's funeral."

Sky returned James' probing and responded with, "Oh, she did? What exactly did she tell you?"

"That she gave the baby up for adoption and you were one of the select few who knew about it."

"Excuse me for a second. I need to use the restroom," she said.

"Ok. You're not about to bolt out on me, are you?" he asked.

"No silly," she said with a chuckle, "I'll be right back. I'll even leave my keys."

* * * * * * *

Once in the bathroom, Sky stood in front of the mirror and smiled at her reflection. *Try to use me. Ha, he got another thing coming. He's gonna be the one being my bitch; a pawn on my chess board.* She washed her hands and let out a villainous laugh, "It's going to be checkmate to you Rayne."

* * * * * * *

James sat nervously as he waited for Sky to return. He had hoped that he didn't go too fast too soon. She returned to the table as if everything was fine.

"So, obviously you're here about Rayne's daughter. Did she send you?" she asked.

James quickly responded with, "No she would flip if she knew I was asking. It's just my curiosity mainly."

"I see, curiosity. Not only are you attempting to play with my emotions, but also want me to share things that were shared with me by a friend. So, what am I getting out of you and your curiosity?" she snarled.

"That is not totally true. This is an added bonus. I'm here and enjoying myself because I find you to be an intriguing woman, smart, ambitious, and beautiful," he said with a smile.

"Ok. I'll buy that for now. Only because you're cute," she said flirtatiously.

She told him everything she knew and then ended the night by allowing him to test his theory of just how good she was sexually. He never once questioned her motive behind telling him the secrets she held for those many years.

James laid in his bed and knew it was imperative for him to find Mrs. Evans. Sky's information, though helpful, turned out to be a dead end. There was no record that an adoption took place. The only documentation that showed that Rayne had any affiliation with Loving Touch was a log book that annotated Mrs. Evans spoke and met with Rayne on more than one occasion, but nothing else. That was very odd to James because both Rayne and Sky's stories were damn near exact.

But why wouldn't she have documentation of the adoption on file? I need to find Mrs. Sheila Evans because she is the only one with the answers I need.

Chapter 2

Sky enjoyed early morning driving; it was cooler and fewer drivers were on the road. Her intent was to leave at six o'clock but because of her long night, she and Jordan said goodbye to Johanna and Orlando at eight o'clock that morning.

Sky decided to make a stop in Valdosta, Georgia on their way to Atlanta. She heard great things about the amusement park in Valdosta, Wild Adventures, so she decided to make the trip a mini vacation. The park opened at ten o'clock, so they planned for a day of fun.

Sky had a lot on her mind as Jordan slept in the back seat. Her last night in Orlando took a surprising turn once they returned to Johanna's after their Dave and Buster's fun.

Jordan went up to bed as Sky and Johanna lounged on the couch, drank wine, and talked. They reminisced about their time together. Sky told Johanna how grateful she was that she was there for her after her husband left her. That conversation brought her back to the prior conversation they had about Sky wanting/hoping that Johanna found a worthy man.

"Sky, that is not going to happen," Johanna said.

"You can't say that, Johanna. Just be patient. You're a wonderful woman," she responded.

"Sky, I have something to tell you." She paused briefly, looked at Sky, and then continued, "The reason that I know that isn't going to happen is because I'm not attracted to men. I'm a lesbian."

"What?" Sky confusedly asked. "For how long and why didn't you tell me?"

"For years and I didn't want to scare you away. Plus, I haven't had a serious relationship since we've met," Johanna said. "I've never felt the time was right."

"The time was right? That's bullshit Johanna and you know it. There's been plenty of opportunities. We're too close for you to not confide in me, so what's the real reason?" Sky asked, matter-of-factly.

Johanna hesitated, "Well... I never told you because I've developed a love for you beyond our friendship."

Wow. That was not what I expected to hear, Sky thought as Johanna looked at her and continued.

"I've never met anyone like you. You are an amazing woman. I did not and still don't want to lose you as a friend, but I do have lustful fantasies about you."

Sky did not know what to say. She sat in silence as

Johanna's news marinated in her mind. The truth was, in the past, Sky had some curious lustful thoughts of women that she was too ashamed to even admit to herself.

Finally, Sky was able to formulate something to say. "I had no idea...wow. It doesn't change anything between us. I've always been strictly dickly, so I can't understand being pleased by a woman."

Johanna smirked at Sky's final statement and responded, "Don't knock it until you try it. I think the delicateness that a woman brings to the sexual experience is fulfilling. I've never felt the type of fulfillment with a man as I do with a woman. It's sensual."

"So, you're saying that a woman can please you better than a man?" Sky asked with her lip twisted to the side.

"Yes, that has been my experience. Think about it; who knows a woman's body better than a woman? I know you've been with men and you've laid there thinking, 'What is he doing?' or you had to coach him around the pussy. I know I had until I experienced being with a woman."

Johanna sat back in her chair and sipped her wine as if she had relived the moment and continued, "She was so gentle but yet aggressive, vulnerable but yet confident. She helped me to develop a whole new outlook on sexuality. I never thought about being with a woman, but almost seven years later, and I'm happy with my decision to explore myself. Like I said, don't knock it until you try it."

Johanna's last words replayed in Sky's mind as she and

Johanna talked and drank more wine. They called it a night just before midnight.

Johanna retired to her room, relieved that her confession wasn't going to change her and Sky's relationship. Suppressing those emotions though was a different story.

Sky had showered and was sitting on the bed wrapped in a towel putting lotion on her legs when there was a soft knock at the door.

"Come in," she said softly.

Johanna stepped into the bedroom. She closed the door and stood by it. Johanna was a Columbian beauty, five feet nine, curvy, dark hair, and stunning green eyes.

"As I laid in my bed, I realized that I may not see you again," she said with her sultry accent.

Sky quickly interjected, "You will."

Johanna moved towards the bed and stood beside Sky. "It's easier said than done. You're moving almost ten hours away, plus you're a workaholic."

Sky laughed and then agreed with her. "Yes, but I'm going to have to make time. You, Linda, and Marie are too special to me to just forget about y'all. So, don't worry."

Hesitantly, she responded with, "Let me make love to you Sky. Let me show you indescribable pleasure." She sat next to Sky, looked her in her eyes and said, "No strings attached, just let me share my passion with you. You don't have to do anything." She inched closer to her and continued, "All I want is for you to clear your mind and give your body to me freely."

Sky sat there speechless. Johanna looked at her and said, "Lay down and let me finish putting lotion on your body while you think about it."

Sky hesitated and Johanna continued, "Go ahead mami, you know I won't hurt you."

Sky laid down on the bed with the towel still wrapped around her body. She laid on her back nervous and unsure as Johanna's small freshly manicured hands applied lotion to her feet. She gently massaged Sky's feet as she placed lotion between her toes.

"Close your eyes," Johanna said softly as she moved to her legs.

Once Sky closed her eyes, she relaxed and enjoyed what was happening versus who was doing it. She enjoyed the much needed attention that her feet and legs had received. From her legs, Johanna moved up and applied lotion to Sky's arms, caressing her gently.

Sky had become so comfortable that she did not flinch or worry when her towel fell and her naked body was exposed.

"You're so beautiful," Johanna expressed softly while she admired every inch of her. "There's nothing more exotic than the curves of a woman's body."

Johanna continued her pursuit to elevate Sky sexually. She massaged the lotion all around her torso.

When Johanna reached Sky's breasts, she showed special attention to her Hershey Kiss nipples. She osculated her lips on Sky's perky breast, just enough to ensure that the sexual tension was being reciprocated. Johanna listened as Sky moaned faintly.

Johanna told her to turn over and quickly put lotion on the back of Sky's body. She got moist as she looked at Sky's perfect, peach shaped ass. Johanna tapped Sky gently and instructed her to raise her ass up. She had a burning desire to taste Sky's sweetness.

Johanna admired Sky's peach from the back before she spread her legs. She kissed both of Sky's cheeks and then Johanna laid on her back and slid her head between Sky's legs.

Johanna looked up at Sky's cherry blossom as she took in the essence of her flower. She dreamt of the day that she would be able to feast on Sky's sweetness.

Johanna took her tongue and danced around Sky's garden. She precisely used her tongue to make love to Sky, who moaned with her every motion.

Johanna placed her mouth on Sky's vagina as she would a mouth. It excited Sky because no one had ever kissed those set of lips like that before. The feeling was a delightful one. For the first time in a long time, Sky had been free from her own thoughts.

The warmth that moved through Sky's body was like that of a gas furnace. Her wetness flowed like a river and showered Johanna.

Johanna smiled as she felt Sky's legs twitch. She wanted to amplify Sky's orgasm. She nibbled on her clit as she used her fingers to entice the already blossomed flower. Sky responded to her touches with hip rolls and wetness.

Johanna slid from in between Sky's legs. She faced her butt and kissed her all over both of her cheeks. She caressed them as if they were the finest silk.

Johanna could not get enough of Sky; her body was picture perfect. She spread her cheeks and used her tongue to navigate around her anal opening. Sky squirmed from the jolting sensitivity of that area. She had only had her "salad tossed" one other time in her life and it had been too long to relate the feeling she felt.

Johanna showed the same dedication to her ass as she did her pussy shortly before. Sky's juices ran down her thighs as Johanna unwound her uptight wound up freaky side.

Johanna fingered Sky's pussy while she licked her ass in a slow motion. She started with one finger but increased with the thrust of Sky's hips from enjoyment. Johanna had four fingers deep in Sky's vagina when she hit her g-spot. Sky's body released her fluids in a continuous flow. Sky did not want to wake Jordan, so she bit down on her pillow to muffle the gratifying sounds.

Sky allowed Johanna to please her sexually for nearly an hour. Her every movement was precise and calculated, from the use of her mouth to the use of her hands, the orgasmic experience was mind blowing.

Afterwards, they laid and had a much needed conversation where Sky reassured Johanna that everything between them was good. As far as Sky was concerned, it was better than good actually.

Sky smiled as she reflected on her night. She always thought being with a woman consisted of pelvis bumping, carpet munching, and dildos, so far from what she and Johanna shared. Johanna was right. "Don't knock it until you try it."

* * * * * * *

"Thank you Mrs. Everson. I am looking forward to meeting with you and your husband today to finalize. You have a great morning. See you soon," Rayne said before she hung up the phone. *Another step in the right direction for Smith & Smith Realty,* Rayne thought with a smile on her face.

Early morning business always made Rayne happy. Too bad her marriage wasn't going as well as business was. David left the day before and their conversations had been forced.

She'd decided to fly to Charlotte to surprise David. His mother was more than happy to watch the children. Rayne barely got the words out of her mouth before she said, "yes".

First, she needed to clear her "To Do" list, which

included calling Sky, pulling some listings, and meeting with the Eversons.

Bill Everson was a local city official. She was meeting with him and his wife to finalize their purchase and discuss offers for their fifty-five hundred square feet home. As early nesters, they downsized to a twenty-five hundred square foot home.

Mrs. Everson had reached out to Rayne because she'd come highly recommended by a few of her peers. Rayne never asked who she was recommended by and remained both grateful and flattered; her hard work had finally paid off.

Rayne browsed her laptop and looked through listings as she grabbed her cell phone and dialed Sky's number. The phone rang and rang; Rayne was about to hang up when Sky finally answered.

"Hey girl. I was about to hang up. What you up to?" Rayne asked.

"Nothing, just driving. I had the radio blasting, getting my Ariana Grande on. I love that song *Problem*," she said.

Rayne chuckled at the image of Sky singing and dancing to that song. "Isn't she like twelve? Where are you on your way to?"

"She is not twelve. I decided to leave Orlando a few days early. I heard the Wild Adventures amusement park was nice in Valdosta. So, Jordan and I are on our way to Georgia to spend a few days, have a little mommy daughter time before I come to Atlanta. I decided to send Jordan to Mississippi for the summer, so I can get settled in. Mom and Dad are meeting us tomorrow, and they're taking her back with them," she said proudly.

"That sounds nice," she responded. "David and I need to take the kids on a vacation. Can't remember the last time we did something like that. Tell your parents I said hi when they get there."

"I understand. We hadn't done anything for real since her father left. So, I figured it was about time. What are you up to?" she asked.

"Well, I'm meeting with some clients at noon and then I'm going to fly to Charlotte to surprise my husband," she said.

"What's he doing in Charlotte?" Sky asked curiously.

"He had a three-day conference there," was her response.

"I can't wait to meet him. It's great that you're still 'honeymooning' after all this time," Sky said.

Rayne sadly confessed, "I wouldn't exactly say that. I'm actually going in attempts to bring some spice back to our relationship. It's been a rough year. Sadly, I can't even blame anyone but me, but I'm confident in our love."

"I know what you mean. I'm sure you'll work it out. The Rayne I know always gets what she wants, taking no prisoners," she said.

Rayne chuckled before she responded with, "Yeah, but

a lot has changed since those days. So, are you still coming on Saturday?"

"Yes, I should be there early afternoon, probably around two," she said.

"Awesome. I'm so excited to see you. I've pulled a few house listings for Monday, if that's not too soon," Rayne said enthusiastically.

"That's fine. I plan to meet with Gary at nine o'clock on Monday to get my office situated and what not. I will be free other than that," she said.

"Great. Well, I hope y'all have fun in Valdosta. I'm about to pack for my trip and then get to that meeting. Talk to you soon," she said with giddiness in her voice.

"Ok. Talk to you later," Sky said before she hung up.

* * * * * * *

"Mommy, what's wrong?" Jordan asked with concern as she looked at Sky.

Sky snapped out of her trance and said, "Nothing Sweetheart. Why'd you ask that?"

"Because you put your mad face on after you got off the phone," she said softly.

"I am not mad Sweetheart, I was just concentrating," she quickly responded.

She had to do better with her emotions. She couldn't even hide her feelings from a child. Jordan was content with her response and went back to playing her video game.

You have to get it together. She'll get hers in due time;

just be patient. That thought brought a smile on her face. With that, she and Jordan continued to Valdosta for their mini vacation.

Chapter 3

James patiently waited at a small coffee shop in downtown Jackson. Jack approached his table as James sipped on his iced coffee.

"Hey Jack. What's up man?" he asked as he stood and shook his hand.

"You know...the usual," he responded with a smile.

James skipped the small talk and asked, "What you got for me today?"

"Mrs. Evans has moved around quite a few times since leaving Loving Touch a few years ago."

Jack paused briefly as he watched the creases in James' forehead form. He swallowed and then continued, "Unfortunately, I haven't found her current whereabouts as of now, but I'm vigorously working on it. Her husband died last year and it's said that after his death, she'd been traveling. I did find an address on her daughter, so I'm working that angle. Hopefully, it does not turn out to be a dud."

"Ok. What about the midwife?" James asked.

"I'm still working on the midwife/doctor information," he said as he watched the grimace look on James' face. "There turned out to be more Evelyns working in the medical field than I thought. Are you sure that there's no way to get her last name?"

"Yes, I'm sure. Keep on working and I'll try a few things on my end," James said with some irritation his voice. "Don't let me down, Jack."

He and Jack said their goodbyes and went their separate ways.

James had hit a brick wall with his search. He knew he needed to locate Evelyn and Mrs. Evans, if he wanted to find his baby girl.

Sky hadn't answered any of his recent calls. They had no contact after their steamy night in Orlando, so he didn't know what was up with her.

He sat in his car feeling defeated. He'd started to obsess about finding the kid and he was not going to allow anything get in his way. He dialed Sky's number as he sat there in hopes of her picking up, but no such luck. He instantly got pissed off and hung up the phone.

I might need to pay Ms. Sky another visit, he thought as he drove off.

* * * * * * *

Sky looked at her phone as James' number flashed across her screen. *This dude needs to stop calling me. He's served his purpose; a good fuck and much needed information about little Ms. Perfect,* she thought as she silenced her phone.

She and Jordan had made it to Valdosta and had just finished eating breakfast. "You ready to hit the park, pumpkin?" Sky asked an overly ecstatic Jordan.

"Yes ma'am!" Jordan exclaimed.

"Alright, let's go then," Sky smiled and said as the left the local McDonalds.

* * * * * * *

"Ladies and gentlemen, we have started our descent. In preparation for landing, please make sure your seat backs and tray tables are in their full upright position. Make sure your seat belt is securely fastened and all carry-on luggage are stowed underneath the seat in front of you or in the overhead bins. Please turn off all electronic devices until we are safely parked at the gate. The flight attendants are currently passing around the cabin to pick up any remaining trash," the lead flight attendant said over the intercom.

Rayne sat in her seat and waited for her airplane to land at Charlotte Douglas International Airport. Her meeting with the Eversons went wonderfully. She was super excited because her commission from that deal was more than enough for her down payment for her new office building. Celebrations were definitely in order.

Rayne could not wait to surprise David. She had contacted David's secretary Amanda and got his schedule.

Amanda also had Rayne added to the room so that she could get a key. She had a little over an hour before he got out of his final session for the day. Just enough time to shower and get sexy, she had her lingerie and pumps on deck.

Rayne picked up her rental car and drove to the Embassy Suites that David was staying at. She admired the lavish lobby as she walked to the front desk. The desk clerk, Cindy, was very pleasant and helpful. Rayne got the key and made her way to David's room in no time. She followed the signs until she reached room two ten.

Rayne inserted her key and walked inside of the room. She entered into a sitting area that smelt of clean linen. She closed the door behind her and moved to the door that separated the bedroom.

As she placed her hand on the door knob, she heard David's voice. *Damn. He must of got out early.* He was on the phone but the only thing she could make out through the door was, "I'll be ready."

Rayne knocked on the bedroom door and said, "Housekeeping."

"Thank you, but my room has already been cleaned," David said quickly.

Rayne knocked again and repeated, "Housekeeping."

David moved to the door and sternly said, "I said my room has already been cleaned," as he opened the door.

He was stunned by Rayne being on the other side of the

door. He asked, "Rayne, what are you doing here?"

"I came to surprise you," she said as she entered the room.

Confused at his reaction, she said, "Not quite the reaction I played in my mind."

"I'm sorry honey. I'm just very surprised, that's all," David said as he kissed her on the forehead.

"Baby, I miss you. I do not like what's going on with us. I want what we had back. I came here for us to have a little alone time. You messed up my plans a little bit by being here already, but I have something special planned for you. I'm going to take a shower first."

David smiled as Rayne grabbed her toiletry bag and went in the attached bathroom. She turned the water on and was humming a tune when she heard a faint knock on the suite door.

She paused and processed the sound through the sounds of the water hitting the ceramic tub.

Rayne stuck her head out of the bathroom door. David was not in the room.

"Nah. I'm not gonna be able to do it. My wife came up and surprised me," she heard David say.

"Well, more ass for me. I'll get one in for you. See you tomorrow," she heard a man respond.

Rayne closed the bathroom door. She got in the shower and pondered on what she had heard. *More ass for me? Who was that guy and what was David up to?*

Rayne finished in the shower and wrapped herself in a towel. David sat up on the bed when Rayne entered the room. "Was that the door I heard?" she asked as she approached him.

"Yes. It was one of my colleagues from group."

Rayne dropped her towel. "I hope I didn't mess up your plans for the evening," she said, fishing for answers to the questions in her mind.

David caressed Rayne's exposed breasts. "Uh-Uh," he stuttered.

He thinks he's slick tryna get me worked up, so I'll stop with my questions. Damn it feels good, but it's not going to work, she thought.

"Uh what?" she said softly as she embraced the stimulation to her breast.

"The guys are going to Club Nikki's tonight...it's an adult club," he said trailing off. He stopped rubbing Rayne's breasts because he expected her to flip out.

Rayne was very protective of what was hers and he'd never spoke of any desire to see any other woman naked. Shockingly, she was intrigued and also relieved that was what was behind the conversation and David's nervousness. "So, you'd planned on a lap dance tonight?"

Unsure of how the conversation would end, he nervously said, "I hadn't even thought about it. The only reason I agreed to go tonight was because everyone from my group is going and they were giving me a hard time about not going."

"Do you want to go?"

"Huh?" he asked with a confused look.

"Do you want to go?" she repeated.

"You're standing in front of me butt naked and asking me if I want to go see some other women. That reads 'set up' all over it," he said with a laugh.

"I'm serious. Let's go."

"What?"

"Let's go. Tell the guys you'll meet them there," she said as she bent down to pick up her towel.

Still confused about what had happened, he said, "So, you're telling me you want to go to a strip club?"

Rayne looked at him and said, "I want my not so uptight husband back and I am willing to provide whatever pleasure needed to get that. We are a team. I don't want you to ever feel that you cannot share something with me. *That's pretty ironic coming from me, seeing as I have so many secrets.* I love you David."

"I love you too Rayne," he said with a sideways stare.

Rayne continued her humming as she unpacked her bag. Within thirty minutes, she was ready to step out with her husband in a gray shirt, black jeggings, and black booties. Rayne handed David the keys to the Toyota Corolla and they held hands as they made their way to the parking garage.

Rayne filled David in on her meeting with the Eversons

on their way to the club. He was very happy that things had played out the way she had hoped they would. Their night was off to a good start.

Though Rayne was nervous about how the night would go, she was hopeful for her marriage. She would rather be there with her husband as he watched some ass and titties versus him going out and screwing some woman. *Lord, I hope I hadn't pushed him there already with all of my foolishness.*

They arrived at the club. Rayne was surprised at the set up because it was not like the stereotypical strip clubs that she'd seen on television. If it had not been for the half naked women on the stage, she would have taken it for an upscale lounge.

Rayne watched the expressions on David's colleagues' faces as she and David walked toward the table they were seated at. They had no idea what to expect because David didn't tell them that Rayne was accompanying him.

David immediately went into introductions; "Hey fellas. I want you to meet my lovely wife, Rayne. Rayne, this is Mark, Arthur, Dean, Chris, and of course, you know Ted." Each stood and shook her hand.

"Nice to meet you all. Hope I'm not busting up your fun," she said with a smile.

They all chuckled nervously, still trying to feel out the situation.

Shortly after they sat down, a topless young lady came

with drinks for the gentleman. The waitress looked at Rayne and David. "Hey sugas. Can I get you something to drink?"

"I'll take a rum and coke," David said.

"I'll take a coke minus the rum," Rayne replied.

She could not help but blush while talking to the woman, who had the most beautiful breasts that Rayne had ever seen. *She had to have bought those because they're perfect.*

The guys loosened up around Rayne after about thirty minutes with the help of liquor and naked girls. Rayne sat in amazement as she watched the girls perform their tricks on the pole. *They'll make any woman think she could be Diamond from "Players Club",* she thought as she chuckled to herself.

The young lady named Mercedes who came onto the stage was absolutely beautiful. She had a stunning exotic look to her. She looked like she was mixed with black and either Japanese or Korean. She totally had a dancer's body; thick thighs, toned butt, and small waist. She wore a rhinestone embroidered outfit with thigh high boots.

Rayne watched as Mercedes got to the top of the pole, flipped upside down, slid down the pole, and flipped into a split. The dollars were thrown and she had not even removed any of her clothes. David tried not to look so amazed but hell, Rayne was quite impressed.

Rayne had just got her buffalo wings when the dancers

began making rounds around the room. Rayne caught Mercedes' attention and she made her way to their table. "Hello gorgeous. You want a personal dance tonight," she said flirtatiously.

Rayne smiled and said, "No, thank you. I actually would like a dance for my husband." Rayne pulled a fifty out of her purse and handed it to her. David's face lit up a kid on Christmas morning.

Mercedes smiled at Rayne. "Which one of these lucky guys is your husband?" she asked.

"This handsome one right here," Rayne said, doing her Vanna White hand motion.

Mercedes told David to move his chair away from the table and commenced to dancing for him. Rayne watched as Mercedes moved sensually on, around, and in front of David. Rayne admired her athleticism as she got into a handstand and clapped her ass in David's face.

Mercedes gave David a kiss on the cheek when she was done. She looked at Rayne with her almond shaped pretty browns. "Can I talk you into a dance beautiful? Free of charge, it would be my pleasure," she said with a wink. That was when Rayne realized that she was being hit on.

Before Rayne could respond, Mercedes slid her chair back and began dancing in front of her in a different manner than she had for David. She rolled her hips in a hypnotizing rhythm.

Rayne never thought she could ever be turned on by a

woman, but Mercedes had her in a trance. She was giving Rayne's hormones a run for their money.

Mercedes ended Rayne's dance with a kiss as well, but hers was on the lips. As Rayne sat there staring into Mercedes' eyes, her lips parted slightly and Mercedes put her tongue into Rayne's mouth. It was like there was no one else in the building at that moment. She was brought back to reality when Mercedes backed away and whispered, "Thank you beautiful," into her ear.

All eyes were on her at the table. Mark turned to David and said, "Man, your wife is awesome. I wish Kim was half as cool as Rayne."

David smiled and said, "Yes, she is something."

Rayne sat there and tried to regain herself. She'd never been turned on by a woman before, she needed a minute. She leaned close to David and said, "I'll be right back. I need to go to the restroom." David nodded his head as she got up and headed to the restroom.

Rayne leaned on the counter as she took a deep breath. She had just reapplied her lip gloss when she heard the restroom door open. She gave herself one last look over before she stepped off toward the door.

When she turned, she was face to face with Mercedes. "Oh. Excuse me. I didn't even see you," she said.

"It's ok lovely," was her response.

Mercedes took a step toward Rayne. "You're so damn fine. I haven't seen a woman with your natural beauty in a minute. I know you're married but I can't help but be forward with you…I want to taste you."

Shocked by her response, Rayne said, "Excuse me?"

Mercedes moved closer and invaded every bit of Rayne's personal space. "I said I want to taste you. I'll bet you taste like strawberries. Or maybe even honey." She kissed Rayne with an intensity that was even higher than the first kiss.

It was something about that woman that instantly heated Rayne down to her soul. She'd gotten so into the kiss that she had closed her eyes. She did not open her eyes until Mercedes pulled her lips away from hers.

She said, "Don't make me beg," licked her lips and added, "I will though."

"I-I," Rayne started.

Mercedes placed her finger on Rayne's lips. "Shhhh, just one quick taste for now."

She turned Rayne around and placed her hands on counter. She whispered, "Just relax lovely," in her ear and then pulled her jeggings down.

"Look at that ass. Beautiful," she said as she looked down at the black laced thong that separated Rayne's cheeks. She placed her hands on each of her cheeks and spread them.

Mercedes used her tongue and shifted Rayne's panties to the side. She moaned as she tasted Rayne's sweet indulgence; it was even better than she expected. She wanted more. She knew she only had a small window to please Rayne before David would miss her, so she made every second count.

Mercedes buried her face in Rayne's pussy and devoured her fruit until her nectar dripped on her tongue. She watched the sheer enjoyment that was on Rayne's face as she came. Mercedes slurped up the wetness. Then she popped her on the ass and pulled her clothes back up. She kissed Rayne on the back of her ear.

"I hope that was as enjoyable for you as it was for me, lovely."

She pulled a card out of her purse and gave it to her. "I put my personal cell on the back for you. Call me sometimes. I want to taste you again. Think about me tonight when you're with your husband. Until later, lovely."

And just like that, she was gone.

What the hell did you just let happen, Rayne? You haven't let anyone but David touch you in all these years and you crossed that line tonight...and with a woman. But it felt so good.

There was no way she could tell David of the acts that took place in that bathroom. She fixed herself and went back to her husband like nothing happened.

David and Rayne hung out with the guys a little while longer and then went back to the hotel room, where they made love with the level of passion they had prior to Rayne becoming an accessory to murder.

The evening they shared together was what they needed

to begin bridging the gap between them, so David thought. David's arousal came from the fact that he was happy to have his friend back for the evening while Rayne's fire was brought on by the one and only Mercedes, whom she thought about the entire time she and David made love.

Chapter 4

James woke to the clapping of pots and pans. He spent the night; he had never spent the night at any woman's home. He rubbed his head as he laid in Angela's bed. *You fucking up man. You getting too comfortable with this broad.*

Angela had become his constant. With all the mess and disappointment in his life, he enjoyed the calm she brought him.

It had been a few days since his and Jack's dead end conversation. He told himself that he would go see Angela to see if she knew anything else about Mrs. Evans and the adoption. That was a lie though, honestly, he just wanted to see her.

James had never allowed himself to feel anything for any woman before. He had no idea what love was. His love only went as far as loving the pussy he got and loving the dick he gave them. He actually had conversations with Angela that he paid attention to.

James got up and sat along the side of the bed. *Am I*

falling in love with this girl? His cell phone rang as he sat there battling his mind.

Jack. He better have something for me before I fire his ass.

"Hey, what up Jack?"

"Morning James. I got some news for you. Can we meet at the spot?" Jack asked.

"Ok. How about one o'clock? I got a few things I need to take care of right quick," James replied eagerly.

"Cool. See you then boss," Jack said before hanging up.

James had some things to take care of alright...with Angela. He got out of the bed and made his way to the kitchen that Angela had scented with maple sausage.

James watched Angela from the doorway with his maple sausage exposed. She was in front of the counter in a t-shirt and panties with plates in her hand. Angela turned and smiled when she saw him.

"Hmmm. Now that's a sight first thing in the morning," she said.

He walked up to her and said, "Oh yeah. Hope it's a good one."

"Always."

"Looks like you're doing your thing in here."

"Well, it's the first time you didn't run out of here like secret squirrel, so I figured I'd make us some breakfast."

James laughed. "Secret squirrel?"

"Yep," she said, joining him in laughter.

"I'll show you secret squirrel," he said as he spun her around and bent her over the counter.

James grabbed her by the ponytail she had hanging to the back and pulled her towards him.

"You want me to fuck you real good this morning?" he asked.

"Yes!" she yelled. She no longer was that timid mouse he first encountered in her office. "Fuck me daddy."

"Then I need you to slide them panties off if you don't want them ripped."

"Rip them," she said seductively.

He smiled, let her hair go, and ripped the panties off of her. By then, he was fully erect and ready to go. He slid the plates to the side and pushed her face down on the countertop.

Angela let out a sexual grunt as he entered her. Her erotic screams of pleasure filled the space as she threw her ass at him. The past few times they'd done it, Angela had given James a run for his money. He'd created a sexual beast and he enjoyed every minute of it.

"I'm coming daddy," she announced. James knew that meant she wanted him to go deeper.

He fought the urge to explode as her walls contracted around his manhood. He slowed his strokes as her wetness engulfed the space between their bodies.

James got lost in her intensifying noises. He could not contain himself anymore. He got another stroke in before he pulled out. He shot his thickness up and down Angela's back and ass.

James watched Angela as she smiled; she'd become a fan of him showering her with his love. He popped Angela on the ass and grabbed the towel that was lying on the counter and wiped his sperm from her skin. *That's that all natural G style moisturizer.*

They got cleaned up and then sat and ate breakfast. Along with the sausage, they had scrambled eggs and orange juice. He appreciated Angela's hospitable gesture.

James ate and got going to prepare for his meeting with Jack. He had to get home to shower and change.

His mind raced as he drove. *I wonder what Jack got. Hope it's something good to jump start this search cause I'm tired of these dead ends.*

He chilled and listened to the radio the remainder of his hour trip to clear his mind. He knew he was done when he didn't mind driving the distance to see Angela, especially when there was so much local willing ass in Jackson. *Was it time to hang up the pimp jacket?*

* * * * * * *

Sky rustled around the sheets of the hotel bed. She was deep in an emotional dream.

The dream started off sweet. She was in her Orlando home with her husband. They spent the entire day together. They were in the middle of a romantic candle lit dinner gazing into each other's eyes when his phone rang.

He spoke briefly and ended the conversation with "I'm on my way." He pulled Sky close to him and told her he had to go in to work.

"Don't leave me," she whispered softly.

He kissed her as he held her deeply in his embrace, "I have to go honey. I'll be back, trust me."

"No, you won't," she repeated over and over again as she watched him leave.

Though she was dreaming, the emotion was very real and came through as she sighed in her sleep.

The scene changed and she stood in a foyer of a strange house. She heard sounds of a heated conversation coming from a back room. She made her way through the unfamiliar house toward the voices.

The door to the room was slightly cracked open. When she peaked in, she saw Rayne, but could not see who she was talking to.

"You said you were going to handle it, now you telling me you can't leave her. You need to get rid of her but for now, come handle me," she heard Rayne say as she motioned slowly with her index finger.

When the man came into Sky's line of sight, she was shocked to see it was Randy. *What?* she thought as she watched Rayne and Randy in that room.

She got angry as she watched Rayne push Randy down and straddle him. *Where is her husband? She's never satisfied with what she got. Skanky bitch!*

Sky busted in the room with her fist balled and snuck Rayne with a punch to the face before Randy grabbed her. "Sky, what the fuck?" he said as she struggled to get free.

Sky was still fighting when she woke up with her fist still clenched. She was panting through a panic attack. *Why am I dreaming of them together? Did they really have something going on before he got killed? Breath Sky, you can get through this.*

Sky grabbed her purse and got her bottle of Lithium Carbonate. She got out of the bed and got a bottle of water from the refrigerator. She poured the pill from the bottle and realized that she only had five pills left.

The closer Sky got to going to Atlanta, the more frequent she had been taking the medication. Good thing her therapist was also her friend, so she could easily get a refill.

The pill kicked in almost instantly and her breathing returned to normal. *You have to get a hold of these emotions, Sky. Now you're having crazy ass dreams. Get it together girl.* "Ok," she said and went into the bathroom for a shower.

She felt like a million bucks after her shower. The Lithium Carbonate had mellowed her out and she was ready to take the day head on. She woke Jordan and they enjoyed their final day in Valdosta.

* * * * * * *

Rayne woke to David getting ready for his final day of

conference. She walked into the bathroom and found him fixing his tie in the mirror.

"Good morning handsome. Let me get that for you," she said as she reached for his tie.

"Thank you baby."

"When does your flight get in tonight?"

"At seven o'clock, I think... what time is your flight?"

"It's at one o'clock. So, I'm going to get some breakfast and hit the mall before I go."

"Don't have too much fun," he said with a smirk. "Try to show some restraint."

That statement went further than just shopping because she had Mercedes on her brain.

"I'll try," Rayne said.

David grabbed his briefcase and kissed Rayne on his way out. "See you later baby. Have fun shopping. Love you."

"I love you too," Rayne said feeling guilty, but not guilty enough to halt her plan.

Rayne went into her purse and pulled out the card Mercedes gave her. She turned it over and the name Imani was written above a "seven-zero-four" phone number. *Imani, nice name.*

Rayne laid on the bed and looked at the phone as she contemplated her decision to call her.

What are you going to say? This is the woman whose coochie you dominated last night? It's eight o'clock in the morning; is it too early to call? Should I text first? Stop acting crazy and just dial the number. She took a deep breath and dialed the number. A woman answered.

"Hello."

"Can I speak to Imani?"

"Speaking."

"Hi. This is Rayne."

"Who?"

Feeling a little played, she said, "Rayne, from last night."

"Ohhh. Lovely. How are you beautiful?" she said, making Rayne at least feel relevant.

"I'm doing good. Hope I'm not disturbing anything."

"Nah. I'm just lying in the bed. So, I was on your mind?"

"I must say, you did leave a lasting impression in my mind."

"Good. That's what I wanted to do."

"Oh yeah?"

"Yeah. Now, tell me a little about yourself."

They talked and talked. Rayne shared about David, the kids, and her career.

Imani shared that she attended the Art Institute of Charlotte for fashion design and wrote poetry in her spare time. In addition to her being artistic, Rayne found out that she was also an athlete. She did gymnastics from elementary to high school, hence her performance the night before. Imani was the modern day Diamond.

"I need to see you again lovely," Imani said seductively.

Rayne was very intrigued by Imani but still unsure about the situation. "I don't know about that."

"There's no need to fight it. I know you felt the same connection that I did. That's why you called me. I respect your situation and am not trying to disrupt it. You're a special woman, Rayne. I thought so last night, but after spending damn near an hour speaking to you, now I know it."

"I don't know what to say. I-"

"Say that you will at least have breakfast with me. I'll be patient. You're too special for a one-night stand."

Rayne blushed and said, "Ok."

"Great. There's an IHOP on Woodlawn. Are you familiar with the area?"

"No, but I have a GPS."

"Ok. How about ten-thirty?"

"Alright. See you there."

"See you lovely."

Rayne showered, got dressed, and packed her bag. She knew she was playing a very dangerous game, but the thrill was like none she had experienced. She loved David and could not see her life without him, but Imani was a breath of fresh air.

Imani was already seated when Rayne got to the IHOP. She smiled as Rayne walked toward her. Imani stood and greeted Rayne with a hug and kiss on the cheek. "Nice to see you beautiful, "she said.

"You too," Rayne said quickly, blushing. Imani pulled Rayne's chair out for her. "Aren't you polite, Ms. Imani," she said playfully.

Rayne fought her urges to let Imani have her way with her. Throughout their conversation, Rayne flashed back to their sexual escapade. She yearned for Imani to place her mouth all over her body, but she heeded David's warning of "show restraint".

The ladies talked non-stop. When Rayne looked at her watch, it was almost noon. "Imani, I have to leave for the airport."

"Ok lovely," she said as she grabbed the check that waited patiently on the table during their conversation.

"You don't have to pay for my breakfast."

"No, I don't have to, but I want to. I'm just glad you graced me with your presence."

Imani walked Rayne to her rental. "Rayne, I'm going to Atlanta in a few days to do an open mic poetic review. It's at Club Envy downtown. I would love it if you came and checked me out."

"I'd love to."

"I'll text you the information when I get it."

Imani sent Rayne off with another one of her moving kisses. *So much for the mall,* Rayne thought as she drove toward the airport.

* * * * * * *

Jack was already waiting when James arrived at the coffee shop. Their greetings were short and they got straight to business.

Jack started the conversation with, "I've located Mrs. Evans. She is at St. Mary's Care Home in St. Mary's, Georgia."

James said surprisingly, "A care home? I thought she was traveling."

"It turned out that she was not traveling and had been in St. Mary's due to post traumatic stress after she witnessed her husband get murdered. The traveling story is the story that her daughter, whom I haven't yet located, had everyone to believe."

"Damn, her husband was murdered?"

"Yeah. They got mugged and in his attempt to protect her, he was beaten to death. It was done by a young kid as his gang initiation. It was really brutal from the details I got. She's coherent but I'm not sure how helpful she'd be."

"I got to try, this is too important to me not to."

"I understand. Here's the address along with the visiting hours."

"Thanks Jack."

"No problem boss man. I'll be working on the daughter."

They shook hands and left the coffee shop. James instantly began developing his game plan for his departure to St. Mary's.

Chapter 5

The Smith house was quiet. David had taken the kids to the park and Rayne was making final adjustments to the guest bedroom for Sky, whom she expected within the hour.

Rayne bounced around happily. Not only was she happy to see Sky, but her life was on the up and up. Since returning from Charlotte, the intimacy between her and David had improved tremendously (Imani being a vital part in that). She and Imani communicated a lot verbally, and she had finalized her lease agreement for her office space. Rayne had no worries.

Imani's poetic showcase was that night. Rayne mentioned to David that she heard about it and wanted to go, never mentioning Imani. He'd agreed to watch the children so that box was checked, she only had to convince Sky.

Rayne finished cleaning and was relaxing with a glass of wine when there was a knock on the door. She placed her wine on the table and went to the door.

Sky was standing there when she opened the door. "Heyyyyyy," Rayne sang as she reached out and hugged her.

"Come in, come in."

Sky looked around and said, "This is a nice place you have. I hope I can find something half as nice as this."

"You will. Seeing as you got the right woman on the job."

Rayne gave Sky a tour of the house, which ended upstairs in the guest bedroom.

"Your house is beautiful. Thank you for accommodating me. Where are the kids?" Sky asked.

"David took them to the park. I expect them any minute now. You need help with anything in your car?"

"No, for now I'm going to just bring out my suitcases and I'm going to get a small storage unit for the rest of the stuff."

"I have some storage space in the garage, if you didn't want to spend that unnecessary money."

"Ok. If you don't mind."

"Of course I don't mind. Have you eaten lunch yet? I'm about to make some sandwiches."

"I'm good, I grabbed something on the road, but I could use something to drink though."

"We have apple juice, water, orange juice, milk, and wine."

"Wine sounds good but I'll take some apple juice."

"Coming right up."

Just as Rayne handed the apple juice to Sky, the door opened and she heard "Mommy mommy. Whose cool truck is that?" Evan asked, running into the kitchen.

"It's mommy's friend Sky's."

"Mommy, we had so much fun!" Eva ran in shouting.

David appeared shortly after with Ethan in his arms. Rayne attempted to tame the chaos. "Hey, everybody come here. I want y'all to meet my friend Sky." They all made their rounds.

"Nice to finally meet you, Sky. I've heard so much about you," David said with a hug.

Eva and Evan were ecstatically talking about their park adventure while Rayne, Sky, and David were talking. The last thing Rayne heard was Eva say to Evan, "Let's go build a tent in my room," before they disappeared up the stairs.

David turned to Rayne. "I'm going to go give Ethan a quick bath because he had a ball playing in the sandbox."

"Ok honey. I'll have lunch ready by the time you are done."

"Ok babe," he said with a kiss. She watched him as he and Ethan went up the steps. When she turned, Sky was staring at her, "What's that look for?" Rayne asked.

"Well, you all bubbly and stuff. Looks like your surprise visit paid off."

"Guess you can say that," she said with a smile as a thought of Imani crossed her mind. "Do you like spoken word?"

"Actually, I do. There was a club in Orlando I'd gone to a couple of times that did spoken word nights. Why?"

"A friend of mine is performing tonight and I wanted to go. That is if you wanted to go."

"Sounds like fun."

Rayne smiled at the thought of seeing Imani again. She made her family turkey sandwiches as Sky went out to her truck to get her bags.

* * * * * * *

Sky hurried out to her truck because she felt some rage brewing within. *So much happy in that house. Happiness that I can't have now. It's not fair.*

Sky got her pills from her purse and took it before she grabbed her bags. *Then there was four.*

She picked her phone up and dialed her friend Phyllis aka Doctor Barnes' number. She did not answer, so Sky left a voicemail. "Hey Phyllis. This is Sky. I'm down to my last four pills and I need a refill. Please call me or text me when you send it in. Thank you. Talk to you soon."

With only four pills left, it was imperative that Phyllis got back in touch with her quickly, especially with her increased episodes.

Sky got her things and went back in the house. On her way to take her bag to the guest bedroom, she passed the bathroom where David was giving Ethan a bath.

David was talking to Ethan as he splashed the water.

Sky checked David out as he kneeled beside the tub. *Damn, he is fine.* She was admiring his toned glut muscles when he noticed she was standing there.

"Oh. I didn't realize you were there."

"Didn't mean to startle you. I enjoy watching a man being involved with his children. It's a beautiful sight," Sky said wrapped in his gorgeous smile.

"I agree. I wouldn't trade the time I spend with my children for a million bucks. I don't understand these men who don't take care of their children." David took Ethan out of the tub and started drying him.

"He is so adorable. He looks like a happy baby," Sky said.

"He is, he hardly cries and is almost always smiling."

"Well, let me take this stuff to my temporary home. Thank you for opening your home to me. I greatly appreciate it."

"No problem."

Sky walked away with an extra bounce in her hip. David was a pawn in her chess game with Rayne.

* * * * * * *

"Hello. I'm here to visit Mrs. Sheila Evans," James said to the counter attendant. The young lady behind the counter grabbed a binder labeled **Visitors**.

"And what is your relation to Mrs. Evans?"

"She's my auntie."

"I will need your driver's license." James grabbed his

wallet and handed her his license as the young lady continued, "Mrs. Evans has not had any visitors other than her daughter. I'm sure she'll be happy to see you, Mr. Black."

No visitors. Poor lady, James thought as he read the young lady's name tag *Tiffany*. She placed his information on the visitor's log and handed him his driver's license back.

"She's in room one nineteen, which is the last room on the left."

"Thank you very much, Ms. Tiffany."

"You're very welcome."

James walked to the room thinking of how to approach her as delicately as possible. He gently knocked on the closed door before opening it. He saw an older black woman with salt and pepper hair sitting in a chair looking out the window. She had a sad expression on her face.

"Mrs. Evans?"

She didn't even turn his way. He continued, "My name is James Black. I'm a friend of your daughter's. She told me to come check on you."

She slowly turned and looked at him, "Angie sent you to check on me?"

"Yes ma'am."

Lord forgive me for this lie.

She gave a soft smile. "Come sit down son," she said motioning to an empty chair. She looked at him. "You're very handsome."

"Thank you Mrs. Evans."

"You and Angie an item? Hope I can have some grandchildren as good looking as you."

He laughed. "No, we're just friends."

Hope this lie doesn't bite me in the ass. Don't even know that broad.

"Oh ok. Well, I appreciate you coming to check on an old hen. Just sitting here looking at the garden and reminiscing on some good times."

"It's a beautiful day. How about we go out to the garden and you tell me about those good times? Do they allow that?"

She said "Yes" as she stood from the chair. James looked at her more closely; she could not have been more than fifty-five but her mental state had aged her. She slumped as she walked and had a drab look about her.

Mrs. Evans grabbed James' arm and they walked to the attendant desk to inform them of the intent prior to walking out of the building to the flower garden. They walked a while and then ended up on a bench that was in front of a fountain.

She spoke about her husband mostly. She told James how she and her husband were high school sweethearts that lost contact when he joined the Army. She got pregnant by another gentleman and reconnected with her late husband years later. She spoke of their adventures together and also of their retirement plans. Mrs. Evans started drifting into sadness as she spoke.

James quickly changed the topic in attempts to not rattle her fragile mind. "So, Angie told me you were a social worker, that you did adoptions. Tell me about that."

"Yes. I had a very fulfilling career. I helped many couples find children to complete their families. The joy those children brought them was priceless. Don't get me wrong, there were some rough times, but I enjoyed it."

"Do you remember a case with Rayne, Evelyn, and the Browns?"

She looked up in the sky as if someone was whispering in her ear, "Oh, yeah...Rayne was such a sweet girl. It's a shame how they tricked her."

Tricked her?

"Who?"

"Acted like they were helping her but in actuality, she was helping them."

James sat confused as she continued rambling. "Money make people think they are superior sometimes. At least that little girl got a chance to live the good life. A life better than Rayne could have provided as a young mother." She smiled, as if pleased with that thought.

James didn't want to push her fragile mind, but he had to know more.

"Who has the child? Why is there no records documenting the adoption?"

"I can't, I can't," she repeated, while getting a little agitated. "Take me back to my room please."

"Ok. I didn't mean to upset you, Mrs. Evans."

He walked her back to her room. She went and sat back into her chair and stared at the garden; the peaceful look returned to her face.

"I'm about to leave, Mrs. Evans. I really enjoyed spending the afternoon with you. Can I come back and visit you again?"

She looked at him and smiled. "That would be nice. Next time, bring Angie with you. She needs to get out of that office sometimes. She works too hard. I hate that she's so much like me. Don't want Loving Touch to take over her life like it did mine, especially with her having a friend as handsome as you. I'm going to need grandchildren."

What the fuck? James stood in shock as he realized his Angela and her Angie were one in the same.

* * * * * * *

Rayne and Sky sat at the table in Club Envy, which was packed. They were between sets and the house band was on stage playing *Killing Me Softly*.

"This place's pretty nice," Sky said, looking around the dimly lit room.

"Yeah, it is nice," Rayne said as she looked down at her phone.

She'd gotten a text message from Imani asking if she had made it to the club. She texted back, **"We're here and**

sitting in the second row of tables in front of the stage."

"So, has your friend been doing poetry for a long time?"

"Honestly, I'm not sure how long she's been doing it."

"Oh" Sky said, pausing as Imani walked towards their table.

Imani's beauty threw both of them for a loop. She floated across the floor looking like a goddess. She wore a black and gold mid-drift shirt, gold hoop earrings, gold armlets on both arms, a long black maxi skirt that accentuated her curves, and black leather strappy sandals. Her makeup was flawless with smooth gold tones that enhanced her olive toned skin and hair that was neatly pulled in a bun on top of her head.

Rayne stood to greet Imani when she reached the table. "Hello lovely," Imani said before kissing Rayne on the cheek. "Glad you were able to make it."

"Me too," Rayne replied grinning. "Imani, this is my good friend Sky. Sky, this is Imani."

"Hello Sky," Imani said, extending her hand.

"Nice to meet you, Imani. I love your outfit," Sky said.

"Thank you. You ladies look lovely tonight as well," Imani said as she stared at Rayne.

"Thank you," Rayne and Sky said in unison.

Imani smiled and sat with Rayne and Sky, never taking her eyes off of Rayne. "I go on next, after Kaci. I'm a little nervous because she's amazing," Imani said nervously.

"You'll be fine," Rayne said.

"Is this your first time performing here?" Sky interjected.

Reluctantly, Imani turned her sights off of Rayne and acknowledged Sky. "Yes. I've had my sights on Envy, but Rayne gave me a little extra motivation to come and check it out."

"That's Rayne for you, always so helpful," Sky replied snootily. "Excuse me, I need to use the restroom."

"Want me to come with you?" Rayne asked.

"No, I'm fine. I'm sure Imani needs a few more minutes of your time to shake them butterflies," she said before walking off.

Once Sky was out of sight, Imani grabbed Rayne's hand. "All I've been thinking about is seeing you, my lovely. I hope I get to see you later, so I can taste your goodness."

"I don't know about that, especially with Sky being with me."

Imani moved closer to Rayne and said, "I'm sure you can find a way to give me a few minutes. I have to go get ready to go on stage. Think about it."

She kissed Rayne on the lips and walked away. Rayne sat and thought about her next move.

* * * * * * *

Sky came from the bathroom and halted when she saw Imani kiss Rayne. *I knew there was something going on with that one. Hmmm...this may work to my advantage. Instead of seducing David, I'll let Lil Miss Perfect ruin her own marriage, with my guidance of course.* A devious smile came to her face as she moved through the crowd back to her seat.

"Hey everybody, let's give it up for the band...thank you all for coming out tonight. Let's show some love to our next mistress of poetry. Welcome the not only talented but also beautiful Kaci." The crowd went crazy with their applauses as Kaci came onto the stage looking like an African queen. Her chocolate skin was radiated under the light. Her honey blonde dreadlocks framed her almond shaped face.

Kaci began to speak with such passion that Rayne did not noticed that Sky had returned to the table. "So, what's the deal with your girl Imani?" Sky asked.

"What do you mean?"

"You know what I mean. A blind man can see she has a thing for you. So, what's going on?"

"Well..." Rayne paused and hesitated before continuing, "I met her when I went to Charlotte. David and I went to a strip club with some of the guys from the conference. She's a stripper at the club. I've never been attracted to a woman before but from the first time I laid eyes on her, she intrigued me. She gave me a lap dance that ended in an electrifying kiss."

"So, all of this is about a kiss? Must have been one hell of a kiss, cause that girl is gone," Sky interrupted.

"It didn't stop there. When I went to the bathroom to

regain my composure, she came in and tongue kissed my *girl* like her life depended on it. Sky, it was mind blowing. That night, David and I made love with so much passion, but I was thinking of her the whole time. You probably think I'm awful."

"No, I don't, you're human. Have you told David?"

"God no," she exclaimed.

"He hadn't questioned the sudden change?"

"I told him that it was because I missed him and what we had. I don't know what to do. She wants to see me tonight."

"So?"

"So what?"

"Are you going to see her?"

"I'm here with you. Are you ok with that?" Rayne asked, sounding as innocent as a child.

"You're my girl. Why wouldn't I be? But you are going to have to figure out what you're doing, and probably be honest with David about your feelings and curiosity of those feelings. Maybe you should convince him to allow you to bring her into your bed. He may enjoy that. You'll never know until you talk to him."

"Ok. You might be right," Rayne said.

"*...I sit inside myself looking out as the scene unfolds from within pure heart wrenching pain and anger seems to consume every molecule of my being why must life deal such unfair blows...*"

Sky watched Rayne as Kaci's words spoke to her spirit. She smiled as she thought of Rayne's demise.

Chapter 6

James took a deep breath before getting out of his car at Angela's apartment. He had not spoken to her since his visit with Sheila, her mother. He felt betrayed ever since he spoke to Sheila. He had slowly been falling in love with Angela and felt that she should have told him, especially with the increased amount of time they'd spent with one another. *Karma's a bitch, James.*

He knocked on the door and was greeted with a hug and kiss from Angela. "What's wrong baby?" she asked when he did not reciprocate her affection.

"We need to talk," James said as he entered the apartment. He stopped in front of her sofa and turned to face her. "So, I went to visit Mrs. Evans on yesterday, at St. Mary's Care Home." He watched as her expression changed.

"She had a lot of interesting things to say, the most being that you are her daughter," he paused, waiting to see if she would attempt to justify her omission of that fact. When she didn't, he continued, "So, you don't have anything to say?"

"Why did you go visit her? Wait, how did you find out she was there?"

"I told you when I met you that she was a big part in me finding the kid. So, why did you keep that from me?"

"First off, don't act like I've been the only one withholding information, because I never believed that sister's kid bullshit. I don't see you doing all of this for a child that's supposedly your sister's. Second, someone like you doesn't just fall for someone like me without motive. But, I'll play your game."

She moved to the sofa and sat down. "Well, as you know, Sheila is my mother. She's been in St. Mary's since my step father was killed. I didn't tell you or anyone else, for that matter, to protect her. I'm hoping she recovers from this so that she can return to her normal life, so I don't want people to look at her as if she's crazy because she's not. If you can't understand that, then too fucking bad."

"Ok. I understand that you're protecting her. I don't expect anything less than that from you, but we've been kicking it for months now."

"Exactly, we've been 'kicking it'. You come beat it down, chill for a few, and leave. The other night was the first time you spent the night, so don't go there with that James. I'm just some willing ass for you."

"First off, you're not just some willing ass Angela. I'm really feeling you. Come here."

They both sat on the sofa. James turned her face toward his and said, "Look, I've never been in love before and really don't know what it feels like, but I know I feel things with you that I've never felt with anyone. You are special to me and I'm not just saying it to say it. That's real. Yes, I haven't been one hundred percent open with you, but the streets have taught me to protect myself and never let anyone get too close. So, how about I start this honesty thing off. You were right, the kid is not just any kid, and she's my kid. I just found out about her last year and I've been trying to locate her for the past few months. I'm not perfect but I'm me, so I hope that's enough for you."

Angela smiled at his final statement. "Well, I appreciate your honesty. I suspected it was something along that line. Mom told me about that case about five years ago when I started in social work. It was more so a warning because that case haunted her."

Angela paused briefly before she continued. "You want something to drink?" she asked as she got up and went to the kitchen.

"No. What do you mean by that?" James asked hesitantly.

Angela went back to the sofa with a wine glass and a bottle of Chardonnay.

"The reason why there is no record of the adoption is because she took a payment from the Browns to not file the adoption through the agency. It haunted her because she said the young lady did not know the plotting that had taken place behind her back. It tore my mother up regularly that she did something as unethical as that, but she did it for me. My father walked out on us when I was eight years old for his secretary, so she had to raise me alone. She didn't reconnect with my step father until I was sixteen. That money put me through college. I owe everything I am to my mother, fifty thousand dollars' worth. That is why I would lie to protect her."

"Wow, fifty thousand dollars is one hell of a secret. So, who has the kid? The Browns?"

"I'm sorry but I really don't know. All I know is they were the money bags of the adoption. Mom even told me they put the mother up during the pregnancy to ensure that she didn't change her mind."

"Thank you for confiding in me. You won't regret it. My intent is not to hurt you."

"Good. Now, can I get that hug and kiss you didn't give me earlier?"

"Of course," he said grinning from ear to ear. "Is that all you want from me?"

"Since you're asking, how about you bend me over the couch and eat my pussy from the back?"

"I aim to please," he responded as Angela giggled the way that drove him crazy.

* * * * * * *

Sky was in the kitchen sipping on some tea when

Rayne came down that morning.

"Good morning Sky."

"Good morning."

"Yes, it is," Rayne said cheerfully. "What are you getting into today?"

"I'm going to meet Gary for brunch so that we can go over how we are going to work my integration into the practice. What about you?"

"I have an appointment with my interior designer to get the office ready to go for my grand opening. I lined up some listings for us today, if you have some time."

"That sounds great. I'll be free around one. I'll give you a call after my meeting."

"Ok. Sounds good."

David joined them in the kitchen. "Looks like y'all are having a good time in here."

"Yep. We're women about our business," Rayne said.

"I second that motion," Sky said. Her cell phone rang and she excused herself to the backyard.

"Hello. Hey Phyllis. How are you?"

"I'm doing good. How are you doing?"

"I'm doing alright."

"Are you sure, seeing as your message said you only have four pills left? What's going on Sky?"

"I've just had a little anxiety lately with the move and all. That's all. No worries, I'm good."

"Well, Sky, I cannot refill your prescription. I believe

there's more going on than just some bipolar and anxiety issues. I can't help you from here but I have sent a referral to one of my close associates in Atlanta, Doctor Ellis. I'll text you the information to her office when we hang up."

"Phyllis, I am fine. I DO NOT need to see anyone."

"Sky, I'm not trying to upset you. As your friend, know that I am only trying to help. As your physician, I want to provide the best care for you. Please trust me."

"I do trust you, but I don't want anybody picking and probing to find something more than some anxiety that was triggered by a traumatic time in my life."

"I think it is more than that, Sky. I believe that Skylar is more than just an alter ego you've created for your 'F' it moments. I think that you may have a case of dissociative identity disorder."

"Get the fuck out of here, Phyllis. I am not crazy."

"I'm not saying that nor do I think that Sky, but after some of our conversation that involved your blackouts and the symptoms that we diagnosed as bipolar disorder, this is my professional educated guess. It is still only a guess and that is why I want you to see Doctor Ellis. She is great at what she does and I trust her. Please Sky."

"Ok. I'll think about it."

"Thank you. I will send you her information. Her name is Cynthia Ellis. Take care of yourself and I will talk to you soon."

"Ok. Bye."

That bitch thinks I'm going to let her go see that chick, she's crazy. I got this. I've been taking care of Sky all this time and I will continue. Skylar reentered the house.

Rayne had her briefcase in her hand and was headed to the door. "I'm about to leave honey. Enjoy your day. Your mom should be here any minute to pick up the kids. Love you and I'll see you later." Rayne kissed David and then turned to Sky. "I'll see you around one, Sky. Good luck this morning."

"Ok."

"So, you think you're going to like Atlanta?" David asked Sky as he made himself a cup of coffee.

"Yeah. Things are looking pretty good. Can't wait to start working and of course, I'm looking forward to the house hunting with Rayne."

"She'll find you something nice. It's amazing what she does in the real estate market; she's like an artist performing their craft."

"Speaking of artist. You missed a great show last night. Rayne's friend was great."

"Rayne's friend?" he said, looking puzzled.

"Imani. The young lady we went to watch perform. Oh, I take it you haven't met Imani. I'm sorry."

"Oh no, it's ok. I'm sure it just slipped Rayne's mind."

"I'm sure. Well, I'm about to hit the road. You enjoy your day."

"Thanks Sky. You too."

She smiled as she left out of the house and went to her truck.

* * * * * * *

David didn't give anymore thought to his and Sky's conversation about Imani. He left the house and went to Trust Bank to do his monthly audit report. He expected the process to go quicker than usual because the head teller volunteered to come in to help him, overtime well paid as far as he was concerned.

She was at the bank waiting when David arrived. By the time he parked, she'd exited her car and walked towards his.

"Good morning Mr. Smith," she said with a glowing smile.

"Good morning Ms. Eugene. Nice ride. Is that the 640i?"

"Yes. It was my birthday present to myself. I've always wanted a BMW convertible. Ain't she sexy?"

"Yes she is. That white on chrome is nice. Congratulations. It's a good look."

"Thanks," she said as they moved to the bank's door.

"Oh yeah, I think I saw your wife last night."

"Oh really?"

"Yeah, she was at the club where I performed my spoken word last night. She was as stunning as I remember her from the Christmas party."

"She did go out to a poetry showcase, so it was more than likely her. So, you're a poet? Ms. Eugene, that's awesome. Kaci Eugene, The Poet, has a nice ring to it. I'm impressed; beautiful, smart, and artistic. You're a triple threat. Hope these guys out here are ready cause you got it going on."

"Thank you Mr. Smith," she said blushing, "You have to come check me out next time. Maybe you can bring your wife. She seemed to enjoy herself, plus Imani spoke very highly of her. She said that she was a great supporter. If it wasn't your wife, I would have thought they had something going on because Imani goes that way," she said, finishing with a giggle.

David gave a small chuckle to hide both his curiosity and confusion. Imani had been brought up two times in less than an hour and never once by Rayne.

He and Kaci's morning was productive, and he completed his reports in half the time.

"Thank you very much for your help, Ms. Eugene. It was a pleasure working with you."

"The pleasure was all Mr. Smith," she said seductively as she walked away to her car.

* * * * * * *

Every second that Rayne had to herself, she spent a portion of it thinking of Imani. Her drive to her agency was not different. She knew that she needed to get it together, but she just could not shake the burning desire.

Rayne thought back to the night before when she and Sky went to Envy. She went to see Imani after they left the club. Sky hung out at the bar in the lobby of Imani's hotel, while Rayne visited.

Rayne knocked on the hotel room's door. She was greeted by Imani, who led her into the dimly lit room. She'd placed candles throughout the room that produced a relaxing atmosphere.

"How much time do I have to enjoy you tonight?" Imani asked.

"Sky is downstairs and I told her I'd be down in an hour."

"Perfect. I can do a lot in an hour. That is, if you're willing to give yourself to me," Imani said playfully as she squeezed Rayne's butt. She pulled Rayne to her and kissed her gently. "Is that alright with you?" Imani uttered softly.

Rayne was totally immersed in the energy that the kiss brought and she could not speak; she nodded her head slowly. Imani led her to the bed. Rayne stood in anticipation of Imani's next move; she was both anxious and nervous.

Imani took Rayne's top and skirt off. Once Rayne's skirt hit the floor, Imani stepped back and admired Rayne's fit body in her pink matching bra and panties.

"Are you sure you have three children? Your body is amazing. Your clothes do you no justice lovely."

"Thank you," Rayne replied blushing.

"Thank you for trusting me with your beautiful body," Imani said as she laid Rayne on the bed.

Imani unstrapped Rayne's wedge heels and placed them

on the floor. She took Rayne's feet and rubbed them before she grabbed a piece of ice that was in a chest near the bed. Imani took one of Rayne's feet and traced it with the ice cube and kissed it down and around to her toes.

Imani took the ice into her mouth and proceeded to suck Rayne's toes. Rayne shuttered from the cold sensation, as well as the pleasure. Imani continued until the ice she held in her mouth melted.

Imani grabbed another cube of ice and used it to move up from Rayne's feet up to her inner thighs. She followed behind every ice trail with soft kisses.

Rayne laid there in a pool of total ecstasy. She embraced everything that Imani initiated. Imani gracefully removed Rayne's panties and explored her genitalia with her hand, mouth, and the ice. Rayne responded with moans, groans, and rolling hips.

While lying there, Rayne's mind drifted to David. She knew she was wrong and should not have been there but the lustful hold Imani had on her was too powerful for Rayne to fight. She had gotten swallowed up by Imani's sexual essence.

Imani consumed Rayne's body in an unimaginable way. Their action packed hour included a blindfold, several fruit, whip cream, and a silver bullet (which turned out to be Rayne's favorite accessory). Imani used the bullet and stimulated Rayne's clitoris as she engaged her body with her mouth and free hand.

Rayne experienced a tingling sensation that made her squirm in her seat as she reminisced. Her thoughts were interrupted by the ringing of her cell phone; it was Sky.

"Hello."

"Hey Rayne. I have something to tell you."

"What?"

"Well, I kind of slipped and mentioned Imani to David."

"What? How? What did you say?"

"We were talking about the club and I said that your friend did a great job."

"How did he respond?"

"He was like it was no big deal, it must of slipped your mind."

"Ok."

"This might be a good time to bring her up."

"Yeah, maybe. Well, I'm just getting to the office. I'll call you later."

"Ok. Sorry."

"It'll be ok; it's not like you did it on purpose."

"Of course not. See you later."

"Alright."

Rayne sat in her car for a minute after the call to regain her thoughts. How was she going to tell her husband that she had a burning desire for another woman? She did not have the answer but she knew she would have to figure it out soon.

* * * * * * *

James made his way to Orlando to see Sky, since she had been avoiding his phone calls. It seemed like the Browns had their hands all in the messiness of the situation and he knew they would never tell him anything. Not only did they not know him but their secret was worth fifty thousand dollars. Sky had to know more than what she'd shared originally.

James was surprised when he got to the clinic and was told that she relocated to Atlanta. He wondered if she'd contacted Rayne. He definitely couldn't call Rayne. Though she played nice in front of others, he knew she still carried some level of hate for him.

It pissed him off briefly seeing as he traveled to Florida, but then plan B came to mind, Linda. She was on him hard the last time he was there and he knew he could get her to spill her guts.

Linda had mentioned that night that she was the guest services manager at the Waldorf Astoria. He called and cancelled his reservations at the Embassy Suites and drove to the Waldorf Astoria.

Waldorf Astoria was a much higher end hotel than Embassy Suites. He'd been greeted by several employees by the time he made it through the grand lobby to the guest services desk.

Once James reached the guest services desk, he was helped by an overly happy woman named Janice. He told Janice that he was extremely pleased with her customer service and would love to speak to her manager. She skipped to the door behind the counter. As James stood there, he hoped that Linda was the one on duty, otherwise his trip might have been a bust.

The door opened and out came Janice with Linda behind her. *Yes!* Linda lit up when she saw him. "Well, well, well. James right?"

"Yes. Linda right?"

"Yes."

"What a surprised. Well, let me tell you that this young lady was a wonderful help and full of energy. I wanted to let management know. Seeing you is an added bonus though."

"Oh, stop it," she said with a huge grin on her face.

"Seriously. You are a beautiful woman. I hope I'm not being to forward."

"No, you're fine and thank you. I'm glad Janice was able to help you. What brings you back to our wonderful city?"

"Business as usual, but I do plan to incorporate some pleasure into the trip as well," he said seductively, showing his pearly whites.

"Oh," she said softly.

He pulled out his business card and handed it to her and said, "Call me when you get off. Maybe we can go have a drink or something. That is, if you man won't mind."

"I don't have that issue. I get off at five."

"Perfect. See you later."

He walked off and left both Janice and Linda in awe.

Damn I'm good, he thought smiling to himself.

Chapter 7

Rayne sat under the gazebo in deep thought. She'd allowed her sexual obsession with Imani to taint her reality. She had lost focus and she knew it. The reality was that she had a loving husband who loved her dearly, a beautiful family, and an up and coming real estate business; all things that any woman would want.

Like so many others, Rayne had got caught up in the "right now". It wasn't until that moment that she realized that the passion she felt with Imani wasn't anywhere close to the passion she and David had prior to her mental shut down. She knew she was to blame for the strain on their marriage.

The conversation with David did not go as Rayne hoped. It was two days before David brought up the Imani conversation he and Sky had. He'd spoke to her about her experience that night several times, giving her numerous opportunities to mention it, which she never did.

Rayne sipped on her coffee as she replayed the

conversation from the night prior.

"What is going on Rayne?" he'd asked.

"Nothing baby. What are you talking about?"

"I'm talking about you floating around here all preoccupied. I'm talking about you constantly on your cell phone. I'm talking about new secret friends you're having. So, I ask again. What is going on Rayne? Are you seeing another man?"

"No, not exactly..."

She paused to gather the right words when David chimed in with "What the hell? What you mean not exactly?"

"Well...I've been communicating with Imani-"

"The girl you went to see at the poetry spot?"

"Yes. Imani is actually the stripper from the club in Charlotte."

"What? Hold up. I'm a little confused, Rayne. The stripper? So when/how have y'all gotten so close?"

"When I went to the bathroom that night, I ran into her there. She gave me her number and we've been speaking ever since."

"There has to be more to the story or y'all had one hell of a conversation for her to travel to Atlanta to see you."

"Well, she didn't travel to see me. She came to perform."

"Yeah ok. You may believe that but I certainly don't. So, how far has this situation really gone Rayne? Don't bullshit me either."

"I've been with her...sexually."

Rayne watched David bite down on his bottom lip and give a slow head shake. She knew right then that she had hurt him with that confession.

"So, what exactly was your plan? Were you going to continue this behind my back or were you going to come at me with that threesome bullshit? Cause y'all women think that's every man's fantasy. My fantasy was to have a faithful woman who would not cheat on me with a man or woman. I'm hurt Rayne, especially since she'd done in a week what I tried to do the past year. I've never thought about being with anyone since the day I met you and definitely have not touched or allowed anyone other than you touch me."

He got up off of the bed and went toward the bedroom door.

"David, wait. Let's talk about this."

"Let's not. I'll be in my office. Don't forget that tomorrow is my fishing trip with my dad. I'll take the kids to mom and that way, you'll have some free time for what's her face."

The heaviest feeling ever moved into Rayne's stomach. David never left a conversation like that before, so she knew she'd messed up big time. For the first time since Imani entered her life, she reflected on her vows and hoped she and David could get past that "for worst". Rayne cried herself to sleep alongside the spot David would normally lay.

* * * * * * *

Sky was smack dab in the middle of an emotional whirlwind. She woke from another haunting dream where Rayne played the leading lady.

Skylar had a lot of hatred toward Rayne. She had secretly been jealous of Rayne since she and Sky became close. She felt as if Rayne took Sky from her. Skylar had been Sky's protector since her accident when she was twelve.

When Sky was a young girl, she developed a passion for horse riding; she started riding at four. Sky had been prepping for her first jump competition the day of the accident. She and her horse, Butterfly, were in the middle of their practice when a rattlesnake slithered from under the stacked jumping logs.

The snake startled Butterfly and Sky was thrown mid jump. She sustained massive head trauma, a broken leg, and a broken arm from the fall.

Sky was in a coma for three weeks. Skylar talked her through those days of total silence. Once Sky recovered, Skylar remained in the background. She only popped in during those "I wish a motherfucker would" moments.

Sky was losing control quickly; Skylar's voice was getting stronger. She stopped Sky several times from contacting Doctor Ellis. Sky grabbed her pill bottle and took the final pill. It was a battle between the two personalities every time she took a pill. If she did not get help soon,

Skylar would be the more dominant personality, which would be total mayhem.

Sky laid in silence waiting on her Lithium Carbonate to kick in. She heard a lot of movement outside of the guest room door as she laid there. She could hear David talking to the twins about getting ready to go to their granny's house.

"Is mommy coming too, daddy?" Sky heard Eva ask.

"No sweetie, mommy has a lot of work to do," David responded.

"Ok daddy," she said.

Sky listened to the twins talk and laugh until she dozed off.

* * * * * * *

James got more than he bargained for from his time with Linda. She went up to his room after her shift was over that evening. They ordered room service and drank wine. James filled Linda's glass every time it got low. The tipsier Linda got, the more she talked. She also became more touchy feely; she touched and/or inched closer to him throughout their entire conversation.

"So, when's the last time you spoke with Sky?" James asked.

"I haven't spoken to her since she left. She texted me and let me know she made it and things were going good."

"What made her move to Atlanta?"

"I guess she needed a change. Things for her hadn't

been the same. Takes a strong woman to go through what she had. I don't think I would have gotten through it with my mind still intact. I'm getting a little warm," she said as she took off her shirt.

Linda sat there with her D cup breasts popping from the top of her t-shirt. Surprisingly, he was not turned on by the beautiful woman in front of him. His thoughts were on Angela and the fact that he could not wait to get back to Mississippi to see her. He knew to do that, he had to handle business first.

Linda continued. "I'm sure they'd probably have my ass in a padded room still. Shit."

James sat confused. At first, he thought Linda was talking about Sky's divorce but when she started talking about a padded room, shit sounded more serious than a failed marriage. He was nervous pursuing the topic more, but he had to know.

"I think I missed something. Are you talking about her divorce?"

Linda tilted her head to the side and looked at James and said, "Divorce. Sky didn't get a divorce. Her husband is dead."

"Dead?"

"Yeah. You didn't know?"

"No. She kept saying that her husband left her. So, I assumed that meant a divorce, especially when she reassured me that she was over it."

"She definitely is not over it. That's for sure. She'd called me crying many of nights. I'm surprised you did not know; y'all being from the same hometown. She talked about your sister knowing about his death."

"What happened? Was he sick or something?"

"He was murdered last year, shot in the head. Sky lived for justice against who committed that god awful crime. Sky obsessed over the case and the fact that it was unsolved. She said something about your sister having pieces to the murder; that she was home when he was killed."

James' thoughts froze on what Rayne could possibly know about Sky's husband's murder. "Man, Sky loved that man. Randy was her world."

"Randy," he stuttered.

What the fuck? Can't be! I need to talk to Rayne like right now.

He had a feeling Sky was up to something and he had to warn Rayne.

"Look, Linda, it's been fun but I'm about to call it a night. I have some work to do. Need me to drive you home?"

She slid all the way next to him and placed her hands on his chest.

"I thought I could stay with you. I've always had a weakness for a handsome man," she said, licking her bottom lip. James had to turn his head because Linda's big bright almond shaped hazel eyes tempted him.

"Sorry sweetheart, as tempting as that is, I just

remembered that I forgot to handle some important paperwork. If I don't take care of it, my business partner is going to be furious. So, would you like for me to take you home?"

"No. My car's here, plus you've been drinking along with me. I'll just grab the hotel's corporate room for the night, if you don't want my company."

"Good deal. Excuse me, I have to use the bathroom. Here's your shirt."

James grabbed his phone from his pocket as soon as he reached the bathroom. He did not have Rayne's number, so he called his father. He knew Bruce would have been asleep but after what he had learned, he felt waking him was warranted. Bruce gave James the number after James assured him several times that everything was ok.

James dialed Rayne's number but it went straight to voicemail. He tried two more times with no answer. A slow throbbing panic came over him. He knew he had to go to Atlanta. Driving that night was out of the question because as Linda pointed out, he was feeling right from the wine as well as the Hennessey that he had prior to Linda's arrival.

Ok, get a few hours of sleep and then get on the road, he sighed. *Sure picked a good time to drive. Damn, I should have flown.*

James left out of the bathroom and went back into the room. To his surprise, not only was Linda still there, but she was butt naked sprawled out on his bed.

Lord, why do you tempt me like this?

* * * * * * *

Sky woke from her nap energized and ready to start her day. She showered and made her way downstairs to the kitchen. Rayne was in the kitchen pouring herself some orange juice.

"Good morning," Sky sang.

"Morning," Rayne mumbled.

"Are you ok? You look like hell."

"Well, thank you."

"Sorry but you do."

"I feel like hell."

"What's wrong?"

"David and I finally had our Imani conversation last night, and he is not happy with me. He has not said a word to me since and he's gone on a three-day fishing trip, so we probably won't talk until he gets home," she said with a sigh.

Sky fought the joy that brewed deep down inside her from that news. "I'm sure it'll be ok. Love conquers all. So, what are you going to do with your free time? You can't spend it moping."

"I'm thinking about picking up my jewelry making hobby. I hadn't had much time to make anything. I'm going to play hooky today and just enjoy some me time."

"That sounds good. I would join you but some of us have to work to make it."

They both chuckled. They chatted a little as Sky ate her breakfast.

Sky's phone rang three times as they sat there; two of the calls were from James and the other was from Phyllis. Sky declined all three of the calls; she had no desire to be bothered by either of them.

"Though this is fun, I have to go finish getting ready for work."

"Ok. I'm about to go in the garage anyways to grab my jewelry supplies."

* * * * * * *

Rayne went to the storage area of the garage. She located her supply tote on a shelf above Sky's things. Rayne grabbed the tote and had started back toward the house when she knocked one of Sky's boxes over. She panicked, hoping that she had not broken anything.

Rayne put her tote down and picked up the contents of the box, which was mainly pictures, knick knacks, some rope, and a blindfold. Rayne laughed as she picked up the rope and blindfold. "Sky, must be into some freaky shit."

Rayne looked at the pictures as she picked them up. She smiled at the pictures of Jordan, Sky, and the Florida scenery. Rayne placed the pictures back in the box and knelt down to grab a keepsake box.

Rayne admired the vintage lace detailed design on the box. The contents included a wedding ring, letters, and pictures. "Ahhh," Rayne said as she looked at the first picture. It was a picture of Sky in her wedding dress. *She was a stunning bride,* Rayne thought. The next few pictures were of Sky and her bridesmaids.

Rayne almost shit herself when she went to the next picture. Her heart raced as if she had just completed a marathon. She heard the garage door close.

"What are doing with my things?" Sky spat at Rayne.

"I knocked your box over on accident," she said with a slight stutter in her voice.

Sky looked down in Rayne's hand and saw her and Randy's wedding picture.

"So, I guess you expect me to explain."

"Yes, I do."

Sky turned away from Rayne, as if she was ashamed and began. "Well, see, it's like this-"

Those where the last words Rayne heard before everything went black.

Chapter 8

James got on the road at four the next morning going to Atlanta. He had no idea where Rayne lived, but he hoped to either get in touch with her or call Bruce for the address when he got closer. The only thing on his mind at that time was trying to warn her.

His mind raced as he attempted to put the pieces of the puzzle together. *How in the hell did Sky and Randy's slob ass get together? That's fucked up, since she knew him and Rayne had a thing. Damn, did she think Rayne killed him or was she just fishing for information?*

James hoped it was that Sky was fishing because she seemed to have had a calculated plan. He blamed himself because while he was using Sky for information, he fed her all the information he had on Rayne.

"Fuck," he exclaimed.

He knew he needed to calm his mind. He grabbed his phone and called Angela.

"Hello," she answered sleepily.

"Hey babe."

"Hey James. It's three here, you never call me this late. Is everything ok?"

"Not really but it will be. Just needed to hear a calming voice."

"What happened?" she asked, perking up.

James could hear her adjusting on the other end.

"I just found out that Rayne may be in trouble. It's a long confusing story but it's bad."

"Wow. So what are you doing now?"

"I'm on my way to Atlanta to warn her about what I found out."

"From Orlando?"

"Yes."

"Wow. It must really be bad. You be sure to be careful."

"I will. So, tell me something good."

"Ok. I saved a bunch of money on my car insurance by switching to Geico," she joked.

"You're funny," James said with a laugh.

"Just wanted to make you laugh, but for real, I want you to know you are very special to me. You make me happy."

"Now that's something nice to hear. Know that you're a very important part of my life. Like I told you, I've never opened myself to anyone, especially no woman. So, believe me when I say it."

"Thank you, that's sweet. I don't take your words

lightly."

"Good."

James and Angela's talk helped James to not over think the situation. By the time he got off the phone with Angela, he was a lot more relaxed. He sang and dance to the radio as he chipped away at the distance between Orlando and Atlanta.

Jack called James along his journey. "Hey Jack. What's up?" he said.

"Hey. A whole heap is up. Can you meet me?"

"No. I'm actually about two hours away from Atlanta. What's going on?"

"Two things. I located the doctor, her name is Evelyn James."

"Great," James interjected.

"Yes. She works at Jackson Memorial Hospital alongside her husband, Doctor Stewart James."

"Ok. Good. What's the other thing?"

"The way that I found Mrs. James is quite interesting. After you told me about the Brown's hefty "hush" donation, I began digging around in their background. I found out that Mrs. Brown was a member of the Zeta Phi Beta Sorority."

"Ok."

"While digging through charity events and what nots, I found an article in the Grenada Post which showcased the Zetas of Grenada during the Mayor's annual banquet."

Will he come on with it. I don't care about who's part of what sorority, James thought getting impatient.

"Guess who were pictured in the story."

"Just tell me Jack."

"None other than Mrs. Brown and Mrs. James. Hot dog! The caption under the picture had Mrs. Brown quoted as saying 'long time friend'."

"You got to be shitting me."

"But wait, it gets better. Then I started digging in their past up to a year prior to the child's birth. Mrs. Brown was pretty much clean, but Mrs. James not so much. About a month prior to the child being born, there was a cashier's check drawn up from her to Mrs. Brown for fifty thousand dollars. Coincidence, I think not, so I dug some more. On September twenty-fourth, two thousand and two, Mrs. James had a birth certificate drawn for her baby girl, Elaina Rose James. I could not find any records anywhere corroborating the pregnancy."

"Well, I be damned. The doctor has her."

"It seems that way to me."

"Good job, Jack."

"Thanks, just doing my job."

"Well, now I have another task for you. Get eyes on Evelyn. I need to know as much as possible about her schedules and habits, her husband's schedules and habits, as well as Elaina's."

"I'll get right on it."

"Good deal. Take care man and thanks again."

"You too."

James was ecstatic by the call and could not stop smiling. He spent the rest of his trip plotting his next moves.

* * * * * * *

Rayne's head pounded as she came to. She was seated on the garage floor propped up on a support beam. Her hands were tied behind her back. She blinked several times in hopes to clear her blurry vision.

What happened? Did she hit me with something?

Rayne's vision slowly returned and she saw Sky pacing back and forth having a conversation with herself.

"This was not supposed to happen. We had a plan...Well, plans change. It's that nosey bitch's fault...So, what do we do now...She has to die...No, remember we said there's no way to do it without being pulled into it. We're going have to convince her to confess to her crime...Sky, that trifling bitch has never owned up to anything...Let's at least try...I say 'try' and snap her neck..."

"Sky," Rayne said faintly, interrupting her conversation.

Sky jerked her neck toward Rayne, like a hunting dog that identified the prey.

"Sky," Rayne said again "What are you doing? Why am I tied up?"

"Seemed like a good idea at the time."

"What is going on? I thought you were my friend. We'd

been through so much. I don't understand! Then you and Randy. What the hell? That's some foul shit Sky, especially since he was my first love."

"Your first love that you stole from me!" she yelled.

"What? You are crazy as hell because I did not steal him from you."

"Do not call me crazy. Yes, you did! We had been together before I moved to Jackson. We spent the summer together and talked through the school year. We were fine until you came along. I broke up with him when I found out that you and him had something going on. But he couldn't live without me, so I let him come back. Once I went to college, he'd come visit me. Life was good until you got pregnant. You had a hold on him that I could never understand, back then and up until you killed him!"

"I did not kill him."

"Stop lying! He told me that he was going to meet with you that day. All you had to do was give him his money; you did not have to kill him."

Tears streamed down Sky's face. Rayne did not know what to say. She sat there in shock.

Sky's tears did not last long and she started to pace again. Rayne heard Sky's contemplation on how to murder Rayne and get away with it.

"Forget that. Bet she didn't do all this thinking when she killed Randy."

"I did not kill Randy! You crazy bitch!" Rayne hollered.

Sky moved quickly toward Rayne. She drew back as far as she could and hauled off and slapped Rayne.

* * * * * * *

James' cell phone rang and he looked down at the unfamiliar four-zero-four area code phone number. He quickly answered it, in hopes that it was Rayne.

"Hello."

"Hello. James?" a male said from the other end of the phone.

"Yes. Who's this?"

"This is David, Rayne's husband."

"Oh. Hey. What's up?"

"Your dad called me worried. He asked if everything was alright because you led him to believe something was wrong when you asked for our address. I'm on the road to South Carolina for a fishing trip but I need to know if I should turn around. I've called Rayne's cell and the house with no answer. What's going on?"

"Rayne hadn't answered any my calls either. I don't know exactly what is going on but I think Sky has it out for Rayne."

"Sky? No way. They're friends. I can't see that."

"I couldn't either until what I found out last night. It's a long story. Trust me when I say it's not a good one. I'm actually an hour away from your house."

"Wow. It must be pretty bad for you to drive hours to tell her because she didn't answer her phone. I'm about to turn around. I'm a little over an hour out. I'll keep trying Rayne."

"Ok. Cool. See ya."

"Oh. You'll need the code to get into our neighborhood. Our visitor's code is five, seven, two, eight."

"Five, seven, two, eight; got it."

"Hope you're wrong James."

"Me too."

* * * * * * *

Sky felt as if she was on autopilot as she moved throughout the garage. Skylar's rage had consumed her. She looked at Rayne and her busted lip with no remorse.

She deserved that and then some. Calling me crazy, she ain't seen crazy yet.

"Who's crazy now, princess? You looking like you got a problem. Is there something you want to say? Huh?"

"You better be lucky that I'm tied up or I would kick your ass."

"Oh yeah? Ha ha. I would drag your ass around this garage like the piece of shit you are. Trust and believe that."

"Whatever, you trifling trick."

"Oh, Miss Goodie Two Shoes is trying to get hood! Fuck out of here with that bullshit. You ain't shit and won't ever be shit. You lying piece of shit. But don't worry, I'll take care of David's fine ass for you when you're gone."

"Fuck you."

"No, fuck you. If you know what's good for you, you

might want to tell me what I want to know cause I'm not as patient as Sky. I don't even like your ass."

"Why are you talking about yourself in third person, Ms. I'm Not Crazy?"

"Maybe because I am not Sky. I'm Skylar, that bitch you never want to meet. So, you ready to tell me about that day you took my love from me?"

"Sky, Skylar, or whatever your name is, I did not kill Randy. But know that I probably would have, given the chance, because he was no angel. He was a sick and dangerous man, but I see now y'all were made for each other. You want to know what happened? What happened was your sorry ass husband tried to rape me!"

"I don't believe you. Randy would never do anything like that. As a matter of fact, he was in Jackson that week helping my grandmother with some remodeling. Randy was a good man and I will not let you taint his good name. You, on the other hand, are a lying, thieving whore who thinks the world revolves around you."

Sky started to pace and mumble to herself. She was determined not to think anything negative about Randy.

While Rayne debated with Sky, she had been working on loosening the rope on her wrist. Luckily for her, Sky was not a professional and had not gotten the rope extremely tight. Little did Sky know that Rayne and David had weapons placed throughout their home, in case of a home invasion. She had a thirty-two caliber handgun less than ten feet away from her.

"You want to know about what happened, so here it goes. Your lovely husband disrespectfully came to my mother's wake to show me how big his balls were. He invited himself into my life and befriended my husband. The stress of it all sent me into a panic attack that resulted in me being hospitalized. Your lovely husband then called me to threaten and intimidate me, at which time I offered to give him what I owed him, what I stole from him, and then some. But that wasn't enough because he asked for our child that he knew I did not lose. Hindsight being twenty-twenty, I now know how he knew that information," she said, cutting her eyes at Sky.

Rayne shifted from her position to release pressure on her butt, as well as to ensure Sky could not see her progress with the rope.

"Surprisingly, he had enough class to not barge in on my mother's funeral, so we met the next day at the rattiest of motels. Probably one that y'all frequented. Anyways, I'm there ready to give him a fifteen thousand dollar check but that was not payment enough. He pinned me up on the wall by the throat and dropped his pants. He said he was gonna use me and then toss me on the street."

"You're a liar!"

Rayne ignored Sky's rants and continued. "As I stood there helpless, all I could think about was my gun in my purse. I wished I could get it to shoot his dick off as I felt it rub against my leg. I prayed to God as he fought to pull my clothes off. Makes me want to puke thinking about his nasty hands on me, groping me. My prayers were answered when James kicked in the door and beat his ass."

"James? Son of a bitch!"

"Yep! He decorated the wall with his sleaze bag brain matter!" she yelled as her hands came free.

Sky was stunned when Rayne jumped up and did not react quick enough to stop her from reaching the gun that was affixed under the step that led to the house. Sky closed in the gap too quickly for Rayne to get a shot off after she cocked the gun. Sky grabbed the gun and they tussled about briefly before the gun went off.

Chapter 9

James arrived at David and Rayne's house and hopped out his car quickly. He ran to the front door and twisted the doorknob. The door was locked, so he alternated ringing the door bell and knocking.

James walked around the house to the backyard after no success at the front door. He moved to the side where there was a cobblestone walkway that led to a door in the wooden fence. He kicked the locked gate until he knocked it off the hinges. *Damn, I hope these folks don't call the cops on me in this uppity ass neighborhood cause I know my black ass will go straight to jail. Do not pass go. Do not collect two hundred dollars,* James thought as he moved swiftly across the backyard.

James reached the door and to his surprise, it was unlocked. Rayne had not locked it after she went in from the gazebo that morning. "Rayne!" he called as he stood in the unfamiliar home. He had no idea where to start his search. Hell, he did not even know if she even truly in trouble.

He called her name again and moved through the kitchen. He noticed the orange juice and half eaten piece of toast that was on the counter top. He'd made it through the living room and was at the stairs when he heard the gun go off in the garage. He took off in a sprint toward the sound.

James snatched open the garage door. There stood Rayne and Sky. "Rayne!" he yelled, confused about what he saw. Rayne turned and looked at him as she and Sky both fell to the ground.

"You stupid bitch. You shot me," Sky said before she spit in Rayne's face.

Rayne turned to James. "What are you doing here?"

"I came to warn you about this crazy broad, but I guess I was too late to save the day this time."

"No problem," she said attempting to force a smile. "Help me get this crazy bitch off of me please and call the police."

* * * * * * *

When David pulled up to the house, there was an ambulance and police cars everywhere. He didn't even turn the engine off before he ran to the house, leaving his father in the truck.

A police officer stopped him as he ran up to the door.

"This is my house. Where is my wife? What is going on?"

"Sir-" the officer started but David was not hearing that.

"Where is my wife?" he asked in a stern, no nonsense tone.

Another officer approached. "Sir, calm down and I will help you. And you are?"

"David. David Smith."

"Mr. Smith, an unfortunate situation occurred this morning. Your wife is fine. She is inside giving her statement and she is also being looked over by the paramedics. Do you know a Mrs. Sky Brown Thomas?" he said as he looked down at his note pad.

"Yes. That's my wife's best friend. Is she ok?"

"Not exactly. She was dead on arrival via a gunshot wound to the abdomen. It appears that your wife was the shooter."

"What!?!"

"We are still getting all the details, but it seems to be self defense. Follow me. I will take you to her, but she is very shaken up, so some comfort is much needed."

David nodded his head as he moved to the house in disbelief. There were people everywhere once he got into the house. It was like a maze as he moved through them.

David finally made it to Rayne in the living room. Tears ran down his face as he saw the bruise on the side of her face and her swollen eye and lip.

"Baby," he called as he went and embraced her.

"Oh," she said painfully as he hugged her. Rayne was sore from the beating she had received from Skylar before she woke up.

"Baby I'm sorry."

"It's ok, honey. I'm glad you're here. I didn't get a chance to call you. Everything happened so quickly."

"I love you, Rayne."

"I love you too, David."

David looked up and saw James off in the corner talking to an officer; it looked as if he was giving his statement. The curiosity of what had happened burned David down to his core, but he knew that at that moment, his position was to be Rayne's rock.

* * * * * * *

Rayne laid on the couch and watched as David walked the last cop and his father out of the house. David had given his father the quick version of the situation and told him he would update him later.

Rayne looked at James, who had begun softening her heart for him. She was still in shock that he traveled hours to warn her. "Thank you, James. I appreciate what you did to make sure I was ok."

"No problem. When I found out that Sky and Randy were married, I had a feeling she was up to no good."

"How did you find out?"

"Long story that we also need to get into, but now is not the time or place. You get better and then we'll hash that out another time. I'm about to head out. You get some rest after you talk to your man cause you know he got all kinds

222

of questions."

"I know. It's time to come clean. It's time to own up to my mistakes, our mistakes," she said giving him a side stare.

"I hope you know what you're doing because I don't think either one of us want to see inside a prison, partner."

"I got this," she said as James moved toward the door.

I think so anyways, Rayne thought. She knew she owed David the truth but the question now was how much of the truth would she tell him.

"Alright David, I'm outta here," James said to David.

"Thank you for everything James," David responded.

"No biggie. Y'all take care."

"Alright man," David said, giving James some dap.

James left and the spotlight was shining on Rayne. David sat on the couch beside her.

"I want to apologize for the way I left this morning. Coming home to all the police and the ambulance was scary. It made me realize that regardless of how mad you make me, my life would not be the same without you. We've been through too much to let anyone or anything come between us. I love you Rayne, for better and for worse. I love you, Mrs. Smith."

"I love you too, Mr. Smith."

David kissed Rayne gently on her forehead. Those words meant a lot to Rayne, especially because she was about to unload some heavy stuff on him. Rayne took a deep breath. *Here goes nothing.*

"What happened today was karma coming full circle by way of a crazy woman because of my lies, deceitfulness, and secrets."

"Rayne, I'm really confused right now."

"I know. Just bear with me while I get into the story. You may not like some of the things I say next, but it will be the truth. The whole truth because I am tired of my past haunting me. You might want to get a drink; I think you'll need one."

David took Rayne's advice. He came back into the living room with a bottle of wine and two wine glasses. Rayne started her story as David poured them some wine.

"The meat and potatoes of the story starts with my first encounter with Doctor James, which was not last year. I was nineteen years old when I met her. I'd woken up in a hospital room, similar to the way I did the day before Mom's funeral. Mom was by my side that time though. I fainted at my job and was taken to the hospital. Doctor James, whose name was Doctor Lamb back then, dropped a bomb on me after she introduced herself. She informed me and my mother that I was almost four months pregnant."

She heard David gasp at that news, but she looked down at her wine glass and continued without looking up at him.

"My mother was hurt and disappointed in me because she thought that I was a virgin, which I was up until the time the baby was conceived. What my mother didn't know was my deep dark secret about the conception. One night James, Eric, and I were home alone while Bruce and my mom went out. James came into my room during his pill popping high and forced himself on me."

David attempted to interrupt her but she shook her head no and continued.

"I was devastated and broken beyond what you can imagine. I never shared this with anyone. Not only was it my intent to save myself until marriage, but I also did not want to come between my mother and her husband. I was dating Randy at that time, the guy who you got all friendly with at the wake. He was my first and only boyfriend prior to me meeting you. I found out today that he was also Sky's husband."

"Rayne, this is a lot to take in. Was he the reason she attacked you? Was there some twisted love affair?"

"I know it's a lot but unfortunately, the story gets even more twisted than any love affair. Please, just let me get everything out."

"Ok."

"I'd become reckless after the incident and started having sex with Randy. It wasn't until the ultrasound was done that I knew the baby had to have been James'. I decided to pass the baby off as Randy's. I moved in with him and everything started off good. I was about six months pregnant when the honeymoon came to an end. I found out that he was the hoodlum that my mom believed him to be. One afternoon, I went home and saw weed and money laid out on the dining room table. I confronted him. We argued and he put his hands on me. I called Sky and went to her apartment in Hattiesburg. I left Jackson that night. I did not step foot back until last year."

Rayne poured herself more wine and continued with her confessions.

"Since things did not work with Randy, I decided to give the baby up for adoption. I'd gotten information from Doctor James and proceeded through the process. Sky's parents had a doctor friend who was unable to conceive. She and her husband wanted to adopt my baby. It was a win win, as far as I was concerned. The Browns opened their home to me during my pregnancy. I delivered a healthy baby on September twenty-fourth, two thousand and two. So, I have a son or daughter out there somewhere. Let's fast forward to our trip last year, which will bring us to Sky and her reason for wanting to hurt me. Randy called me while I was in the hospital demanding his money and his baby."

David interrupted with, "His money?"

"Oh yeah, I guess I left that part out. When I left Randy that night, I took seventy-five hundred dollars in cash from his safe. I'm sorry that I'm ruining your image of me."

"Me too but I love you, so go ahead and finish."

"Anyways, I told him that I had a miscarriage, which he

called me on. Now that I know that he and Sky were married, I understand his cockiness. I apologized to him for my theft and told him I would give the money back to him with interest. He agreed and we hung up. The next day when I went to Bruce's for the will reading, he called me and told me to meet him at a local motel. When I got there, he was being all pleasant and such. I expressed just how unimportant he was to me and he needed to take the money and forget about me. He flipped out and pinned me to the wall by my throat. He dropped his pants and was pulling at my clothes in attempts to rape me. I fought as much as I could between gasping for air. I got tunnel vision and felt myself passing out when there was a crash from the door. At the time, I didn't see what was happening because my vision was still impaired. I heard tussling and cursing and later, a gunshot. I was scared because I didn't know if I was next. I tried to get up to get away, but my body was not cooperating. The guy bent down and helped me up. It was James. He said he overheard my conversation and felt that I was going into a bad situation, so he followed me. He wiped the hotel room down so there was no evidence of either of us being there. As much as I hated him, I was grateful for him at that moment. If he hadn't of come, I wouldn't be here right now. So, that is the story of the past. The present was Sky knew about the meeting and took part in Randy's revenge plot. Once he was murdered, she set her sights on ruining me. While I was in the garage grabbing my jewelry supplies, I knocked one of her boxes over that had her and Randy's wedding pictures. She came in and saw me with it. She acted as if she was going to give me an explanation but instead, she hit me with something and knocked me out. She tied me to one of the support beams. She was planning on getting rid of me and living happily ever after with you. The only thing that bought me some time was that she was looney tunes and she couldn't get her thoughts together. She had like fifty personalities, she called herself Skylar. I maneuvered out of the rope she tied my hands with and ran for the gun under the steps. We wrestled with the gun and it went off and resulted with me telling the story and her in the morgue. So, there you have it."

David sat speechless. Rayne did not know how to take his silence. Did she say too much? Was her past too much for him to handle?

"David? Say something, please."

"What do I say when I find out that the man who saved my wife was actually only the solution to a problem that he caused? Or should I say something about you having a long lost child with this man? Or should I say something about you withholding the fact that you are an accomplice to murder? How about the fact that you were planning to take thousands of dollars from our household to cover up your lies? What exactly do you want me to say? Huh, Rayne?"

"I want you to say something along the lines of even

though I have laid a lot out on you, you love me enough to work through it. I want to know you still have my back. At least say that you won't turn me in to the cops."

"First off, stop being silly, not only are you my wife, you're the mother of my children. I will never turn you in to the cops. Secondly, I've told you it's you and me forever. But I do need time. I wish you would have confided in me before now. I'm hurt that you didn't, but I'll be ok. Is there anything and I mean anything else I need to know about your past or present?"

"No. That's everything."

"Good, from this day on, no more secrets. Let's go to bed and start fresh tomorrow."

Rayne smiled as David helped her up from the couch. *Lord, please be with us through this journey. We need you more than ever before,* Rayne thought as she turned the lights off and went upstairs.

Chapter 1

RAYNE

Life for Rayne was crazy after the shooting. Yes, she shot Sky in self defense but her heart was hurt because she still could not fully process the betrayal. As far as Rayne was concerned Sky was her best friend. It wasn't until she woke tied up in her garage that Rayne realized that Sky was crazy. Well sick, because technically it was her other personality Skylar that hated Rayne. Skylar was the crazy bitch that lived in her, but either way the incident haunted Rayne.

David had been supportive as usual after finding out about the rape, the baby, and the murder but Rayne knew it would only had been a matter of time before he'd get tired of her and her shit. She feared that she'd pressed her luck with him because he had become distant. There was no doubt in Rayne's mind that anymore blasts from her past would result in their divorce.

* * * * * * *

KACI

A man like David Smith is one in a million. There was not one woman at Trust Bank that had not fantasized about him at some point, but none yearned for him the way Kaci Eugene did. Kaci had been having a secret affair with David in her mind for months. She envied Rayne and wanted to be her. What she'd do to have him even for just one night, was unimaginable. Kaci had David set in her cross hairs and she was determined to get him.

Kaci strategically set her desk to watch David inconspicuously. She'd get to the bank early to get a lengthy show. She would watch as David glided across the bank lobby smiling at everyone he encountered on his way to his office. One morning David did not go to his office and instead came toward Kaci's desk. *Damn is he coming over here?* She thought as her heart raced with excitement.

"Good morning Ms. Eugene," David said.

"Good morning Mr. Smith," Kaci replied.

"Thank you for all your hard work and dedication. I appreciate you coming in on your days off to help me get the reports done. That means a lot to me. Here is a little something to show my gratitude."

David handed Kaci an envelope. She opened the envelope and found a gift certificate for an hour massage at Sherrie's House of Relaxation.

"Thank you, Mr. Smith."

"You're very welcome Ms. Eugene. I hope you enjoy it."

"I will."

David smiled and said, "You have a good day," as he went to his office.

David had no idea what he'd done in that quick interaction. Kaci sat there and daydreamed all day of how life would be as Mrs. David Smith. But first she had to deal with the current Mrs. David Smith. *Wife or not, he will be mine,* she thought as visions of him danced in her head.

* * * * * * *

JAMES

James patiently waited to discuss the baby situation with Rayne. Due to the Sky shenanigans, James was not able to share the information that his private investigator Jack had given him.

James had been patient to let Rayne deal with things on her own time, but his patience had worn thin. He felt he came too far in his investigation to let it go so calling Rayne was high on his priority list because Elaina Rose James constantly stayed on his mind.

His girlfriend Angela came into the bedroom from the bathroom. "Good morning baby," James said as he motioned for her to come to him.

"Good morning," she said before he tongued her down ready to share the morning wood he had with her. Angela pulled back from him; which threw James off because she was always down for his freakiness.

"What's up Angela?"

"We have to talk."

Fuck. Those words out a woman's mouth is almost never good.

"What's going on babe?"

"My period was late. So I took a pregnancy test and I'm pregnant."

James sat quietly processing her words as Angela carried on in a panic.

"What are we going to do? I'm not ready to be a mom. Hell I don't even know *how* to be a mom. We just made "us" official; talking about bringing a baby in the world. Fuck."

"Babe breath," he said embracing her. "It's going to be ok. For the record I think you'll be a great mom. We can do this."

James was ecstatic. For the first time in his life he was in love and it felt good. Angela smiled and kissed him.

James made a vow then to not let her down. He would do whatever he needed to, to take good care of Angela and their unborn child. James laid her on the bed and showed her how happy he was that she was giving him an opportunity at fatherhood.

Chapter 2

One year later...

Rayne was back to business as usual and was on her daily mommy duty. Her morning started with her dropping the twins off at their elementary school and then dropping Ethan off at daycare. Eva and Evan had just started the first grade and Ethan was almost two, so shutting down was not an option for Rayne. She knew she had to remain strong for her children, if for no other reason.

She made her way to her office to start her work day. Rayne was proud of her accomplishments at Smith and Smith Realty. She had three real estate agents that helped her build her company.

Rayne was greeted by her top seller April when she reached her office. "Good morning Rayne. You're looking lovely as usual. Oh my, I love those shoes."

"Thanks girl. You are here early."

"Yes and I brought gifts!"

April handed Rayne one of four Starbucks cups out of a carrier that sat on her desk.

"Thank you. You're awesome."

"Well, what can I say?" she said with a giggle. "So, I have the Walkers coming in for their closing this morning. That's why I'm here a little early."

"Great! You are on it this month."

"Well I learned from the best. Plus I'm working on that bonus. I only need two more sales so get your checkbook ready."

"It's ready. You've been putting in work so it would be my pleasure to sign that check."

The other two agents Bobby and Karen came in shortly after. Rayne had a quick meeting with them and then started her day by returning client phone calls.

* * * * * * *

"James, I enjoy being on your payroll and all but when are we going to move forward with this Elaina case? I've watched the James family so much that I feel like I'm part of their family," Jack said to James.

"I know Jack. I've been so busy focusing on Angela and Angelica. It seems like yesterday Angela told me she was pregnant and now Angelica is four months old. She's changed my life man. It's kind of fucked up to say but I feel like I should leave well enough alone. Hell, Elaina's been fine without me and Rayne for this long."

"I understand. You're the boss so if you want me to stay

on it I will, if not I won't."

"For now stay on it."

"No problem. Will do."

They said their goodbyes and left the coffee shop. James rushed back to Angela's apartment. He moved in after Angela told him she was pregnant. His and his brother Eric's house flipping was going exceptionally well. He went to Jackson often to check on his dad and handle whatever business he couldn't handle over the phone. James replayed his and Jack's conversation on his way to the apartment.

* * * * * * *

Kaci watched David carefully during the time Rayne revealed all of her secrets. Though David kept his personal and professional lives separated, she knew something was not right. She just couldn't get close enough to him to pry. She wasn't worried though because she had an ace in the hole that neither David nor Rayne knew about; her cousin Imani, known to many as Mercedes.

It wasn't an accident that Rayne and Imani hooked up for their brief but electrifying affair. David and his colleagues went to Imani's strip club during the annual conference as a result of a recommendation Kaci made to David's secretary. The initial plan was for Imani to try David and test his character, but that changed once Kaci over heard his secretary on the phone with Rayne. Kaci informed Imani of the change and like she'd hoped Imani pursued Rayne and eventually turned her out.

Kaci picked up the phone and called Imani.

"Hello."

"Hey cuz. What are you up to?"

"Nothing much. Just watching a little TV. Is everything ok? You don't normally call me this time of day," Imani stated.

"Yeah everything's alright...I guess. I've been noticing that David has been acting strange. Has Rayne said anything to you about them having any problems?"

"Rayne doesn't talk to me anymore," Imani said sadly. "She distanced herself after that shit with her crazy ass friend trying to kill her. She was on that her life's fucked up and she'd done enough fucked up things so she had to end communication with me bullshit. She said otherwise she'd never be able to fix her marriage."

"So they're having marital problems. Interesting. Thanks Imani. I have something I have to do."

"Are you about to be messy?"

"Nope. Just seizing an opportunity."

"Ok Ms. Opportunity Seizer, be careful."

"Ok cuz. I will."

"Ok. Later."

Imani felt a certain kind of way after they hung up because she was in fact not over Rayne. She wanted Rayne in her life. There was not a day that went by that she did not think about her.

* * * * * * *

"Ms. Flores? Yes I do remember you. I have an opening tomorrow at noon," Rayne said to the lady on the other end of the phone.

"Noon would be perfect Mrs. Smith."

"Great. I'll see you then. Thank you for choosing Smith and Smith Realty," she said before she hung up.

Rayne's phone immediately started ringing again. She looked down as Imani's name flashed on the screen. "Decline," she said as she declined the call.

Rayne exited her office and hopped into her vehicle to meet with a client. She never noticed she was being watched by an individual in a black SUV.

* * * * * * *

Look at her. I hate that bitch. Queen Rayne it's time for you to be knocked off your high horse. It's time for you to pay for all your shit. You dirty whore.

Chapter 3

David was at his desk working on his computer when Kaci softly knocked on his door.

"Come in," he said as he looked up from the monitor.

"Ms. Eugene what do I owe the pleasure of this visit?"

Kaci smiled. "I have some exciting news that I wanted to share with you. I'm a semi-finalist in the Atlanta's Young Poet competition."

"Congratulations. That's great."

"Well since you seemed pretty excited when I told you I did spoken word I was coming to invite you to the show."

"Nice. When is it?"

"It's Saturday at eight at Club Nigeria."

"Congratulations again and I will try my best to come check you out."

"Cool. Hope you're able to make it. I'll go now, I'm sure you're busy."

"Crazy busy. You know how the end of the month gets."

"Yes. Don't hesitate to call me if you need me to help

with the audits."

"Sure thing."

David knew that Kaci had a crush on him and was flattered. He thought that she was a beautiful girl but he felt no woman was worth losing his wife over. There had been a slight strain in his and Rayne's relationship after she unloaded her secrets to him, but he loved her none the less. Though David decided to honor their commitment, he was mentally exhausted. *An evening of poetry may not be that bad,* he thought as he put Kaci's event in his PDA.

* * * * * * *

Rayne returned to her office after an afternoon of meeting with clients and potential clients. April was at her desk and greeted Rayne with a smile.

"Somebody is loved today," she sang.

"What are you talking about April? All chipper and stuff."

"I'm talking about you getting gifts in sexy wrapping from the hubby. I've been dying to know what is in it so come open it."April pulled her to a box that was on her desk.

Rayne admired the flower box. The wrapping was black satin with a hot pink lace ribbon. "The box is very nice," Rayne said with a huge grin on her face. "I can't wait to see what David sent." She looked at the attached card, "*With all my heart.*"

"Awwww," April said looking over Rayne's shoulder.

April was a hopeless romantic who hadn't found love yet so she lived through Rayne and David's relationship. Rayne picked up the box and gently shook it before she slid the ribbon off and carefully unwrapped the box. April was shaking with anticipation.

"I can't believe you have not ripped into this box yet."

"My dear April, these things must be handled with finesse. When you get presents from your significant other you can't just be tearing into them like a mad woman. Trust me," Rayne said as she jiggled the box. April gave Rayne the "yeah ok" look and began tapping her foot.

"Ok. Ok," Rayne said as she tore the last piece of paper off.

Rayne smiled as she lifted the top off of the box. She expected to see long stem roses but to her surprise the content was very different. Rayne screamed, dropped the box, and ran towards the door.

"What," April began before she screamed as well.

Inside of the box were not the long stem roses that Rayne expected. The box was filled with spiders that begun spurring out of the box all over the table. Rayne ran outside and April was close behind her. They both were afraid of spiders; Rayne deathly.

Once outside April called Bobby, the police, and an exterminator. Rayne was crying by the time Bobby got there. She tried to contain herself, but she could not shake the feeling of the spiders crawling on her.

Bobby and April were going over possible scenarios when a police car came to the office. They met the officer at his car while Rayne stood off to the side.

Rayne's mind was racing a mile a minute. *Who sent the package and why did they send it?* Then she thought about David. Rayne knew she should tell him about the incident but she did not want to worry him. They had enough problems that they were working through and she did not want to add one more thing.

Rayne and April made their statements to the policeman; Officer Jennings. He'd asked her if anyone had any animosity toward her, business or personal. Rayne said no but she thought about Imani, who had coincidently called her earlier that day. Imani had expressed on several occasions that she was not happy about Rayne cutting her off. She was convinced that she and Rayne were supposed to be together. "No," Rayne said choosing not to mention her brief lesbian affair.

"Ok ladies. That will be all for your statements. I need to see the box," Officer Jennings said.

"I'll show you," Bobby said before he escorted him into the building.

"I'm leaving. My nerves are shot. I need a drink. Call me on my cell if you need anything," Rayne said to April.

"Ok. You be sure to relax. Don't worry about anything over here. Bobby and I will handle it. The exterminator should be here soon," April assured.

"Thanks April."

"No problem Rayne."

Rayne forced a smile, said a last goodbye, got into her car, and left. She was a block away from her office when her phone rang; it was Imani. Rayne answered the phone with no pleasantry in her voice. "Don't call me anymore you crazy bitch! You better stay away from anything that belongs to me or you will be sorry!" Rayne hung up before Imani had the opportunity to say anything.

She drove home, took a hot bubble bath, and drunk a few glasses of wine. Lucky for her that day was a day her mother-in-law had planned to pick the children up from school.

She was still in chill mode when David got home. He asked her how her day was and against the faint voice of reason she omitted the special delivery in her recollection of the day. *So much for not withholding information Rayne.*

Chapter 4

Bruce had eagerly been waiting to meet Angela and baby Angelica. He'd waited so long for a grand baby (a biological one) and he was ready to spoil her. Bruce was a Type 2 diabetic with bad circulation. His diabetes hindered him from driving long distances so he was unable to visit them on his own.

James put off Bruce meeting Angela for as long as he could. Every time Bruce suggested a visit James would always come up with an excuse. Not because he did not want Bruce around but because he wanted to hide the incidents of the past. Angela knew of Rayne but not their relationship and definitely not the rape. Bruce called James and told him he was going to get on the road to see the baby if James wouldn't bring her to him; definitely not what James wanted with his condition. With him not having a relationship with his mother, outside of his brother Eric, his father was all the family he had.

James battled with how he was going to pull off the

meeting. He decided to pick up Bruce and bring him to their apartment versus taking them to Bruce's house that had pictures of Rayne everywhere. James was sweating bullets the whole ride while Bruce continuously expressed his excitement. James became nervous of his decision when Bruce started going on about how he was glad James finally gave him a grandchild though he was grateful for Rayne allowing him to be a papa to her children. *Lord please let us get through this visit. I know I need to tell Angela that Rayne is my stepsister, but please don't let her find out by Pop's lips.*

James pulled up to the apartment. He grabbed Bruce's bag and lead him to the apartment. Angela met them at the door with Angelica in her arms.

"Hello Mr. Bruce. So nice to finally meet you," Angela said with a huge smile on her face.

"Likewise young lady," Bruce said as he reached out and gave her a hug and kiss on the cheek. "Oh, and this must be little Miss Angelica. Come to your Papa," he said reaching for the baby. "Oh, my goodness she's beautiful."

"Thank you," Angela said. "Come on in. The living room is this way."

Bruce followed Angela never looking up from Angelica, who looked back at him. Bruce sat on the couch, while James and Angela watched from the loveseat.

"She looks like my mama. Our Indian genes run deep. We gonna have to keep a shot gun on deck," Bruce said still looking at Angelica's innocent face.

Angelica looked up into Bruce's face, smiled, and cooed.

"I ain't playing angel. Your Papa is going to be ready for them knuckle heads."

"Don't worry her daddy will be ready too," James quickly added.

"You better stay ready because she's beautiful," Bruce said before he turned to Angela. "Ms. Angela you are beautiful yourself."

That she was. The woman James met who had the boyish figure was no more. She'd put on twenty good pounds after having Angelica. Her hips were more defined, her ass was plump, and her boobs had grown to a full C cup.

Angela smiled, "Thank you Mr. Bruce. You're so kind."

"Thank you for not only putting up with James but also for bringing such a precious jewel into the world. I'm so in love with her," Bruce said as he brought Angelica to his face and snuggled her belly. James couldn't remember a time he'd seen Bruce that happy. It made his heart full to see his pop's enjoyment.

* * * * * * *

"Nice to finally meet you Ms. Flores."

"Likewise Mrs. Smith."

"I've pulled several listing from your specifications." Rayne spread the stack of listing sheets on the meeting table at Smith and Smith's. "These are the ones that I feel will best suit you. Therefore the ones I would like for you to see first," Rayne said pointing to four pictures.

"Oh my goodness this one is gorgeous."

"Yes it is; three bedrooms, three bathrooms, two car garage, basement and pool all within budget. The current owners have done beautiful upgrades in the kitchen and bathrooms," Rayne explained.

"I'm so excited. I can't wait to get started," responded Ms. Flores.

"I know our appointment was set for tomorrow but I had a cancelation. So I'm free this afternoon if you'd like to start today."

"That would be great!" Ms. Flores exclaimed.

"Wonderful. We will start with these four," Rayne said as she stacked the listings.

"Sounds good."

"Let me let my colleague know that I'm leaving and get my purse. Then I'll be ready to go."

Rayne touched bases with April then she and Ms. Flores headed out in her Chevy Tahoe.

* * * * * * *

James let out a sigh of relief as he and Angela laid in the bed.

"What a day. I'm beat," he said.

"Yes, me too. It was a good day though. I'm glad I finally got to meet your dad. He's great."

"Pops is a pretty amazing dude. He's in love with

Angelica. She doesn't even know it yet but she's going be able to get whatever she wants from that guy."

"Yeah, I can see that happening. She's going to be spoiled rotten. I don't know who's going to be worse; your dad or my mom."

"Oh hell. We're gonna have one rotten ass kid." They both chuckled.

"Angelica has given Mom life again; a reason to live. I'm so glad she's getting better and will be able to come home soon."

"Me too," James said as he held Angela close. "So how about you give daddy some of that good loving?"

"Baby, your dad is across the hall," Angela whispered.

"So."

"So I don't want him to hear us."

"You don't want him to hear us? So you think you gonna hold the good good from me all weekend?"

"Uh..."

"Uh no. We can be quiet and if not we got plenty of pillows for you to bite."

"But baby..." her words were lost as James kissed her softly on her neck.

James pressed his hardening penis on her, "You gonna tell him no? You know he has a mind of his own."

"But..." she started.

"Shhhhh...You're thinking too much. You're tripping so I'm going to talk to my girl; me and her be on the same sheet of music."

James shifted in the bed and got to where he had a clear view Angela's entire body. He peeled off her panties and talked to the lips that he knew would see the situation as he did. Angela moaned as he used his tongue to spread her lips. She tried hard but she could never resist James.

"So are you still saying no?" James lifted his head and asked.

"No," Angela said panting.

"Good. Now grab that pillow," he said as he flipped her over.

* * * * * * *

Evelyn sat in the corner of the hospital's chapel crying. "Lord this cannot be happening. She's my baby girl. Are you punishing me for the deceitful way I got her? I know I was wrong for befriending Rayne and tricking her into giving Elaina up, but please don't let my baby die. I'm sorry God. Please forgive me," Evelyn prayed in between the tears.

Two months prior Elaina was diagnosed with acute lymphoblastic leukemia. Her symptoms went undetected from Evelyn and her husband Stewart. They'd equated her fatigue, weight loss, and bone pain with her extensive extracurricular activities that included soccer, softball, and tennis.

Elaina had started chemotherapy immediately to destroy the cancer cells. The treatments were going well; so Evelyn thought until Elaina's doctor told her differently.

"The cancer has produced at an accelerated rate and though the chemotherapy is working, it is not working fast enough to combat these infections. Until we cure Elaina's infection we are going to hold off on chemo," he'd said to Evelyn and her husband Stewart.

"Ok Bob. Cut to the chase on what's happening," Stewart said to his colleague.

"Elaina is going to need a bone marrow transplant once her treatment is complete otherwise I believe the cancer will return IF we are even able to get rid of it. The chance for success is greater when the marrow is donated by a relative. I'm telling you both now to prepare you mentally to provide that marrow," Dr. Whitman said. Evelyn and Stewart looked at each other realizing their lie had finally caught up to them.

Evelyn knew she had to contact Rayne and come clean if she wanted to save her daughter. That is how she ended up in the chapel stuck in her guilt. She wiped her tears and made a decision to call Rayne the next day once she got her feelings a little more under control.

Chapter 5

Saturdays were usually good days for David and Rayne. He hardly worked on Saturdays and Rayne only worked appointments on Saturdays, so they had a little cuddle time before the kids started demanding their attention.

With the heighten tension between them they didn't cuddle much anymore and David missed their closeness. He rolled over and woke Rayne with soft kisses and gentle caressing. She woke up with a smile on her face.

"Mmmm. Good morning Mr. Smith. I haven't been woken up like this in a long time. Mmmm…It's nice," she said softly as David set his sights on her breast.

David's touch made her melt on the inside; she became putty in his hands. "Oh baby."

Rayne missed the sensual way David touched her. Though they still made love occasionally, it wasn't as passionate as it once was. Rayne got lost in the moment and yearned for David. Her entire body warmed when he finally kissed her. She anticipated feeling him as he did her.

He caressed her hair as he entered her. Rayne looked up at David as he slow grinded her walls loving every second of their closeness.

"I love you David," Rayne said with tears in her eyes as she released her juices.

"Hmmm. That's what I'm talking about," David said as he felt the warmth of her fluids. "I love you too Rayne. Til death."

David worked Rayne over as he commanded her hot juicy vagina. After thirty minutes and what seemed like a gallon of sweat between the two of them, David was ready to explode. He embraced Rayne as he thrusted deep inside of her. A tear escaped from Rayne's eye as David came inside of her. David kissed her on the forehead and she was on cloud nine. They shared a brief kiss before he pulled out and laid beside her.

"Damn. We haven't started a Saturday off like that in a while," David said in between some pants. "You got me out of breath girl."

"That's good. You better get your cardio up old man," she said jokingly.

David laughed. "I got your old man," he said as he tickled Rayne.

"Ok. Ok. I'm sorry grandpa," Rayne said as she laughed hysterically as David continued tickling her. "Ok, I stop. You're not old," she added.

David stopped tickling her and said, "That's what I

thought."

Rayne gave him a peck on his cheek, "I'm about to hop in the shower. I'm sticky."

"Ok babe. I'll be in there in a minute."

Rayne gave him a big smile and went into the bathroom. David laid there for a minute. Rayne's cell phone rang just as he sat up. He reached over to her night stand and answered it. "Hello, Rayne Smith's phone."

"Good morning this is Officer Jennings from the Clayton County Sheriff's Department. Is Mrs. Smith available?"

"This is her husband David. Is there something I can help you with?"

"Well I was calling to check on your wife after her incident to ensure there had not been anymore strange occurrences."

"Strange occurrences?"

"Yes," Office Jennings said hesitantly.

"Officer, was it Jennings?"

"Yes."

"I have no clue what you are talking about. What incident?"

"Well sir I think you will have to speak to your wife about that. I'm sorry if I've caused any inconvenience but like I said I was calling to do a follow up. Please have Mrs. Smith call me if she's had any more issues."

"Ok. I will relay the message," David said feeling both

worried and furious.

"Thank you and I'm sorry for any inconvenience I may have caused."

"No problem officer. You have a good day."

"Thank you and you do the same."

David hung up the phone and immediately went into the bathroom.

"I was starting to think you weren't coming," Rayne said from the shower.

"I thought we were starting over. No secrets."

Rayne turned the shower off and said, "We are."

David paused, bit down on his lip and said, "Then why in the fuck is a police officer calling to check on you after an incident I know nothing about!"

"Babe-"

"What the fuck Rayne?" he said shaking his head.

Rayne knew she'd messed up. David hardly raised his voice at her and never ever cussed at her.

"I'm trying Rayne. Through all the bullshit, lies, and secrets I'm still here but damn it Rayne. How much more do you expect me to take?"

"Baby please calm down."

"Calm down? Fuck all that Rayne. I'm tired of your deceitfulness."

"Just let me explain. Please," Rayne said as she grabbed David's arm. "I did not tell you because I didn't want you to worry. So please take that into consideration.

The other day there was a flower box delivered to the office. I thought you sent me flowers because the card said 'with all my heart'. When I opened the box it was filled with hundreds maybe even thousands of spiders. April called the police. That's it," Rayne said with the inability to meet David's eyes.

"That's it? Let me get this right, on top of all the other crazy stuff now you have a what? Stalker?"

"I really don't know David. I'm trying to figure it out myself."

"Exactly...yourself," he said with a hard sigh. "Thanks for telling me," he added before he walked out of the bathroom.

Damn. I fucked up again, Rayne thought as she sat on the ledge of the tub.

* * * * * * *

Today is the day, James thought as he watched Angela sleep. His mind raced with many thoughts as she woke up.

"Good morning. Watching me again?" she asked with a smile.

"Of course. Good morning beautiful," James said with kiss. Angela scooted close to James and he held her as they spoke.

"What are you going to do today baby?" Angela asked.

"I'm going to take Pops home and then I want to have a special evening with my lady. How does that sound?"

"Sounds good to me."

"Good. I love you Angela Arnold."

"I love you too James Black. Forever and ever."

"I hope so," James whispered as he held her close.

* * * * * * *

Kaci danced around her bedroom getting ready for her poetry competition. She sang with Lauryn Hill as she switched her outfit for the second time. Kaci smiled at her reflection in the mirror; pleased with her selection of the black strapless jumpsuit and gold pumps. The jumpsuit's heart shaped top showcased her breast nicely as the waistline showcased her coke bottle shape. Kaci turned and smiled at the way the outfit displayed her apple butt. *Damn I look good. Hopefully David comes and without his wife. He will not be able to resist me tonight,* Kaci thought as she touched her breast.

"I need you David, if it's quite all right. I love you David, you warm a lonely night. I need you David. Trust in me when I say 'it's ok'. Oh, oh pretty baby..." Kaci sang. She put on her makeup and headed to the club.

* * * * * * *

David left Rayne at home with the kids and went to club Nigeria. He hadn't been out alone in a long time but after Rayne's continued deceit he felt he needed to get out.

David entered the club, got himself a drink, and found an empty table. Smooth R&B played in preparation for the show; he vibed to the Maxwell that was being played as he sipped on his drink. The club began to fill up quickly. David watched as the people flowed into the space. *I'm glad I got here early and avoided the crowd of people.*

David was tapped on the shoulder. He looked up at a beautiful woman who was five nine, curvy, olive skinned, with long black wavy hair. David was taken aback by the woman's exotic beauty.

"Hello. Sorry to bother you but is anyone sitting here?"

"No."

"Do you mind if I sit with you?"

"No, be my guest."

"Thank you," she said as she took a seat.

"I'm Anna by the way and you are?"

"David."

"Nice to meet you David. Thank you for your kindness. I did not want to stand."

"You're welcome," David said with a smile. Anna smiled back at him.

* * * * * * *

Kaci peaked through the curtain on the stage and was happy to see David center stage. She watched as Anna tapped David and sat with him. *No bitch. I hope you don't have sights on that one. I already have one bitch to deal with.* "Alright guys the show starts in ten minutes so get y'all stuff together," the event host said back stage.

Kaci pulled her head back through the curtain and prepped for her performance. She tuned out the rest of the world and filled her creative space in her mind. Kaci was the fifth act to go on and she was ready! When she heard the host say, "Now we have the talented and beautiful Kaci with *Sexuality of a Dream,*" along with the snaps, she strutted her stuff onto the stage. Kaci smiled as the guys whistled and cheered.

"Thank you everyone. I hope you enjoy," Kaci said making eye contact with David.

"Everlasting is how I describe the lust that lingers inside of me, Ride him I must, Looking into his eyes when I climax, Destiny is calling for us, We are prisoners of a fantasy that we created, but can't control, My soul is burning for more, Why me, Why now, Why here, Will he respect me in the morning, Do I respect him now, Lights out, Candles lit, Close the door, and pour your pleasure on me, Is this what he wants, Is this even what I want, Let me stop playing games, Am I dreaming, Could he be the one, This all has to be dream, And as I wake he enters me."

Kaci was engulfed in her words and closed her eyes during her performance; making her words and motions sensual. When she opened her eyes people were on their feet snapping and cheering. She was happy to see David among them. He shot her a head nod and "good job" when their eyes met.

Kaci bowed and exited the stage as the host returned. She exhaled once she got back stage and relaxed until the end of the show. As Kaci waited for the winner to be announced by the host all she could think about was the woman who was cozying up with David. She didn't know who she was or what she was doing with him, but she didn't like it. Kaci got angry thinking of the possibility of her not being his choice outside of Rayne. "No bitch, you will not come up in here and snatch him from under my nose," Kaci whispered.

"And the first runner up is the beautiful and ultra-talented...Kaci." the host exclaimed. Kaci stepped from behind the curtain; everyone whistled and clapped. She felt like she'd won by the love the crowd had given her. Her smile shined bright from the stage. Kaci was overwhelmed by happiness, especially when she looked at David. He had a huge smile on his face and gave her a thumb up. Nothing could take away the high Kaci had at that moment...except for Anna and her growing comfort with David. She did not like the too friendly shoulder and arm touches from Anna.

* * * * * * *

Rayne put the children to bed and attempted to watch a movie. She could not concentrate though because of how David left things. She feared that she may had lost her husband. He left out of the house looking good and smelling good with no word to her; something that had never happened in the ten plus years of being with him.

Rayne fought the thoughts of David going out to see or be with another woman. There was no way she pushed her husband in the arms of another woman. Or was there?

Rayne was in deep thought when her cell phone rang. She quickly reached for the phone hoping it was David; instead she saw an unfamiliar Mississippi phone number.

"Hello," Rayne said.

"Hello. Rayne?"

"Yes. Who is this?" she said curiously.

"This is Evelyn."

"Hey Evelyn. What a surprise. How's things going?"

"Honestly things are not going well."

"What's wrong?"

Evelyn took a deep breath and said, "Well I have something to tell you. It's not only difficult for me to say but it's also going to be difficult for you to hear."

"Evelyn you really have me nervous right now. Is it Bruce? Has something happened to him?" she asked panicked.

"No it's not Bruce. He is well as far as I know. It's about your baby."

"Ethan?"

"No. The one you gave up those many years ago."

Those words upset the pit of Rayne's stomach.

"Evelyn you know better than anyone that is a part of my past that I plan to let remain in the past. Therefore I will not discuss that with you," Rayne said with infliction in her voice.

Evelyn knew the situation was a sore topic for Rayne but she had no choice but to tell her about Elaina if she wanted to save her life. "Rayne I understand that but she is very sick and you as her biological mother can help her."

"Wait. She? Sick? How do you know all of this?"

"Because she is my daughter."

"What? What are you talking about Evelyn?"

Evelyn got quiet as the shame surfaced.

"Don't fucking get quiet now. What do you mean Evelyn?"

"I've been raising your daughter. I was the doctor friend that Sarah and Bill spoke of."

"You got to be fucking kidding me," Rayne said as her rage began to brew.

"I'm sorry Rayne."

"No the hell you are not! Y'all bitches probably planned that from the beginning. First my best friend tries to kill me. Now the other friend I thought I had used me for my baby! Y'all hoes weren't shit! This shit's adding up now; you being so helpful with the adoption, the Browns being so concerned with the well being of the baby, and them wanting to move me in. I can't with this right now Evelyn."

"I'm sorry Rayne. I truly am but please don't let our daughter die."

"I agree. You are sorry," Rayne said as she hung up the phone.

Rayne was furious with Evelyn. She grabbed a bottle of wine and popped the cork. One and a half bottles later her anger subsided and she was overwhelmed with sadness for the child; her child. She cried herself to sleep.

* * * * * * *

James rushed home after dropping his father off at home. He was excited about the evening because he planned to propose to Angela. He'd lined up the babysitter for Angelica, made reservations at a downtown restaurant, got the two-carat diamond engagement ring sized, and bought flowers for the special evening.

James was on cloud nine when he arrived at the apartment. That feeling quickly went away when he got into the bedroom where Angela was sitting on the bed. James went to hand her the flowers but instead of being greeted with love he was greeted by Angela's red eyes and wet face.

"Baby, what's wrong?" he asked concernedly as he dropped the flowers on the bed and went to hold Angela. Angela snatched away from James. "What's up baby? Why you pull away from me?"

"Because you disgust me," she exclaimed.

He stood in shock looking confused. "What? Disgust you?"

"Yes! How could you?"

"How could I what?" Angela began to cry. "Angela talk to me. What did I do? Baby please talk to me," he pleaded almost in tears because he knew he hadn't done anything to hurt Angela. "Baby please," he pleaded once more.

Angela handed him an envelope that she had laying on the night stand. She crossed her arms as she watched him pull out the contents. James' eyes got big as he looked at paperwork on his rape conviction, old family pictures of Bruce, Sonya, him, Eric, and Rayne (one of the pictures had "BROTHER AND SISTER, COPARENTS, OR BOTH" written on it), and a note. James read the note, "*How well do you know the man that you sleep beside every night? The manipulator. The rapist. The felon. The murder.*"

"Baby," James said reaching for Angela once more. Not only did she pull from him she slapped him.

"Stay away from me," she said walking to the bedroom door. "Pack your shit and go."

"Baby no," he said as she walked out. He went behind her and met her in the kitchen. She had grabbed her keys and was picking up her purse. James grabbed her by her waist. She fought him telling him to let her go.

"I'm going to Jessica's to pick up Angelica. Be gone when I get back."

"No Angela. I'm not leaving. I love you. Please let me explain."

"Explain what? That you've kept some serious shit from me? Or that I really don't fucking know you? Fuck that and you too!" Angela spat.

James' heart broke with that statement and the level of anger she said it in. She broke him. Tears fell from his eyes. Shocked that he could even cry he quickly wiped them. "Ok Angela. Listen to me. You are the only woman I've ever loved and I'm not trying to lose you. I love you and you have my daughter. How about I move into the spare room to give you space? Please don't break up our family. You're all I got."

Angela was having an internal battle between her heart and her mind. "Please," James said again as she contemplated.

"You better stay out of my way," Angela said before she stormed out of the apartment.

Chapter 6

"Oh David. Give it to me baby," Kaci screamed from her bedroom as she came.

"Damn, Kaci. I'm about to cum."

"Call me Ms. Eugene," Kaci said as she felt the cum forcefully shoot into the condom.

Kaci's celebratory sex had come to an end and she felt good. Kaci was in her own world as she laid on her bed and attempted to slow her pulse. She was oblivious to what was going on around her.

"You hear me Kaci?"

"Huh?" she said coming back to reality.

"What did you say?" she asked looking at the sexy chocolate man in front of her.

"I said, I'm feeling you Kaci. You're a talented and beautiful woman," he paused as if looking for the words to say, "I get you being into role playing and shit but who is this David that you're so into?"

"Derrick..."

"Come on Kaci. We've been doing this song and dance for months. Don't get me wrong the sex is the bomb and I want to continue what we got going but obviously you're into buddy. So who is he?"

"He's my boss."

"Your boss? Man," Derrick said shaking his head.

"Other than him being your boss, what's the deal?"

"He's married," Kaci said.

Derrick sat next to her on the bed and said, "Baby girl I think you're setting yourself up but I'll be your David anytime."

"Good. How about one more round?"

"Shit I'm down."

Kaci straddled Derrick and slipped her tongue in his mouth as he gripped her ass.

Chapter 7

Rayne woke to an empty bed and puffy eyes from crying. She got up and went to the guest bedroom, David's office, and then the kitchen looking for David. He was nowhere to be found. *I know good and well he did not stay out all night*, she thought as she stomped up the stairs.

Rayne went back to their bedroom and grabbed her cell phone. She called David's phone but he did not answer. She looked at the time; it was just before eight o'clock. Yes, it was early but not too early to call her in-laws' house. *For David's sake he better be there,* Rayne thought as she dialed the phone.

Her mother-in-law answered the phone, "Hello."

"Good morning Beverly. I didn't wake you did I?" .Rayne asked.

"No darling. I just came in from the garden. Is everything alright?"

"Yes. I woke up and David wasn't here. I got a little worried. Is he at your house?"

"Yes. He's asleep though. Do you want me to wake him?"

"Oh, no ma'am. Just let him know I called when he gets up."

"Ok honey. Is it ok if I come get my babies today?"

"Of course. As a matter a fact I'll bring them to you. That way I can stop by the office and handle a few things."

"Good. How long?"

"It'll be within the next hour."

"Ok. I'll make them breakfast so don't worry about that."

"Yes ma'am."

"See you after awhile."

"Ok. Bye."

Rayne appreciated Beverly's involvement in her children's lives. When she ended the call with Beverly, Rayne felt relieved. Relieved that her husband was at his parents' house and not laid up with another woman. Eva came into the room as she sat on the bed.

"Good morning Love Bug," Rayne said as she hugged her.

"Good morning Mommy. Where's Daddy?"

"He's over to your Grandma and Papa's house. Go wake Evan up and y'all get dressed. Y'all are going to spend the day over there."

"Yay!" Eva said as she ran out of the room.

Rayne showered, got herself and Ethan dressed, and

left for her in-laws'.

* * * * * * *

David shamefully laid in the bed at his parents' house. He watched his phone as Rayne called and choose not to answer it. He heard the house phone ring shortly after and knew it had to have been her as well. Yes he did end up at his parents' house but he had not been there the entire night.

David decided it would be best to shower before Rayne got there; to wash any remnants of his night away. He got up and hopped in the shower. He replayed the night as the water ran on his body.

David and Anna got real acquainted during the poetry showcase. He congratulated Kaci on her performance and briefly talked to her. He kept the conversation brief because he had made plans to meet Anna for coffee.

They sat at Starbucks and talked for over an hour. She shared with him that she moved to Atlanta to start over after a bad relationship. David enjoyed how easy it was to talk to Anna. She brought him a calm that he had been missing with Rayne. David got so comfortable that their night cap ended at Anna's hotel room. The small voice in David's head told him it was a bad idea, but that voice was dulled by the burning desire that Anna had awaken in him.

David sat on a loveseat near a balcony. He looked at the city lights through the slightly opened curtain. "Excuse me," she said as she went into the bathroom.

What am I doing? I should not be here, he thought. His guilt overtook him and he decided to leave. When he got up from the chair Anna came out of the bathroom in her bra, panties, and pumps. David wanted to move but the sight of how her perfectly put together body looked as she stood there paralyzed him. He admired the red hot underwear set that sat on her olive skin.

"I hope you weren't going to leave," she said throwing her hip into a sexy pose.

"Well..." he started.

"Well?" Anna asked moving closer to him. She kissed him gently on his lips. "Well?" she said again with another kiss. The final "Well" came from her lips before she and David engaged in a full-fledged passionate kiss. By then his man had betrayed Rayne with the hardness he had for Anna.

Their tongues danced together as David undressed with help from Anna. She led him to the bed where she used her tongue as she plotted to keep his attention on her and not his wife and children.

"You like that Papi," she asked exotically.

"Oh yes," David mustered up.

"Good," she said.

David's dick throbbed in the shower as he thought about Anna's mouth on him. "Shit," he said as he massaged himself. He thought back to the way Anna felt with his initial entry. The tight new pussy took him perfectly and he enjoyed every moment of it. David sped up his tempo in the shower until he once again released himself on Anna's account.

David knew he opened Pandora's Box, but he didn't care. With all Rayne had put him through, he felt justified.

Chapter 8

James sat in his Impala in front of the coffee shop he and Jack usually met at. It had been a week since the anonymous package was delivered to Angela. She had not spoken to him and overlooked him whenever they were in the same area. James was tired of it and was ready to do anything to win her heart back. When Angela went out, he snatched the envelope. He intended to have Jack look into its origin.

He watched as Jack pulled into the parking lot of the small coffee shop. James grabbed the envelope from his passenger seat and met Jack inside.

"How's it going?" Jack asked.

"It's going," James replied dryly. "I got another task for you."

"Alright. Lay it on me."

"A week ago my girl got this delivered," he said as he handed Jack the envelope. He continued as Jack went through the contents, "I want to know who sent it and why."

Jack shook his head as he looked at the pictures and the note. He wanted to question James about the reliability of the "truth", but choose not to because of James' demeanor.

"Alright boss I'll handle it."

"Good deal," James said as he stood up.

"One other thing," Jack said. "I know you haven't been pressed on the Elaina situation but I have some information that I think you need to know. She has been in the hospital for almost a month now."

"What?" he said as he sat back down.

"She has leukemia. The word I got is that she is awaiting a bone marrow transplant."

"Damn."

"Yeah. So you know, those take better from a blood relative; just some food for thought."

"Alright. Thank you man."

James sat for a minute after Jack left, letting the news marinate in his mind. He knew he had prolonged having the needed conversation with Rayne long enough. They needed to talk and quickly.

* * * * * * *

Rayne was at a lunch meeting with her client Taylor Barksdale. She and her husband were in the process of purchasing a foreclosed mansion. Rayne was excited about the half million dollar home. Rayne helped her purchase her first home when she relocated to Atlanta and appreciated her loyalty with her second home.

"So everything is going as planned and all we are waiting on now is the final signature from the bank," Rayne paused as her phone vibrated. She silenced the vibration without looking and continued, "After that we will be ready to do the closing."

Her phone rang again; James had hung up and called right back. "Excuse me. My apologies," she said as she powered the phone off. *What the hell does he want?* She thought briefly before continuing her meeting. "I foresee you having your keys by the end of the week."

"Great," Taylor said.

Rayne and Taylor ate lunch with Rayne not giving James a second thought.

* * * * * * *

James sat pissed but not surprised that Rayne didn't answer his call. His mind raced with thoughts. He already felt lost about possibly losing Angela and the family they'd built and refused to lose another part of himself. He made the decision to take the situation head on. He started his car and made his way to Jackson Memorial.

Chapter 9

David and Anna's relationship got hotter than he expected it to. He knew it was wrong being with her, but it felt so right when they were together. Besides the sexual attraction, she stimulated his mind with their intellectual conversation. Not that he could not get the same from Rayne, but with all she put him though he honestly did not want it from her.

David sat at his desk anxiously awaiting his and Anna's lunch date. He finalized all of his open documents and texted Rayne so that he could leave. He'd ensured that Rayne was busy with clients so that he would not get caught up in his love triangle.

David told his secretary that he was leaving for lunch and may or may not return to the office. She smiled and gave him a head nod with no worries.

* * * * * * *

Kaci sped through the Atlanta traffic as smoothly as she could ensuring that David did not see her. Immediately after David walked off from the secretary's desk, Kaci went and asked questions. She'd noticed the changes in David and was both curious and suspicious of the reasoning behind it. She ran scenarios in her head; not liking any of them.

After thirty minutes of travel, David pulled up to Rosie's Italian Eatery. Kaci watched from a distance as David parked in the quaint parking lot. He got out and moved to an SUV that was next to him. David opened the vehicle door and Anna step out.

"That bitch! What the fuck?!?!"

Kaci's insides cringed as she watched David and Anna kiss. Her legs twitched as they embraced, smiled at one another, and walked to the restaurant door hand in hand.

"I knew that bitch was going to be a problem. She has to go," she spat as she peeled off.

Chapter 10

Elaina was asleep in her hospital bed when James walked in. He let out a faint sigh as he looked at Elaina's fragile body. He'd envisioned their first encounter several times since his search began, but never imagined it being in a hospital room. He took in the features of her face looking for similarities to his own. Looking at her reminded him of himself when he was young.

Evelyn entered the room as James took a step closer to Elaina. "Who the hell are you and what are you doing here?" she spat.

"Oh, excuse me," he said jumping back. "You must be Mrs. James."

"Yes. Now, who the hell are you?"

"My name is James Black...I'm Elaina's father."

"Father?" Evelyn asked with her hand to her heart.

James nodded his head. "Lets go talk in the waiting room," Evelyn said.

James followed her to the waiting room that was down

the hallway. "I know you probably have a lot of questions, but just know that I am here to help."

"Thank you and yes I do. Did Rayne send you?"

"No. I'm not sure if you're aware of mine and Rayne's relationship, but she is not very verbal with me. She only told me about the baby, Elaina, when her back was against the wall."

Evelyn sat silent as James continued, "I've had an investigator in place looking for Elaina ever since I found out about her a little over a year ago. Today he told me that she was sick and in need of a bone marrow transplant. I'm here to be tested to see if I'm a match."

Evelyn let out a sigh of relief, "Thank you Lord! Thank you so much for coming. I'll let Doctor Whitman know so we can get you tested quickly because it takes a few days for the results to come back. I didn't know what to do when Rayne didn't call me back. I know she's upset, but I thought she'd at least call me back."

Evelyn contacted the doctor and within an hour James was in a hospital gown being prepped for the sample to be taken. As he sat in the room in the hospital gown thoughts of Elaina's frail body filled his head. He was determined to be a part of her life.

Chapter 11

Kaci waited in her car for Imani to come out of the old fashioned ice cream shop where David and Anna were inside of. It had been a week of her spying on David's frequent rendezvous with Anna.

She was on pins and needles by the time Imani opened the door and got into her car. "Soooo..." Kaci probed.

"So I go up in there and they're at a table up in the cut. I walked up and said 'Oh, hello. David right?' He says 'Yeah' looking all crazy. Then he asked, 'Do I know you?' Guess he didn't recognize me with my clothes on," she added with a chuckle. "I said 'Yes I'm Imani or Mercedes as many call me.' He almost shit bricks when I said that. The whole time old girl looked confused as shit. Then I asked, 'How's Rayne doing? I haven't spoken to her in a minute.' He was like 'She's good.' I said 'Good, let her know I moved to Atlanta and I'll get at her soon.' I know I pissed him off but he couldn't show it in front of his Barbie. I said it was good seeing him and left him sweating."

"Good," Kaci said with a sneaky grin on her face. Shortly after, David and Anna were exiting the ice cream shop. Kaci and Imani watched as they moved to their cars, prematurely ending their date. The two of them sat in the car with smug looks on their faces; Kaci thinking of her desired relationship with David and Imani of hers with Rayne.

Chapter 12

James sat in his car with a somber expression on his face. He'd just met with Elaina's doctor and was not happy with the conversation they had. Dr. Whitman informed him that not only was he not a match for the bone marrow transplant, but there was no possible way that he was Elaina's father. Evelyn had allowed him to interact with Elaina as "one of mommy's friends" during the days that they were awaiting the test results. He grew fond of her. She was a great kid and he would have been proud to call her his own.

James was crushed by the results. He was hurt on many levels, the main being that Randy was her father and he killed him. "Fuck," he said as that thought crossed his mind. Randy was a piece of shit true enough but James felt awful because he took away one of her two possibilities for a healthy life. This especially bothered him because Rayne was being such a bitch. James shook his head when he thought about how selfish she was being. He had become tired of making excuses for her behavior. He picked up the phone and called her.

* * * * * * *

Rayne was sitting at her desk looking over some documents for her client Taylor when James called her. *What the fuck?* She thought as she sent him to voicemail. He immediately called back. *Why is he calling me so much these days?* She thought as she answered with an attitude.

"What?"

"Hello to you as well. I've been calling you."

"Whatever James. What do you want?"

"Do you have a few minutes because what I have to say will take a few minutes?"

"Not really but what do you want?"

"Alright Mrs. Nasty Attitude. I'd been calling you to talk more about the baby, but since then I've taken things into my own hands."

"The baby? What did you do?" she said in a slight whisper as she got up from her desk and walked towards the door not wanting to be heard by her agents.

"After you told me about the baby I hired a private investigator-"

"What?" Rayne said, but James did not stop.

"That along with my own digging is how I found out about Sky and Randy. But anyway, I found out about Evelyn and Stewart James and little Elaina; who I've heard that you recently learned of as well. When I called you a few days ago it was because I found out that she had leukemia and needed a bone marrow transplant. I went to the hospital; something you might want to do as well but that's neither here nor there right now. I went and got tested so that I could donate my marrow. Well, surprise surprise I was not a match. Unfortunately, the reason I was not a match was because I am not her father." Rayne let out a gasp. "So if Randy and I were the only two in the lineup, then his crab ass was her dad."

Rayne sat silently on the other side of the phone. "Are you there?" James asked.

"Yes," Rayne replied softly.

"I committed and you covered up the murder of the only other person who would be a match to that innocent little girl. So what do you have to say since your shit is coming back around?"

"Fuck you James!"

"Don't get mad at me because the truth hurts. I know and you know that your ass is not perfect. So the question is, will you stop being selfish and do the right thing by Elaina now? Chew on that. Later."

James hung up and Rayne stood outside of her agency in complete shock. James' words cut her to her core. Was she being selfish? How could she treat a child that she birthed so coldly?

Chapter 13

James was mentally exhausted from all the events he'd went through. Angela was still acting distant with him and that was tearing him apart inside. He walked into their apartment and there was a cold drab feeling that left him with an uneasy feeling. The blinds were all drawn and everything was still. He looked at his watch and it was only six pm; a time too early for the home to be settled for the evening; especially since Angelica had become a busy body.

James moved down the hall to Angelica's room. He peaked in and noticed that she was not in her crib. From her room James moved to the room he and Angela once shared. He slowly opened the closed door and found Angela on the bed with her face wet with tears.

"Baby what's wrong?" he asked. Angela looked up at him and then turned her head away. "Baby what's wrong?" He repeated as he moved to her.

"Nothing," she whispered.

"You don't cry for 'nothing' baby. Hell, I've never seen

you cry period until recently. Please talk to me," he said as he embraced her. He needed her and it was obvious to him that she needed him. He held her as she wiped her tears.

After a few minutes she said, "This is not how this was supposed to be. Everything was perfect and now it's not," she paused as more tears fell. "Why did you keep all of those secrets? I've never judged you. You could have told me. Do you not think that I knew you did not always fly right? Hell, you fucked my brains out after knowing me for all of ten minutes. I'm hurt that after all we've been through you still don't trust me. We have a daughter for pete's sake. I can't..." Angela began crying uncontrollable.

"Baby I'm sorry. Please stop crying. I'm sorry. I'm sorry. I need you to believe me. I love you so much. Please believe me." James started to cry, which shocked him and Angela. "Baby please. I need you. I will do whatever I have to, to make it right. Baby please," he pleaded.

Angela wiped the tears that were on James' cheeks and kissed his lips. "I forgive you, but no more secrets or I'm gone," she said.

"You don't have to worry about that. From now on I am an open book."

"Good." They sat silently enjoying the closeness they'd shared until Angela broke the silence with, "Now please make love to me. I've missed you."

James smiled, kissed her, and then said, "Wait I have something I have to do first."

Angela sat confused as he hopped up. He got to the door and then stopped, "Where's Angelica?"

"She's with Sarah."

"Oh ok," he said and then rushed out of the room. He went to where he'd been holding his things since Angela put him out of their bedroom and grabbed the engagement ring. He went back into the room to Angela.

"Are you alright?" she asked curious about what he rushed out for.

"I'm better than alright because I thought I'd lost you. Angela you've brought life to a very cold man. You've given me hope when I had none. I was serious when I said I can't live without you." He got on one knee and exposed the ring he had behind his back. "Will you be my wife?"

"OH MY GOODNESS," she exclaimed as she put her hand over her mouth. "What? Oh my goodness. I can't believe this. I don't know what to say."

"Say yes," James said with a smile.

"Yes."

"Yes?"

"Yes!" she exclaimed.

James put the ring on her finger. Then he scooped her up in a kiss and made love to her in a manner they both needed.

Chapter 14

David slid out of Anna's bed and grabbed his clothes off of the floor.

"Do you have to go Papi?" Anna asked with a kiss to his back.

"Oh baby quit. You know I like that."

"Exactly," she said laying more kisses along with soft gentle licks to his back.

"Oh baby…" he moaned. "I have to go. It's already after six. I have to get home."

"Alright," Anna said with a pout.

David turned to her and kissed her pouted lips, "I'll make it up to you. I promise."

"I'll make sure of that."

Damn she's beautiful, he thought as he looked into her eyes and saw the mischievousness behind her words. He got dressed and left Anna's.

David's thoughts were racing as he drove home. He loved Rayne but he'd developed a love for Anna as well; he wanted his cake and wanted to eat it too. For the first time he realized the struggle Rayne went through and why she lied to him about some of the things that had taken place. Though he felt guilty for what he was doing, he had no intent of stopping.

* * * * * * *

Rayne was in the kitchen cooking while Eva and Evan sat at the table finishing up homework and Ethan sat playing when David walked it.

"Daddy," the children yelled as they dropped what they were doing and ran to him with hugs.

"I missed you Daddy. What took you so long?" Eva questioned.

"Baby Girl I had some paperwork to finish at work," he said reciting the lie that he told Rayne prior.

"Daddy. Daddy," Ethan said hopping to be picked up.

Rayne watched the scene with a smile on her face. She loved watching David interact with their children. "You better stop working late or these three are going to get you," she said playfully.

"I see," he said.

"I know I haven't been your favorite person lately but can I get some love too? I'm just saying I am in here slaving over the stove for you."

"It sure smells amazing," David said as he went over and kissed Rayne on the cheek. "What are you cooking?"

"Pan seared steak, mushrooms and onions, mashed

potatoes, and green beans."

"Mmmm. That sounds good. Don't it Ethan?"

"Uh huh," Ethan cosigned from David's arms.

"Let Daddy go take these clothes of and take a quick shower Baby Boy and I'll be right back down."

"Ok," Ethan said,

"Daddy I'll get your case," Evan yelled as he ran for David's briefcase.

Rayne watched as David going upstairs became a family affair as all the kids escorted him to their bedroom. There was so much cheer in the house at that moment. Rayne hoped that mood would continue after she told David about Elaina and her decision to visit Jackson.

Chapter 15

James watched Angela sleep as he held her in his arms. Though he was thrilled to have mended their strained relationship, he could not completely enjoy the moment because of thoughts of Elaina.

He was in deep thought when Angela woke up. "What's on your mind?"

"Oh...nothing," he said startled by her question.

"Really? We're doing this already? I've been watching you for almost a minute and you were spaced out. Open book...remember?"

"Yes I do. Well I'd recently been in contact with the young lady that I believed was my daughter," he paused briefly to watch Angela's response. Other than her ear perking up with the news, she showed no emotion either way. "She has leukemia."

"Oh no," Angela interjected with her hand over her mouth.

"She needs a bone marrow transplant to save her life. I

got tested so that I could donate mine, but when the test came back I was not a match."

"I'm sorry honey," Angela slid in.

"Well," he said with a sigh. "The reason I was not a match is because I am not her father."

"Oh no baby. Come here," she said as she embraced him. Her touch helped him feel better, though he could not help think about Rayne and how she was going to handle herself in the situation.

* * * * * * *

Rayne sipped some wine as she waited for David to return home from dropping the children off to his parents'. Her intent was to discuss Elaina while the children were gone, but that all changed when she received a phone call from Imani. After several attempts to ignore Imani's calls, Rayne finally answered pissed that Imani had not heeded her warning.

"Didn't I tell you not to call me anymore? Are you deaf or stupid?"

"First off Lovely, I'm neither so there is no need for name calling."

"What do you want?" Rayne sternly asked.

"Well Lovely, I was calling to help you but if you truly don't want anything to do with me I will leave you alone," Imani bluffed knowing good and well she had no intent on leaving Rayne alone.

Rayne rolled her eyes, "Again I ask, what do you want?

I don't have time for your games. Just say what you have to say before I hang up."

"Damn I miss that sassiness."

"Imani!"

"Ok. I don't want to hurt you but I love you too much for you to not know. Your husband is having an affair."

"Get the fuck out of here. I don't believe that."

"Why because King David is better than you? You had an affair so why it is hard to believe that he could do the same?"

"Whatever. David loves me and values me and our family too much."

"Ok. If you say so. I did my part by telling you. Just know I'm here for you Lovely. I'll let you get back to your perfect life," Imani said before she hung up the phone.

Rayne sat in disbelief battling her emotions on what Imani said. *David wouldn't do that? But can I blame him if he did?* "Fuck!" she blurted out as she threw the half full glass of wine across the room.

* * * * * * *

David walked into the house at that moment. *What the hell?* He thought as he looked at the mess. "What's wrong babe?" he asked confused at the scene he had witnessed. Rayne stared at him without saying a word. "What's wrong Rayne? You were fine and not throwing things when I left." The little voice in his head was saying that Imani told her about his infidelity but he hoped that it was wrong.

"You tell me what's wrong David. You're Mr. No Secrets. Right?"

David took a seat on the opposite side of the couch. He took a deep breath and said, "Well, I'm sure Imani couldn't wait to run to you. The truth is I messed up."

"So it's true that you're cheating on me? Wow. Messed up? Nah, you fucked up!" She got up and went upstairs.

David was on her heels, "Baby."

"Fuck that baby shit. I can't believe you. You gave me so much grief about my shit and then you do this."

"Baby," he said again as he grabbed her.

"Get the fuck off of me!" She grabbed her suitcase from the closet and laid it on the bed.

"What are you doing?" he asked.

"What does it look like I'm doing? I'm packing."

"Where do you think you're going Rayne?"

"I don't THINK I'm going anywhere. I KNOW I'm going to Jackson. I also KNOW that by the time I get back you better have ended whatever the hell you got going on with that bitch!" Rayne spat.

David wanted to know more about her trip to Jackson, but he felt it was in his best interest to let her calm down. "Ok baby. I love you til death do us part," David said before he left out of their room.

"Keep fucking with me and that will be sooner than later," she mumbled as she went through her drawers.

Chapter 16

"Hey man. What's up?" James said to Jack over the phone.

"I got some news for you boss. The package that your lady received originated in Atlanta."

"Atlanta? The only ties to Atlanta I have is Rayne and I know she didn't send it. Hmmm...odd," James said thinking of any other connection he could have had to Atlanta.

"I'm still working to see if I can isolate a pick up location so I could possibly get some camera footage."

"Sounds good. Anything else?"

"No, that was it."

"Ok. Well I have to go and deal with my sexy ass fiancé."

"Whoa fiancé? Congratulations man!"

"Thanks," James said proudly. "Keep me posted."

"You bet."

Who the fuck is hating on me from Atlanta? He thought as he made his way home to make love to his woman.

* * * * * * *

Kaci acted as if she was furious with Imani when she told her that she told Rayne about David's affair. The reality of the situation was that she knew Imani couldn't have resisted the opportunity to tell Rayne. That was her main reason for including her in on the plan. She bet on Imani not being able to control her emotions for Rayne. They both had it bad for the Smiths.

* * * * * * *

David regretted having to hurt Anna, but Rayne made her point of view loud and clear to him. She did not give him an indicator of when she'd return from Mississippi, but he knew he had to break it off with Anna. There was no way to get pass that if he wanted his family. Unfortunately for Anna, David had love for her but not nearly as much as he had for Rayne or his children.

He took a deep breath before he got out of his car to enter the Starbucks where they often meet. His feet felt weighted down as he walked up to the door.

Anna had already ordered and was waiting when David walked in. Her face lit up when she saw him.

"Hey sweetheart," she said with a kiss to the cheek. "I ordered you a chai latte. I hope that was fine."

"Yes, thank you," he replied unenthusiastically.

"Are you alright sweetheart?" she asked concerned about his lack of excitement.

"Yeah I'm good. I just have a lot on my mind, but we

can talk about that when we get a table."

"Ok. I have something to tell you too love. It's pretty exciting."

They got their drinks and moved to a table in a corner. "So I close on my house next week," Anna said as she was taking a seat. "I'll be glad to get out of that hotel. It's extended stay, but I think I've over extended my stay."

"Congratulations, that is pretty exciting news."

"Yeah it is, but that wasn't even the exciting news I was talking about. It's even bigger than that, but I'll wait until you unload. You look stressed love."

That statement made what he had to do even more difficult. Anna was beautiful but what he liked the most was the genuine concern she had for him. He began contemplating the situation. Was there a way to keep her? Could he at least be with her one last time before he broke it off? *Shit,* he thought as he looked into her almond shaped eyes.

"David are you ok?"

"Yes."

"Are you sure? You were in lala land."

"Sorry," David said regaining focus on the situation at hand. "Anna baby, I love what we have been doing but it has to end."

"Why?" she interjected.

"Because I have a wife."

"So. We both knew you had a wife when we started this.

I love you and don't want to lose you."

"Well, my wife found out that I'm having an affair and told me to end it."

"Found out? How? Does she know who I am?" Anna asked with a worried look on her face.

"She only knows of the affair. She didn't ask the specifics of it. I will never let you get caught up in my mess. So no worries."

They both sat in silence consumed by their thoughts. "Well..." was all Anna could muster up to cut the silence. "That bit of information puts a damper on my news."

"I'm sorry."

"No need to be sorry. We'll be alright."

"Yes we will."

"The 'we' I'm speaking of does not include you David. I'm speaking of me and our baby. I'm pregnant."

At that moment the reality that he fucked up hit him like a ton of bricks.

Chapter 17

Karma's a bitch, continuously played in Rayne's mind while on her flight from Atlanta to Jackson. She'd been on autopilot ever since Imani's phone call the night before. She and David had a brief conversation before she departed. After a failed attempt at a good night's sleep she came to the conclusion that she did not want to leave Atlanta with things as they stood.

Rayne went into the guest bedroom where David stayed that night. To her surprise he was awake. "We need to talk," she said.

"I agree," he said as he sat up in the bed. "Rayne I'm really-"

"Don't," she said as she threw her hand up. "I'm still upset and don't want to talk about how sorry or whatever you are right now. I came in here only because I owe 'us' more than just walking out. Last night before all of the shenanigans I wanted to talk to you about my discovery about the baby I gave away. Come to find out Evelyn had

299

her the entire time."

"Evelyn? The doctor from the hospital?"

"Yes, another lie that has surfaced. But anyway, she has leukemia and needs a bone marrow transplant. I am going to see if I'm a match to help save her life."

"Wow," David said shocked.

"I know I've done wrong and you have forgiven me, but I need some time. Me going to Jackson will give me time to deal with my skeletons and time to allow you to deal with yours." David agreed and they left the conversation at that.

Once the plane landed she put on her shades to cover her puffy eyes and picked up her rental car from the terminal. When she got into the car she called Evelyn.

She never called Evelyn back after her initial phone call so Evelyn was shock to hear from her. "Hello," she answered eagerly.

"Hello Evelyn. I just got to Jackson and I am on my way to the hospital. What room is my daughter in?"

Evelyn's motherly instinct kicked in and she wanted to correct Rayne but she decided against it. "Elaina is in room four seventeen."

"Are you there?"

"Yes I am."

"I will see you shortly. If you were wondering, yes I am still pissed off with you. I am only here to help Elaina."

"Understood," Evelyn stated.

"Good. See you."

Rayne was a ball of nerves by the time she arrived at the hospital. She took several deep breaths but it still felt like she had a frog in her throat. "Ok Rayne you got this," she said giving herself a pep talk. After what felt like an eternity she exited the rental and entered the hospital in search of the room.

When she approached the room the door was partially closed. She tapped softly on it. "Come in," Evelyn said. Evelyn was in a lounge chair next to Elaina's bed. "Elaina I have someone for you to meet. This is one of my longtime friends. Her name is Rayne. Say hi."

"Hello Ms. Rayne. Nice to meet you," Elaina said in a soft frail voice.

"Hi sweetie. Nice to meet you too."

Rayne was taken aback by how much Elaina looked her and her other children. She suddenly understood why Evelyn was so taken by Eva and Evan when she met them. It blew her mind what a beautiful child she and Randy had made.

"Baby, Ms. Rayne and I are going to go out in the hallway to talk. We'll be right back ok?"

"Ok."

Evelyn got up from the chair and she and Rayne moved out to the hall.

"Thank you for coming Rayne. I really didn't know what to expect once you didn't call me back. I'm sure you hate me and I can't blame you, but know that I am appreciative for you coming here."

"You're right about that," Rayne hissed. Evelyn let out a sigh that did not phase Rayne what-so-ever. "James told me that she needs a bone marrow transplant. I'm here to help so what do you need for me to do?"

"I'd have to contact the doctor to get you tested first. Once you're cleared as a match then he'll schedule the procedure soon after."

"What is the procedure like? Is it outpatient? Because I need to get back to Atlanta as soon as possible."

"Doctor Whitman has said the recovery varies between a few days to a week depending on the person."

"Hmmm...ok. Go ahead and call him. I'm sure Bruce won't mind company for a week."

"Thank you Rayne."

"No need to thank me. Like I said I'm not doing this for you but for Elaina."

Chapter 18

Kaci walked into David's office. He looked up from his computer as she entered. "Hello Ms. Eugene. How can I help you?"

She smiled as she said, "Oh yes you can," under her breath.

"Excuse me?"

"Yes. If you're not too busy I wanted your opinion on a piece I was working on."

"Sure. I need a break anyways," David said as he moved from his desk to the sitting area of his office. She took a deep breath and closed her eyes.

"Why can't I get you to love me, Love me like I love you, Days go by with my love for you, Hanging out on the line, To lay by your side at night, And hold you tight is a dream of mine, I want to tell you, How everyone else is wrong for you, Open your eyes, And see how perfect we could be, Stop fighting all of the positives of love, With so many negatives from the world, Allow me to give you my all, And become a part of my world, Let's battle things together, Ignite my flame, And be my fire, Rub your hands against my cheeks, Caress my legs as you kiss me, Love me all over with every touch, Tease my mind with your words, Let your fingers walk all over my body, Feel my hot spots with lips, Take me as I over flow with ecstasy, Have fun with every inch of my bare body, Make me long for you no more, Rub me, tease me, and take me as yours." Kaci exhaled and opened her eyes.

"Damn," David said as he adjusted in his seat.

Kaci caught a glimpse of his bulging hardness through his slacks. "Did you like it?" she asked seductively as she moved toward him.

"Yes..."

"Oh yeah?" she asked standing over him. "How about you show me how much?" Kaci squatted down and touched his hard penis through his pants.

"I don't think that would be appropriate Ms..."

"Shhh..." she said while she unzipped his pants freeing his erection.

"But I'm your boss and..." he trailed off once Kaci placed her mouth on him. She longed for that moment so she showed each part of his penis love; not leaving a millimeter untouched.

David moaned with pleasure. At that moment she knew she won. He had no thought of Rayne or Anna. Wetness seeped through her panties as she moved her mouth up and down his rod. He sat there filled with lust; eyes closed and hips grinding. *Damn I need to feel that,* she thought taking in the sights. She used her free hand and pulled her soaked panties off from under her skirt.

She lubricated her prize really well with saliva before she moved onto the chair with David to mount him. Kaci threw her leg over his legs anticipating him filling her walls. She parted her lips greeting his head.

Beeeeeeeeeep...Beeeeeeeeeep...Beeeeeeeeeep...   "NO!" Kaci yelled as she hit the snooze on her alarm clock. She laid in her bed damn near in tears. "I have to get that man!"

Chapter 19

Rayne spent a week in Jackson. As suspected she indeed was a compatible bone marrow donor. The procedure was conducted successfully with no hiccups. She spent her recovery in her old room in her childhood home. Bruce was excited that she was in Jackson and did not mind waiting on her hand and foot.

Rayne enjoyed the break; it was nice to escape the drama of her life. It would have been ideal for her to have spent a few extra days because she was still a little achy, but business called. Her very picky client Ms. Flores had finally after months of working with her settled on a home near the Kennesaw Mountains. It was imperative that the closing happened that day per the bank stipulations. Though she was still sore, she was not sore enough to trust such a difficult sale to her colleagues.

Once she returned to Atlanta, Rayne went straight to her office. "Hey April. How's it going?"

"Good. How did things go in good old Mississippi?"

"It went well actually, but I'm glad to be back. I'm a city girl now," she said with a chuckle. "Plus I can't wait to see my babies. I'm making a B-line to my in-laws' as soon as this closing is over."

"I bet you can't with their cute selves. I put the paperwork the bank sent over on your desk."

"Thanks. I'm about to go freshen up so I can head out." April nodded her head.

Rayne walked into her office to her closet. In the closet she kept several suits and pairs of shoes. She grabbed a navy blue pants suit, pumps, and her toiletries and headed to the restroom. Her phone rang in the process. It was David. They'd communicated some while she was gone but it was primarily about or for the children. She debated about answering the call but decided it would be best to answer it.

"Hello."

"Hey Babe. How's your day so far?"

"It's going good."

"That's good. So when are you coming home?"

"When I get there so you better have that situation taken care of," she hissed.

David let out a sigh, "How much longer are you going to treat me bad? I messed up Baby. I'm sorry. I need you now more than ever."

"Oh you do?" she said slyly not knowing that he was referring to his mental state.

David was still a wreck since Anna's blow about the pregnancy. Deep down he hoped she was lying in hopes of holding on to him. "I do, but I'll let you get back to whatever you're doing. I love you Rayne."

"Yeah. I love you too." She hated treating David wrong but she needed him to know that he fucked up.

Rayne got dressed and headed to Kennesaw to meet her client at the local Dunkin' Donuts. Ms. Flores was there when Rayne arrived.

"Hello Ms. Flores. Good to see you. I hope you're ready to be a home owner."

"Yes I am!" she exclaimed as she stood and gave Rayne a hug. "I have a gift for you. Here's a mocha latte."

"Well thank you. And it has the caramel like I like," Rayne said grabbing the cup. "You know how to make my day."

She laughed, "It's the least I can do with all the hard work you've done. Not to mention putting up with me and my indecisiveness."

"It was my pleasure." Rayne pulled the paperwork from her briefcase. "First, the not so exciting paperwork. Then we can go to the house and make sure all the things that were fixed are to your standard."

"Ok."

"I need you to sign here...here...here...and here," Rayne said going through the mounds of papers. "Whoa," Rayne said wiping her forehead.

"Are you ok?"

"Yes, I'm just a little hot."

"From the latte or are you feeling under the weather?"

"I don't think it's the coffee. I've been a little under the weather but I'll be alright." She felt queasy and wanted to hurry to finish business to get home. Rayne quickly had her sign the remaining locations. "Congratulations. You are now a home owner."

"Thank you. Thank you," she said excitedly. "You are looking a little flushed. Are you going to be alright to go to the house with me?" Ms. Flores asked as she looked at the sweat beads that sat on Rayne's forehead.

"Yes. I'll grab some water and I'll be fine."

"Ok if you're sure," she said with concern. "How about we leave your car here and I drive that way you can get it together?"

"That would be great."

Rayne got a bottle of water and then joined her at her Lexus SUV. Rayne sipped on her water in between their light conversation on the ten mile drive to Ms. Flores' new home. To Rayne's surprise she had not felt any better by the time they pulled into the drive way; she actually felt worst. "Home sweet home," Ms. Flores said as she got out of the vehicle.

Rayne took a minute to gain her composer before she opened the door. She stood up and her head began spinning. She felt weak and stumbled with her first step.

Before she fell, Ms. Flores caught her, "Easy does it. Lets get you into the house." Rayne collapsed in her arms as she moved her to the door. She struggled to hold Rayne up and unlock the door. Her struggle was brief and she got herself and Rayne into the house where she took her into the den area. She laid Rayne on the carpet and smiled. "Got you bitch."

Chapter 20

David sat at his desk contemplating how to fix his life. He could not figure out what to do to regain what he lost with Rayne. During the time she was gone, he realized that he did not want to live his life without her. Rayne did not believe it but he truly was willing to do anything to keep her. His brain was on overdrive trying to come up with a plan of action to convince Anna to have an abortion. *I need to talk to her. I need to show her that this situation is too messy to bring a child into. Maybe...* His thoughts were interrupted by his phone ringing.

"She must have known I was thinking about her," he said when he saw Anna's number. "Hello."

"Hello David. How are you?"

"I'm doing well and you?"

"I'm alright. I've been doing a lot of thinking since our last conversation and I think we need to talk. Can you meet me?"

"Of course. Where?"

"At my new place."

"I don't know about that."

"I'm not going to bite you David. I think it is best to not be in public. My house is secluded. Talk, that's all."

"Ok."

"I'll text you the address."

"Ok. See you soon."

* * * * * * *

Life was good as far as James was concerned. Bruce had mentioned to him that Rayne was in Jackson when she was there. Rayne told Bruce that she had donated bone marrow to her friend's child; an act that had Bruce puffed up with pride. James was just happy that she finally took her head out of her ass and realized that the sun did not rise nor set on her. That along with his home life had James floating. In his mind nothing or no one could ruin his high.

He was in the kitchen making lunch for himself and Angela when Jack called. "Hey boss. After some digging I found that the package was sent through an account set up by a Johanna Garcia Flores. Do you know her?"

"The name sounds familiar but I can't place it."

"Well, she lived in Orlando until six months ago. I'm expecting some more information to come through momentarily." *Orlando? Where did I hear that name?* James thought running through all of the connections he'd made in Orlando. "As a matter a fact my fax just went off. Hold on one second."

James was spreading Dijon mustard on sandwiches when he remembered where he heard the name. "Fuck!"

Jack got back on the phone, "Holy shit man! I got some news for you. Seems like she was close friends with the crazy broad Sky."

"I'm going to talk to you later. I have to call Rayne."

"I think that's a good idea because she just bought a house from Mrs. Rayne Smith at Smith and Smith Realty."

"Thanks man," James said rushing Jack off the phone.

He hung up and strolled through his phone for Rayne's number. He called it but there was no answer because it was still in the SUV. "Fuck," he said having déjà vu from when he tried to warn her about Sky. He tried several more times before he thought about calling David.

Chapter 21

David pulled up to the address Anna gave him after being led by his GPS. *She was right about this place being secluded,* he thought as he took in the mountainous views. He was impressed by Anna's choice of home. David admired how unlike their subdivision there was distance between the homes.

He got out of his car and rang the doorbell. Johanna came to the door with a calm smile on her face as if she did not have his wife handcuffed and gagged in the other room. "Hi David. I'm glad you came. Come in. Welcome to my home."

His phone rang at that moment. He did not even look at it before he silenced it. He followed her into her front room when the phone rang again. The immediate call back stood out so he looked at the strange Jackson number not knowing if it was Rayne or not.

"Excuse me Anna let me answer this real quick."

"Ok. I'll be right back," she said as she walked toward

the garage.

"Hello."

"David?"

"Yes, who's this?"

"This is James."

"James? What do you want?"

"Is Rayne ok?"

"Yeah, she's in Jackson by Bruce."

"No. She left this morning."

"What?" David asked shocked that she didn't mention that when they spoke.

"Rayne's in danger."

"What? Not this shit again. What have you gotten my wife into this time?"

"Angela got a package from Atlanta outlining my dirt. When I got my investigator on it he tracked the package to Atlanta from a Johanna Garcia Flores. She-"

"Wait. What did you say that name was again?" he asked realizing that Anna's name was Anna Garcia.

"Johanna Garcia Flores. She has been working with Rayne to get a house apparently and she was a close friend of Sky's."

"Holy shit," David said before Johanna knocked him out with a bat.

"Hello. Hello. David? You there?" James said from the phone.

Johanna picked up the phone. "I'm sorry David is no

longer available," she said before she hung up. "Damn baby. Why did you make me do that?" She said as she grabbed David's arms. "You were supposed to come by so that we could talk about our family," she continued as we drug him into the room where Rayne was. "Then I would have killed this bitch and dumped her ass for the animals to eat. Now you've made me hurt you."

* * * * * * *

Kaci kept her eyes on David after Imani's "slip up" to Rayne about his affair. She still occasionally followed him. That day was one of those days. She followed him to Kennesaw, curious of where he had been going at such a strange hour.

She sat outside of Johanna's house peeping trying to figure out whose home it was because Johanna had pulled her truck into the garage. She scooted down enough to watch him and avoid being seen when she saw David standing in front of the bay window on the phone.

"What the hell?" she said when she saw David fall. She thought her eyes were playing tricks on her. She sat there for a minute contemplating what to do.

* * * * * * *

Rayne panicked when she woke up with her hands and legs bonded and tape over her mouth. *What the fuck? Not again. Calm down. Calm down. Breath through your nose,* she thought as she coached herself through a panic attack.

Unlike Sky, Johanna knew what to do. She had Rayne's

hands handcuffed behind her back and her legs were tied in front of her. There was no way for Rayne to escape Johanna's grips. *What are these chick's problem? What the fuck?* Her heart dropped when she saw Johanna dragging David.

"Oh, you're up. I thought my surprise in your drink would have lasted a little longer but it's ok," she said as she continued to drag David. "Look what you made me do. You made me hurt my baby."

Baby? This bitch is bananas.

"You're looking a little confused over there. So let me enlighten you. You took my love from me so I took your love from you."

"What?" Rayne mumbled behind the tape. "What the fuck are you talking about? Crazy bitch," she continued mumbling, rolling her neck with attitude.

"You killed her," Johanna said sadly.

Oh shit. I hope this bitch isn't talking about Sky's crazy ass.

"So I'm going to kill you. Then David, our baby, and I will live happily ever after."

Baby?

Johanna laughed. "The crazy part is I never liked men. I only slept with him to get at you, but the dick was too good to let go." Rayne was fuming as Johanna went into details of hers and David's sexual encounters. "He was like Rayne who when we were together." Johanna said as she laughed some more. "Don't worry you trifling bitch. I'll take good care of him and your kids for you." Johanna went into her waist and pulled out a gun. "Tell my baby Sky I love her," she said as she pulled the trigger.

Rayne twisted in fear; anticipating getting shot. All she could think about in that moment was that her past decisions had taken her from her children. She let out a muffled scream as she felt the impact of the bullet hitting her in the side. She heard a second shot as she fell back on the ground. The shot was followed by a "fuck" and broken glass.

* * * * * * *

Kaci's contemplation ended with her calling the police, putting on her sneakers, and grabbing her gun from the glove compartment. The 911 operator told her to hold tight but she was worried about David. She had no idea about Rayne being in there until she saw her through the window.

Kaci saw Johanna raise the gun, but was unable to get Johanna before she shot Rayne. Kaci shot Johanna in her right shoulder and she dropped the gun. Once Kaci did that she broke the window and climbed in.

While Johanna was wallowing in pain, Kaci grabbed her gun. *What in the fuck?* She thought as she took in the sights; David was still knocked out, Rayne was doubled over bleeding to death, and Johanna was laid out grunting in pain. In that moment she wanted both of them to die to free David of both of his leeches, but the sane side of her wouldn't let her think that way.

She kept her eyes on Johanna as she moved to Rayne. Kaci took the tape off of her mouth and said, "It's going to be alright," as she put pressure on the wound. The police kicked the door in at that moment.

"Kennesaw Police Department!"

"We're in here! We need an ambulance!" Kaci yelled.

Three officers rushed into the room. David began to regain consciousness from his blow. "What?" he asked dazed with confusion. Kaci moved to David and filled him in as the police officers took the hand cuffs off of Rayne and attempted to stabilize her until the ambulance came. He could not believe what had happened. "Lord please save my wife," he prayed. He cried as he watched Rayne's eyes close and her blood left her body.

Chapter 22

Karma has a way of knocking you on your ass, Rayne thought as she sat in her chair and watched her children as they ran about. Her mother in law entered the room as she analyzed her situation.

"You want anything suge?"

"No ma'am. I'm ok."

"Holla at me if you need anything. I'll be in the sitting area reading."

"Thanks Beverly. I appreciate you being here."

"No problem. That's what family's for." She smiled as she exited the room.

Rayne's gratitude went further than one could imagine. Beverly took care of the children and David while Rayne laid in a hospital bed for almost four months. Tears fell from her eyes as she thought of the mess that her secrets and lies caused. *Those damn skeletons,* she thought as she wiped her tears.

"Beverly," Rayne called.

"Yes suge?"

"I changed my mind. I do want something."

"What is it babes?"

"I would like to go outside for some fresh air. If that's not too much trouble."

"Of course it's not," Beverly said going for a wheel chair that was in the corner of the room.

The shooting left Rayne immobilized. She was going through rehabilitation in hopes of regaining full mobility of her legs.

Rayne looked at life totally differently after she left the hospital. She took nothing for granted. She and David were doing well also. Rayne was willing to do whatever it took to maintain her marriage. After all she and David had been through she knew beyond a shadow of a doubt that they belonged together. Their bond was tighter than ever. She had no concerns other than the baby and how he or she would change the dynamics of their household.

* * * * * * *

Johanna sat in her cell at the Cobb County Sherriff's Department where she awaited trial for attempted murder, kidnapping, and assault with attempt to do bodily harm. She rubbed her growing belly as she wrote David the hundredth letter since she'd been there.

"Don't worry honey your daddy will take good care of you while I'm here. That witch can love on you until then, but when I get out I'll be back for our family. Trust me my sweet baby." She gave a deranged smirk as she signed her name on the paper and folded it into an envelope. "Sealed with a kiss," she said as she left her lip balm imprint on the envelope. "I love you David Smith."

Epilogue

JAMES

For the first time in his life James could honestly say he was happy. He and Angela were in a great place. They had a small spring garden wedding surrounded by family and friends. The guest list included Angela's mother who finally got out of the home in St. Mary's and Rayne and her family.

Once Rayne came to in the hospital David told her about how James had once again attempted to save her; an act she could no longer disregard. Even though she was a bitch to him almost always, he cared about her and her wellbeing, so she buried the hatchet and did more than "tolerated" him.

Outside of wedding bliss James and Angela moved out of their apartment into a home and were expecting their second child; James Black Jr.

* * * * * * *

KACI

Kaci's heroics during Rayne's attack changed her perspective on things. Witnessing the love that David had for Rayne while she laid on the floor fighting for her life made her feel guilty about wanting to destroy that. It wasn't until then that she realized that she had love under her nose. She and Derrick, her make shift David, became an item. She left Trust Bank and it wasn't long before David Smith was a name of the past.

* * * * * * *

JOHANNA

Johanna was sentenced to twelve years at Arrendale State Prison in Alto, Georgia. The prosecutor had it easy proving his case because after the search of Johanna's hotel room, there was evidence of her stalking and luring of Rayne through her real estate transactions. The only issue that briefly worried the prosecutor during the trial was the jury possibly showing compassion to Johanna and her round protruding belly. He quickly crushed that sympathy by exposing her affair with the victim's husband.

Johanna gave birth to a healthy baby girl just three days before Christmas giving Rayne and David a Christmas present that they would never forget. "Only eleven years and one hundred and seventy days to go my sweet. Then we will all be together like a family should be," Johanna said speaking to the picture taken of her baby before she was turned over to her social worker. She sat in her cell still very delusional about her relationship with David.

* * * * * * *

RAYNE

Rayne recovered well after her rehab; minus a slight limp that she embraced as a reminder of her strength. Her mental state was spectacular which she credited to meditation, yoga, counseling, and loving life. She decided to be a part of Elaina's life from a distance by way of regular updates and pictures. She was happy that Elaina was able to complete her treatment and was on the winning side of her battle with cancer. Those things also helped her deal with the decision she and David made to raise his and Johanna's baby versus her being put into the system.

She and David went to pick the baby up once Johanna delivered her. Rayne thought it would be hard to go through with the plan, but when she looked into the baby's eyes all of that changed. She was a beauty with jet black wavy hair, olive toned skin, big gray eyes, and dimples.

"Welcome to the family Edith Destiny Smith," she said as she smiled at her. Rayne looked at the baby as the bridge from the past to the present. She decided on the name Edith because the name had a Teutonic origin meaning rich gift; which her life as well as Edith's were.

THE END

About the Author

J. Asmara is a national bestselling author of several works of fiction that includes, romance, erotica, action, and suspense. The Beaufort, South Carolina native grew up as a small town girl destined for great things. As with most people, her life was not always fair, however she endured and overcame adversity. Her passion for writing evolved in March 2014 with her debut novella When It Raynes and she has no plan of stopping.

59900162R00182

Made in the USA
Charleston, SC
16 August 2016